OTTO PENZLER PRESENTS
AMERICAN MYSTERY CLASSICS

MURDER BY AN ARISTOCRAT

Mignon G. Eberhart (1899–1996) wrote dozens of mystery novels over nearly sixty years. Born in Lincoln, Nebraska, she published her first novel, *The Patient in Room 18*, in 1929 and by the end of the 1930s she was one of the most popular mystery writers on the planet. Eight of her books—including *Murder by an Aristocrat*—were adapted for film; later in her career, she was awarded the Grand Master Award by the Mystery Writers of America for lifetime achievement.

Nancy Pickard is the author of nearly twenty novels, including ten in her Jenny Cain series. She is a four-time Edgar Award nominee and winner of the Anthony Award, the Macavity Award, and three Agatha Awards. Her short stories have also won numerous accolades. Pickard has been a national board member of the Mystery Writers of America and president of Sisters in Crime, and she is a member of PEN. She lives in Charleston, South Carolina.

MURDER BY AN ARISTOCRAT

MIGNON G. EBERHART

Introduction by
NANCY PICKARD

AMERICAN MYSTERY CLASSICS

Penzler Publishers
New York

Published in 2019 by Penzler Publishers
58 Warren Street, New York, NY 10007
penzlerpublishers.com

Distributed by W. W. Norton.

Cover image: Andy Ross
Cover design: Mauricio Diaz

Paperback ISBN 978-1-61316-148-7
Hardcover ISBN 978-1-61316-147-0
eBook ISBN 978-1-49765-551-5

Library of Congress Control Number: 2019906537

Printed in the United States of America

9 8 7 6 5 4 3 2 1

MURDER BY
AN ARISTOCRAT

INTRODUCTION

FOR CONNOISSEURS OF CLASSIC mystery novels, those written by Mignon G. Eberhart are "must haves," and certainly "must reads." This one, *Murder by an Aristocrat*, originally published in 1932, gives the reader a wonderful taste of her talent because it contains virtually all of the dramatic ingredients that made her books so well-loved that she became one of the most popular mystery writers of all time. She was one of a golden trio of authors that included Agatha Christie and Mary Roberts Rinehart.

Ms. Eberhart was, in fact, the best-selling mystery writer in America in the 1930s, and this novel goes a long way toward showing why. It is also a fascinating glimpse into the mystery reading preferences of that time that has come to be known as the first Golden Age of Mystery.

This novel stars Eberhart's only series "detective"—a nurse, Sarah Keate, who describes herself as middle-aged, stout, and "no beauty." But she is a beaut at keeping secrets and at ferreting out the fatal secrets of suspects. Nurse Sarah Keate calls this adventure "the Thatcher Case," so I will, too.

As with many mysteries from that era, the Thatcher Case comes adorned with: inherited money, a charming mansion, squabbling aristocratic relatives (and a few not quite aristocratic), an intimidating servant, a gun that goes missing, a possible jewel theft, lies, red herrings, twists, turns, psychological acuity on the part of the author, good manners, bad manners, and, of course, dead bodies. What it does not come with are: cell phones, texts, social media, seat belts, or emails. If that's not enough to lure you in, consider the provocative words and descriptions Eberhart uses in just her first two chapters: *silent old walls, depths unplumbed, horror, frightened witless, dread, every nerve tense, darkness, listening, shock, danger, terrifying, twisted, blood, haunted eyes, strange grave. . .*

No wonder then that *The New York Times* noted a "dangerous" element in her writing; their reviewer praised the atmosphere of suspense that permeates her work. Carolyn G. Hart, the multiple award winning author of best-selling amateur sleuth novels, seconds that opinion by recalling that she enjoyed Eberhart's novels for their "appealing heroines, fascinating locales, and the sense of impending danger." But Eberhart was more than a "good read." She was important to the development of the mystery novel, in general. Best selling mystery writer and mystery historian Dean James has said of her: "[She] raised the profile of the domestic suspense novel. She and Mary Roberts Rinehart paved the way for writers like Margaret Millar, Patricia Highsmith, and Dorothy B. Hughes."

In other words, she was a bold writer for her times.

There is a small, but telling, example of that boldness on the very first page of *Murder by an Aristocrat*. (If you worry that the title gives the end away, you can relax. Almost every character in this novel is an aristocrat!) The great challenge of this kind of a novel, an amateur sleuth novel, is to make it believable that someone with no logical reason to investigate a mystery—when there are police available right down the road—not only does investigate it, but solves it! Every now and then in real life, one hears of such things and marvels at the courage and perseverance of the "amateur" who persists and succeeds where professional crime-solvers may have come up short for years or even decades. But that's *rare*, and seems an obsession on the part of someone who can't stop until the crime is solved, the victim honored, the true perpetrator brought to justice, and perhaps someone else set free. There's a bit of that obsessive quality about Nurse Keate, but she's also the most honest and intelligent character and the one with the most common sense, and that sense tells her this crime *must* be cracked open, so she cracks it.

"Suspension of disbelief" is the literary term for this fictional magic.

In amateur sleuth mysteries, it boils down to, "How *did* Sarah Keate manage to stick her nose into all those homicides and outwit the pros every time? And why *do* we willingly suspend our disbelief, even if only to the end of the novel?"

Partly, we believe it simply because we want to.

But the writer's skill at luring us into wanting to believe is equally important for the task. In this novel, Ms. Eberhart goes about it in the most direct way imaginable, in a manner I've never seen any other author use. She lets her heroine simply tell us, essentially, Look, I know this is impossible, but I'm telling you it happened, so even though I feel silly saying it, you'll just have to take my word for it.

And we do!

Mignon G. Eberhart was born Mignonette Good, in 1899, in Lincoln, Nebraska, and died in 1996 in Greenwich, Connecticut. For her more than fifty novels, beginning with *The Patient in Room 18* (1929), which introduced nurse Sarah Keate, and for her many short stories, she was, in 1971, named a Grand Master by the Mystery Writers of America, for which she served as president in 1977. Eventually, Eberhart, abandoned Nurse Keate to write stand-alone suspense novels. She was awarded the Scotland Yard Prize and the Agatha Award for Lifetime Achievement by Malice Domestic.

Murder by an Aristocrat was filmed in 1936, four years after its publication, with Marguerite Churchill as the amateur sleuth, now named Nurse Sally Keating. Several other of her novels were also made into films, including *While the Patient Slept* (1935), *The Patient in Room 18* (1938), which starred Ann Sheridan, *The Mystery at Hunting's End* (titled *Mystery House*, 1938), with Sheridan again playing nurse Keate, and *The Dark Stairway* (1938).

She was enormously popular, critically acclaimed, and a powerful influence on other writers. I hope you enjoy reading or rereading this novel by one of the greats!

—NANCY PICKARD

MURDER BY
AN ARISTOCRAT

A NOTE BY MISS SARAH KEATE

My nursing practice is beginning to suffer. It is with regret that I arrive at that conclusion. But it is true.

My patients are beginning to grow nervous when they discover that my name is Sarah Keate. They say "The Nurse Keate who—" and check themselves abruptly and watch me thereafter with a faintly wary look. They are restless and ask to have the night light burning. There is something about them which says mutely: "I don't want that red-headed nurse. She's had too much traffic with murders."

But I am a nurse. I am not a detective, and I don't want to be a detective. Nursing is my profession. And—there's no getting around it—there seems to have been a certain fate, a regrettable proximity, involving me and murders, and no one wants a murder in his immediate vicinity. Especially a patient.

I admit that, on occasion, I have felt it my duty to do what I could do in the cause of justice. But I do not relish the growing custom of the doctors to ask for me when the case is what they blandly call "extraordinary." That is what, I later learned, Dr. Bouligny said when he telephoned the registry office. He also said something about a nurse "with discretion." So, I was called!

I have nothing against humanity. But I can only hope for a long succession of appendix or tonsil cases to offset the effect of the Thatcher case.

Thus I have been reluctant to tell, in this manner, of the Thatcher case, even now that, for various reasons, I am at last free to do so. And I wish to express my earnest hope that any prospective patient will perceive that the case was literally thrust upon me. Heaven knows, my only desire was to escape it.

And the pity of it was, there was nothing I could do. My hands were tied. I still feel that there were depths unplumbed, soundings only guessed at.

Well, it is completely over now. And here is the record exactly as it occurred and exactly as I made it shortly after I left the Thatcher house.

It is the story of what happened among the Thatchers during one summer week. And it might be the sum of the life the Thatcher house and its entangled lives had known.

Inconsistently I liked the Thatchers. By them I was held virtually a prisoner; I was frightened half out of my wits; I was forced to eavesdrop; I was obliged not only to read a letter which was certainly not mine to read, but also to return it in a clandestine fashion to its owner, and thereby, in a manner of speaking, to condone something I could not approve and yet could only pity—and all this without a shred of compunction on my part. In the end, even, it was I upon whom was placed the burden of the secret which must still haunt the silent old walls of the Thatcher house.

Yet, inconsistently, I liked the Thatchers.

But knowing what I now know, I could never again force myself to cross that green and tranquil lawn, pass the step where Emmeline stood and screamed, and enter the wide and gracious door.

A door which led to horror.

—SARAH KEATE, R. N.

CHAPTER I

LAST WEEK I HAD my telephone disconnected, and I am sleeping better. I no longer find myself suddenly awake, staring into the darkness, listening. Listening, every nerve tense, as if I dread what I am about to hear. And then coming slowly to the realization that the telephone is not ringing, that the Thatcher case is over and closed. It is always with a feeling of shock that I arrive at this realization; I invariably feel tired, exhausted, and faintly terrified, as if I had just escaped some impending danger.

Having been more or less interested in the simpler aspects of psychology for some time, I strove to analyze my own thoroughly annoying trouble and came to the conclusion that I feared the telephone.

So, as I say, I had it disconnected and have slept much better.

Though as to that there are many things far more terrifying than the telephone that I have stored in my memory. There was the singular way Bayard Thatcher's head was twisted. There was the blood on the wrong rug. There were Dave's haunted eyes when I met him at last at that strange grave. And there was, curiously, the heavy fragrance of summer night rain on roses.

But after all, it was the telephone which summoned me to the Thatcher case to nurse Bayard Thatcher who, Dr. Bouligny said, had accidentally shot himself while cleaning a revolver. He

3

was not seriously wounded, said Dr. Bouligny, but Miss Adela Thatcher had insisted on calling a trained nurse. From the way he spoke, I received a distinct impression that Adela Thatcher's will was law.

The telephone call aroused me at exactly half-past two of a cool summer dawn; I know the time because I remember rubbing my eyes with one hand while I stretched the other toward my alarm clock and wondered whether it was an accident or a baby. The doctor explained the matter rather hurriedly, saying the accident had occurred about half an hour ago, he had dressed the wound and would leave orders for me, and would I please come at once. I resisted an impulse to tell him I would far rather get my sleep out, scrambled some things into a bag, caught a suburban train, and was presently walking along the turf path, raised a little, and so velvety thick with close-cropped grass that my feet made no sound at all, which led diagonally from the crossroads across the spacious lawns surrounding the Thatcher house.

It was that cool, lovely gray hour before the sun, and I recall very clearly but with some incredulity the feeling of peace and tranquillity and serenity induced in me by the wide green lawn, spreading into misty gray, the dim outlines of the shrubbery, the sleepy twitter of the birds in the great old trees, and the house itself, which loomed half clear, half shadowy ahead of me. It was an old house of mellowed brick with clean white trimmings, sprawling contentedly there amid its trees; a house of undecided architecture with a turret here, a bay window there, an unexpected wing somewhere else; a house that, once neat and compact, had been added onto during several generations. It was now a rambling mixture of many modes of architecture, but the effect, somehow, was still gracious and possessed a mellow and charming dignity.

The wide front door was open, with only a screen door across it; a light shone in the hall beyond. As I took a last breath of the sweet morning air which mingled the scents of sleeping flowers and dew-drenched, recently cut grass and stepped on the low porch, a woman came from the stairway in the hall to open the door. She was a small woman not much past fifty, I thought, in trailing lavender silk with lace falling about her wrists. She looked worried and anxious but was not flurried.

"Miss Keate?" It was a soft, rather high voice, delicately modulated and very deliberate. The kind of voice that in my girlhood was called elegant. Or refined. It continued: "I am Adela Thatcher. Will you come this way, please?"

She gestured toward the stairway, and I followed. The light above had fallen directly upon her face and her gray hair, which was in what, I instinctively felt, was an unaccustomed state of disorder. The arrogant curve of what I came to know as the Thatcher nose was softened in her face to a line of not unpleasant dignity, and her somewhat faded blue eyes squinted near-sightedly. She was not tall and, save for a thickness about the waist and hips, was rather slender, but she gave an impression of stateliness and assured dignity. Her hand on the polished railing was white under its laces, but a little broad and thick knuckled; it was a generous but not a sensitive hand.

At the moment I saw very little of the darkly gleaming stairway and hall. I saw little of it, but at the same time there were things I knew about that house immediately. I knew there were glittering bathrooms, lavishly supplied, and generous linen closets delicately fragrant with lavender; I knew that there were many books and good old rugs and ancestral portraits carefully hung; I knew that a stain on the silver—which would be solid and old—was like a stain on the family honor, and that somebody in the household had perpetually red knees from polishing floors and ancient mahogany.

We emerged into a wide, well aired upper hall. At a door almost opposite the stair well a girl in a yellow chiffon negligee stood, apparently waiting for us. One slim hand was on the doorknob of the room she seemed to have just left; her dark hair was pinned back in a remarkably becoming dishevelment, and even at that hurried moment I was conscious of what was almost a shock. The girl was amazingly beautiful.

Now beauty is a rare word, a delicate word, one which may not be used carelessly, but it is the only word for Janice Thatcher. But I do not know to this day exactly why she was beautiful. I suppose she had regular features and a graceful body. I know her black hair was soft and wavy and had a warm brownish tinge. I know she had a creamy magnolia-like skin, very dark gray eyes which were direct and grave under well defined eyebrows and, I believe, long-lashed. But many, many women have all that and have not beauty. No, it was something subtle; something elusive; a sort of inner flame, a something that glowed occasionally like the lambent flashes of a fire opal when you turn it in the light.

Since I am of the generation which quotes Browning, I found myself thinking, "All that I know of a certain star"—and then Miss Adela was saying a little breathlessly:

"How is Bayard? Is he better?"

The girl nodded.

"Is this the nurse?"

"Miss Keate. Mrs. Dave Thatcher," said Miss Adela. "Are you sure it was all right to leave Bayard, Janice?"

"Quite all right," said Janice briefly, looking steadily at me. "He is going to get well. It isn't anything serious."

Something about her, intangible yet positive and definite, too, told me that she had just had some sort of shock. Probably it was a scarcely definable air of rigidly maintained poise, a look of emotions held sternly in leash. At any rate, I knew it at once.

It was just then that it struck me for the first time that two o'clock of a summer morning is an unusual time to be cleaning a revolver.

Both women had been looking steadily at me, and even as I became aware of the odd intensity of their scrutiny, they exchanged between themselves a communicative glance.

"Miss Keate will do very well," said Janice.

"Yes, I'm sure of it," returned Adela Thatcher in a reassured way.

They both looked, I thought, subtly approving. And I didn't see any reason particularly to approve of the appearance of a sleepy, middle-aged nurse who is stouter and crankier than she likes to admit.

Then Miss Adela's faded blue eyes went past me to a door farther along the corridor and became suddenly bleak.

"Where is Dave?"

A little veil dropped over Janice's dark eyes, and she said crisply: "I don't know, I'm sure," and opened the door beside us.

I followed them into a large, airy bedroom with long open windows. A bedroom of fresh ruffled chintz, heavy old mahogany dresser and bed, gleaming floors, and ivory-painted woodwork. On the wide bed lay my patient, Bayard Thatcher. His eyes were closed, but he opened them as I approached, looked narrowly at me past his arrogant Thatcher nose, said, "Hell," quite distinctly, and closed his eyes again.

Well, of course, three o'clock in the morning is a trying hour, and I am no beauty at best. Still, I must admit his candor affected me most disagreeably.

Janice caught her breath sharply.

"Bayard! This is your nurse, Miss Keate."

"I know it," he said, still with his sunken eyes closed and his hard dark face and thinning brownish hair very vivid against the white pillows. "Listen, Adela, I don't need a nurse. It's only a scratch. Doctor can dress it every day——"

"There's a bedroom next door if you'd like to change into your uniform, Miss Keate," said Adela, ignoring Bayard in the blandest way in the world. "Show her, Janice. Dr. Bouligny left a note over there on the table for you. I think he gave Bayard something to make him sleep——" Her gentle, deliberate voice stopped without a period, and she moved with a soft whisper of silk to make some adjustment of the sheets.

Well—that was my introduction to the Thatcher house and household. A house which in its dim fragrance, its gracious dignity, its feeling of ancestry, its every evidence of an age when family tradition was held in honor, was to grow as familiar to me as the palm of my own hand. And a household which—no, I can't say it became familiar to me: there were things about the Thatchers which I accepted but never understood—but which was to engage and hold my strongest interest. Adela, perhaps, in her dignity, her tenacity, her strongly maternal feeling toward her two brothers, Dave and Hilary, and her determined effort to preserve an unbroken surface of amity toward the world, I came the nearest to understanding. It was only toward the last that I really knew Janice.

When I returned to my patient's room, my fresh white uniform rustling and a starched cap concealing the gray streak in my abundant reddish hair, Janice had gone, and Miss Adela, with a parting word about the doctor's orders, soon left us. I glanced at the chart Dr. Bouligny had left, noted a few directions, took my patient's pulse, which was only a little over normal, and his temperature, which was barely ninety-nine, looked at the dressing on the wound, and settled myself at length in a comfortable chair near one of the open windows, yawned and relaxed. While a nurse is quite accustomed to being called from her sleep at all hours of the night, still, it never grows pleasant.

The house was very silent, and I could hear the waking calls of the birds in the trees outside very clearly. It was growing lighter, so I turned out the lamp at my elbow. In the quiet semigloom my patient appeared to sleep, and his sharp profile looked dark and hawk-like. His face was narrow and thin with deeply sunken eyes, rather high cheek bones, a high forehead, and a thin mouth. It was neither a kind nor a lovable face; his eyes were set a little too close together above that arrogantly curved nose, his thin mouth had a sardonic look even in sleep. It was altogether a relentless face. I thought a moment and changed the word: it was a predatory face.

"You don't like my looks?"

"I wasn't thinking anything about your looks," I said, startled. His eyes were a peculiar light yellow-gray, which looked very light in his dark face, and it had taken me a little by surprise to discover that he'd been watching me all the while I stared at his mouth and hunted for a word to suit it. "You must go back to sleep again."

"I don't want to sleep. The doctor's pills are as ineffective as everything else about him. Do you know Dr. Bouligny?"

"Slightly. He's brought a few cases to the hospital. The nurses call him Dr. Bolon——" I checked myself, but he smiled again.

"Dr. Boloney, of course. Irresistible to the average young woman's mentality. But in this case quite applicable. He is also—" he continued in a leisurely way that was not exactly nice—"he is also a piece of cheese, a feather bed, and a Thatcher." His unpleasant light eyes went past me to the elms outside the window, which were beginning to glow in the coming sunlight.

"A Thatcher?"

"A Thatcher. And therefore blessed. When a Thatcher is born the key to heaven is automatically placed in his hand."

"You'd better go to sleep."

"Our doctor's mother was a Thatcher. Several times removed from the present incumbents of the honor, but still a Thatcher. And to be a That——"

"You must try to sleep," I said crisply. "If you keep talking, your pulse will go up and you'll get a fever. We don't want any trouble with that wound."

He smiled.

"Oh, yes. My wound. We must be careful of that. By the way, Miss—Keate, is it?—you might just glance about the room. If the revolver is anywhere, pick it up and put it away."

I did so willingly; I might even say with alacrity. Loaded revolvers lying casually about are apt to make me a little nervous. But though I looked all through the room and the adjoining bathroom, neither room yielded anything in the shape of a revolver. There were some bloodstained towels in the hamper, and some swabs of cotton and gauze stained with blood and mercurochrome in the waste basket, but no revolver. I even looked at his direction in the drawers of the great old-fashioned bureau, which offered a faint smell of lavender, an abundance of well laundered shirts, at least fifty ties, and a square bottle marked Gordon's gin and wrapped carefully in some extremely nice white silk underclothes. But no revolver.

"H'm," murmured my patient, who had been watching me with a sort of eager look in his light eyes. "Now, I wonder—I wonder who took it."

"What in the world," I asked rather sharply, my curiosity overcoming my prudence, "what in the world were you doing, cleaning your revolver at two o'clock in the morning?"

"What's that?" he said quickly, and when I repeated it he laughed. It was not, however, a pleasant laugh.

"Cleaning my revolver. Is that what Adela said?"

"That's what Dr. Bouligny said."

"So that's it." He paused, looking fixedly at one of the tall pineapple bedposts. "So that's it. Oh, clever Adela. Well, if she says so she's probably right. But don't ask me why I was doing it. To my notion that's the last thing in the world to do at that hour. There are so many nicer ways to pass the night. And if you want to know," he added abruptly, "why I hid that bottle of gin, it's on account of Emmeline."

"Emmeline?" I said, bewildered.

"Emmeline. Emmeline of the well known gimlet eyes. Emmeline of the communicative tongue. Emmeline of the unbribable virtue. With two deaf ears she hears much better than most people with two good ears. Emmeline," he said cruelly, "is Adela's trusted maid. Adela thinks she rules the household, but it's really Emmeline. And as to the gin—Emmeline thinks it her duty whenever I'm here on a visit to see that I've not fallen into any bad ways, and that all the buttons are on my shirts and my socks neatly mended. But she is still maidenly and modest at fifty-odd, and my underwear is immune."

"On a visit? I thought you lived here."

"Not by a long shot," he said. There was an acrid undertone in his voice. "I'm a sort of cousin. What is known as a connection. A connection but still a Thatcher, which is why Adela took me on when I was left without resource at a tender age. She tried to bring me up along with her two brothers. It didn't go so well," he added in a musing way. "Dave and Hilary were even then particularly nasty little snobs, and I was never anything to——"

"You really must try to go to sleep," I interrupted hurriedly. At the moment I had no wish to be told the inner politics of the

Thatcher family. Later I was to wish I had overcome my scruples and listened avidly to every word he might say in the hope of discovering in retrospect some hint, some word, that would give us a clue to the dark mystery that was so soon to involve us.

This time he closed his eyes.

"My shoulder's beginning to throb. Can you shift the bandage a little? The adhesive pulls like hell!"

I bent over him, endeavoring to arrange the dressing less tightly. The wound was in his right shoulder, a flesh wound and not serious but apt to be painful. An odd place, I thought idly, accidentally to shoot one's self.

"Still," said my patient, his light eyes so close to mine faintly mocking, as if he'd read my thoughts, "still, it can be done. By holding the revolver with my left hand, pointing it at my right shoulder, and pulling the trigger. Always assuming it was loaded."

This time I definitely disliked his laugh.

"That's better, isn't it?" I said. "Now, do try to sleep."

I pulled the sheet straight, and as he closed his eyes again, sought my chair.

Probably we both dozed for some time, although I was not as comfortable as I had expected to be in the cushioned chaise longue, feeling, indeed, a little restless and uneasy and retaining an impression of not having closed an eye. But I roused at length to a sudden realization that the lawn was bright with sunshine, vividly green and cool-looking, the birds singing blithely; that the fragrance of coffee and broiling bacon was somewhere about, and that a car was racing furiously up the drive.

I got rather stiffly to my feet, straightened my cap, went to the long window, and stepped through it onto a sort of balcony, vine twined. Down below me ran a graveled drive coming in from the road straight past the house and probably to a garage which I couldn't see. The car, a long yellow roadster, had stopped with a swish of gravel directly under the balcony, and a man was getting out of it. Even allowing for the foreshortening of my view of him, I judged him to be considerably stouter than a man of his age—which was probably in the early forties—should be. I caught only a glimpse of a smooth pinkish face, rather pompous, and thin darkish hair, as he tossed his hat into the seat of the car and ran around the corner of the house.

"That," said my patient's voice back of me, "will be Hilary."

"I thought you were asleep," I said.

He frowned.

"Really, Miss Keate, I can't have this. You seem to have some complex about sleep. It's all you can talk of. Go quietly out into the hall and lean over the staircase and see if you can hear what Adela's telling him."

"I'll do no such thing. The very idea. I——"

"Never mind. Never mind. I didn't think you would. All the same, I would like to know. But he'll be up in a moment. Miss Keate, you are about to meet Hilary Thatcher, an ornament to the banking profession, the family, and the county. A man of the bluest of blood and proud of it. In short, a small-town aristocrat, than which there is nothing more aristocratic. Nothing more assured. Nothing more blissfully contented. Nothing," he said, with a curious note of truth, "so effortlessly real. Well—" his voice lost its momentary sincerity—"I do hope you are sensible of the pleasure you are about to have and—— Oh, hello there, Hilary!"

Hilary Thatcher stood in the doorway. He was fleshy, as I had seen, pink, a bit pompous, and nearly bald. His face was freshly shaved, his tie gray-blue like his eyes, and he was too well groomed. There wasn't a thing awry about him, but something in his wary eyes and quick breathing made me feel that he was distinctly alarmed, really violently disturbed, and doing his best to conceal it. There was, however, so far as I could see, not one shade of affectionate concern in his expression.

"Adela tells me you've—had an accident," he said, closing the door. He had looked only at Bayard on the bed, and as I moved to pull down a window shade against the sun he turned with a little start to me. "Oh—is this the nurse? How do you do? Do you mind stepping out of the room for a moment, please?"

He spoke in a nice enough way, and I was about to comply with his request when my patient spoke sharply:

"Stay exactly where you are, Miss Keate."

"But I——"

"*Stay here!* Now, Hilary. Won't you sit down?"

"Thanks, I—can't stop. I just heard that you were—hurt. Adela phoned my wife. Evelyn—sent me right over. I—Adela says it isn't serious."

Curious that there should be such anxiety in his voice and yet no affection.

"No," said my patient. "It isn't serious. A little painful, but that's all. I shall be well again in a very few days. Odd how I get involved in accidents when I'm here. Do you remember the last time? I got a cramp while we were swimming out on Thatcher lake and couldn't—" he paused to shift the pillow under his head—"couldn't make you hear me call for help."

A bar of sunlight striking Hilary's face made it look paler. He said in a nonchalant way:

"You'll curtail your visits if this keeps up."

"It does begin to seem a sort of fatality," said Bayard. "But I won't stay away. No, I couldn't do that."

"Anything I can do for you?" asked Hilary.

"Nothing, thanks, Hilary. I'm doing very well. Nice of you to stop and inquire."

Hilary's plump pink hand with its wide seal ring closed rather tightly on the doorknob. He opened his mouth as if about to say something further, gave me an annoyed look, hesitated, said, "Well, so long," and left.

My patient laughed softly. His light eyes were narrow and fastened on the closed door with a look that was not friendly, not cousinly.

"It's after seven o'clock," I said, glancing at my watch. "Shall I have your Emmeline bring you up some coffee?"

"Not now. I believe I can sleep some more. You might give me a drink of water."

I brought the water and held his head so he could drink it.

"And, by the way, Miss Keate," he said, leaning back on the pillow with a sort of sigh, "don't let any of the family bring that revolver back into the room. You see," he added, closing his eyes, "the next time it might be a success. The shooting, I mean."

It took an appalled moment or two to discover my voice.

"You don't mean someone—you don't think someone shot you—on purpose?"

"I know damn well somebody did," he said.

CHAPTER II

AND AS I STOOD there aghast, entirely unable to credit my own ears, he looked up and said:

"I wish you wouldn't talk so much. You won't let me sleep. Breakfast is at eight. You might go down, now. There's a key to the door. Lock it after you and keep the key to yourself. I don't wish to be—disturbed."

"You can't possibly mean what you've just said!"

"Can't I? It's true."

"It can't be true! You are—it's that opiate Dr. Bouligny gave you. You're talking nonsense. Why, you are in the midst of your family. People who love you. People who——"

"As Hilary loves me?"

Well, it was true that Hilary didn't seem especially fond of my patient. But an ambitious and prosperous young banker, such as one felt Hilary to be, does not shoot a man simply because he has no love for him. Besides, there was Miss Adela Thatcher with her elegant voice and her lavender silks and her well bred face. And there was the air of the house: that indescribable quality of dignity and simplicity and honesty and—I hesitated and finally used Bayard's bitter word—of aristocracy. No, I could not reconcile Bayard's accusation with what I had seen of the Thatchers. I said:

"You don't know what you are saying."

"My dear nurse," said Bayard Thatcher, "I don't care whether you believe me or not. It doesn't matter in the least. Now, do go away and let me sleep."

"Who," I asked, "shot you?"

"I don't intend to tell you," he said, smiling again. "Run along and get your breakfast."

With which he closed his eyes firmly and disregarded a further question or two, and when I emerged from freshening myself up with the aid of the mirror in the bathroom, he was apparently sound asleep. I drew the shades further down to keep the room cool, put a glass of fresh water on the table beside his bed, and tiptoed to the door. I remember the key in the lock caught my eye, and finally, feeling rather silly and ashamed, I locked the door behind me and put the key in my pocket.

I felt sillier when I glanced along that wide, pleasant hall with its windows opening upon a placid summer morning, its worn old rugs, its open doors which gave glimpses of airy bedrooms, fresh and lovely in their delicate chintzes and crisp curtains. Along the wall opposite was a mirror, beautifully polished, and here and there were bookshelves laden with worn books which I learned later were the overflow from the generous library downstairs. No, decidedly it was not the kind of place where the thing Bayard had suggested could possibly occur.

On the landing of the stairs I came upon a housemaid in fresh green chambray and snowy apron. She was on her knees polishing the steps and looked up to say a pleasant good-morning. Apparently she knew of my presence and my mission, for she showed no trace of surprise and told me breakfast would be served in a quarter of an hour. She was a rather plain girl, solid and very neat: exactly the housemaid one would expect Adela Thatcher to select. Her name was Florrie.

After a placid breakfast with Miss Adela and Janice—Adela looking a bit more austere in gold-rimmed eyeglasses and crisp white linen, and Janice unbelievably lovely above the pink roses she brought to the breakfast table—during which the conversation was politely and blandly held to gardens without a word of Bayard or revolvers or wounds or doctors, I returned to my patient's room.

That day, which was Thursday, July seventh, I spent in his room or out on the small balcony. He slept most of the day, and I watched the various comings and goings of the household and thought of his incredible suggestion—statement, in fact—that someone in the family had tried to murder him. I decided against it. It was true that the accident had certain peculiar aspects, but none of them was exactly convincing. It occurred to me, too, that it was a little odd that Hilary had not asked a single question about the accident; he had not asked how it happened, or when it happened, or with what revolver, or didn't Bayard know it was loaded, or made any of the obvious comments. But Miss Adela had already told him of the affair, and, at any rate, it was a trivial matter.

The small balcony overlooked the rose gardens and part of the lawn, and as I lounged in the long steamer chair with which it was equipped I caught various glimpses of the household. A trellis ran up to the balcony, and the vines were laden with roses, and the whole place was almost unbearably fragrant. To this day when I smell sun-warmed roses I think of the Thatcher case—which is, when I come to think of it, a rather strange anomaly.

Janice, slim and very lovely in pale green dimity with the sunlight on her warm dark hair, worked in the garden for some time, digging around the tall gladioluses, which were beginning to bloom, with competent, ungloved hands and directing, with a certain cool efficiency which I liked, a man who appeared to be a sort of gardener and handy-man and whose name I later found was Higby. Once Adela, followed by an old and too well fed bird dog, joined her, and the two talked for some time in what I thought was a rather agitated manner.

And once during the morning the yellow roadster again sped up the drive. There were two occupants this time, a woman whom I surmised to be the Evelyn I had heard mentioned, Hilary's wife, and a young man. They too talked to Janice for some time, and I had an opportunity to observe them lengthily, if not very closely. Evelyn was a tall, remarkably handsome woman of around forty, with smooth gold hair done in a simple knot on her neck, a brown face, a fine profile, and eyes that I found later were very dark blue. She too had a look of race; the well poised simplicity of manner, innately dignified yet simple and gracious and direct, which characterized the other Thatcher women. I found myself employing that ill-used and outdated word aristocrat again: it was the only word to describe the Thatchers.

The young man who accompanied her and who lingered to talk to Janice when Evelyn Thatcher went into the house, bore such a striking resemblance to Evelyn that I thought at first he might be her son. As I looked closer, however, I saw that he was too old for that, and came to what was also a correct conclusion, that he was her brother. Later I knew his name was Allen—Allen Carick—and that he was on a visit in the Hilary Thatcher household up on the hill. If I had guessed what an important part he was to play in the strange and terrible drama that was even then, unknown to me, unfolding, I would have paid more attention to him. As it was I only noted him casually, although it did strike me that once when Janice scratched her hand on a thorn of the roses she was then cutting, he caught her hand and examined the scratch with rather more anxiety than the occasion demanded. And I was quite sure a bit of color came into Janice's face, though it may have been due only to the heat of the sun.

Dave Thatcher—who, of course, was Janice's husband and younger brother to Adela and Hilary—did not appear at either lunch or dinner. At lunch I heard Emmeline tell Miss Adela that he had gone to the cemetery, which somehow increased the little mystery that was beginning to surround him. Especially when something Janice said told me that the cemetery referred to was the family burial plot and only a quarter of a mile or so from the house. Not exactly an all-day pilgrimage.

And I must not forget Emmeline, who brought fresh linen to my patient's room about noon. She was a dark, tall, unbelievably spare woman with iron-gray hair combed tightly back with old-fashioned side combs and a way of watching your mouth instead of your eyes which was quite comprehensible in view of her deafness but was not exactly nice. Not nice either was a curious way she had of twisting and working her hands, rasping her fingers eagerly and constantly against her palms, while otherwise standing rigidly still.

She asked Bayard how he felt in the oddly harsh and inflectionless voice of the very deaf, nodded briefly as he shouted "Better," gave me an extremely sharp look, and left, looking from the back rather like a remarkably tall black clothes-pin with a cap on its head.

It was altogether, so far as I knew, a drowsy, pleasant day. The doctor paid us a brief visit shortly after lunch; Bayard had got over his garrulous spell and lapsed into a taciturn silence, and I napped in the steamer chair on the balcony most of the lazy, warm afternoon.

Hilary came in for a moment after dinner, but made my patient only the briefest call; it began to rain about nine-thirty and at ten I prepared my patient for the night and, at his curt request, locked the door to the hall and settled myself again on the chaise longue. I felt decidedly resentful about that: he didn't need night care at all, and I had anticipated an undisturbed rest in the cool bedroom next door.

But after more years of nursing than I care to acknowledge I have grown accustomed to the whims of my patients. I made myself as comfortable as might be among the chintz-covered pillows. I had turned out all the lights in the bedroom and the adjoining bathroom, my patient appeared to be sound asleep, and the house, quiet all day, had sunk into a heavier, more poignant silence. Almost, I thought drowsily to myself, as if it were holding its breath.

The balcony window was open, and I could hear the soft sound of the falling rain, and the sweet fragrance of the roses filled the room. Through the misty darkness I could see the outline of the window, a long, faintly lighter rectangle. From some water spout rain dripped with soothing, dully beating monotony. An ideal night for sleep.

But I couldn't sleep.

I turned and twisted. I took off my cap, and the hairpins out of my hair, but the cushion under my head was just as hard. I was too cool and fumbled for and drew over my feet a soft eiderdown. I was too warm and tossed it off again. I was thirsty and tiptoed to the bathroom, turning on the faucet with care so as not to wake my patient, but the drink did not satisfy me. I tried counting sheep, I tried making my vision a blank. I tried thinking of the virtues of my family, as someone advised me to do as a cure for insomnia. The latter expedient was almost my undoing. My accumulating rage reached a small climax with the thought of my cousin's gift to me last Christmas—six pairs of gray woolen bed socks, knitted and inexpressibly spinsterish—and I found myself farther from sleep than ever. I became calmer, however, thinking of some of the more entertaining surgical operations at which I had assisted, and was pleasantly drifting off to sleep at last when a clock somewhere downstairs struck twelve in a deep muffled boom and roused me, and I stared at the window again and listened to the rain.

It was some time after that that I became gradually aware that the balcony window was no longer a perfect rectangle, faintly lighter than the room. I had not heard a sound, but there was certainly a blacker shadow in it.

I was sitting upright, leaning forward, straining my eyes and ears. It seemed to me the shadow moved and that I heard a faint sound. Someone was outside on the balcony, cautiously attempting to enter the room.

All Bayard's hints and outright statements swept with a rush back into my consciousness. Who was out there? Why was he trying to enter the room in so furtive a fashion?

My heart was pounding so furiously that I felt sure the thing at the window must hear it. The door to the hall was much farther from me than the window and was locked. If I screamed, would I succeed in rousing the sleeping house before I myself could be silenced? Was I to sit there as if frozen and let my patient be murdered? Was I——

There was another faint sound from the window, and then a pause, as if the intruder were listening again to be sure no one had discovered his presence. Through the breathless silence came the soft beating of the rain and the overpowering sweet scent of the rain-wet roses.

It was then that I knocked the lamp off the table.

I did not do it purposely. I was trying to get to my feet, fumbling blindly for support with my eyes fixed on the shadow at the window. The lamp went over with a dull crash on the thick rug and the bulb in it smashed and there was a sort of scrambling noise on the balcony. The shadow was gone.

"What's that? Nurse! Miss Keate! What's the matter?" It was my patient, of course.

"N-nothing," I said shakily. "Nothing."

"What was that noise?" His voice grew sharper as he grew wide awake. "Turn on the light. What was that noise?"

My trained instinct for protecting my patient's rest asserted itself.

"Nothing," I said more quietly. "I put out my hand and accidentally knocked the lamp off the table. The bulb in it broke. That's all."

"Oh," he said, and after a thoughtful moment repeated in a less doubtful way, "Oh."

And after all, how could I be certain it was anything else? It could so easily be some deceiving play of lights and shadows on the rain-drenched balcony. And windows have been known to creak before now.

It was then, however, that I made a mistake. Instead of going to the window, watching and listening for any sign of a retreating figure, I went to the bathroom, turned on a small light, and left the door into the bedroom ajar. My patient, drowsy with the opiate Dr. Bouligny had ordered for the night, had gone back to sleep at once, so the light did not disturb him, and I felt infinitely safer and more normal. I am not as a rule afraid of the night.

But it is not surprising that I still did not sleep, and I think it was around two o'clock that a second attempt was made to enter Bayard Thatcher's room. It came this time from inside the house, and I was first aware of it when I heard some faint sound of motion in the hall and then the barest click of the latch. The door was, of course, still locked, and I cannot describe my feelings when I sat there in the soft light watching that polished doorknob turn and twist. Finally I walked quietly to the door and bent my head to listen, and I'm sure I heard a kind of panting sound—like a dog on a hot day.

This time the desperate courage of extreme terror moved me. I clutched for the key and turned it in the lock, although I don't know what I intended to do. But my fingers shook and were clumsy, and the key stuck, and it was a long ten seconds before I managed to get the door open.

There was nothing there.

A dim night light burned in the empty hall. Its rows of closed doors and the shining stairs descending into blackness told me nothing. Or—no! Had not my eyes caught some motion there along the opposite wall? But there was nothing—— Ah, the mirror!

It hung at an angle opposite me so that it reflected to my point of vision the wall and doors on a line with my own door but toward the front of the house. And one of those doors was moving. Moving slowly and stealthily, but moving.

There was no light in the room beyond. But I was sure that in the narrowing black aperture there was a face, a pair of eyes. Someone watching me, witnessing my terror—some pair of eyes I could not see actually meeting mine in the mirror.

It was an extraordinarily terrifying moment. But the door closed finally, and remained closed, while I stood as if rooted to the spot. I have always felt it a distinct credit to my nerves that I retained the presence of mind to step into the hall, count, and find it was the second door from the windows.

Probably I would not have had that presence of mind if I had known that while my eyes had been riveted on the reflection of that closing door I was under observation from an entirely unsuspected quarter. Only when I turned from counting the doors

did I discover that a man had come silently from somewhere—
up the stairs, I supposed—and stood on the landing of the stairs
watching me with languid, half-closed eyes.

I very nearly screamed. I would have screamed had not my
throat been suddenly paralyzed. For a moment that seemed at
least ten we stood there, I with my hand on the door of my patient's room, ready to flee inside, and he clinging to the railing of
the stairs.

He was a young man, around thirty, with more than a faint
resemblance to Bayard Thatcher about his nose and forehead; his
chin, however, was undecided, his mouth pale and a little loose,
and his eyes heavy lidded and languid. Gradually my fear subsided. This must be the mysterious Dave Thatcher of whom they
had spoken—Janice's husband.

It was a strange encounter. Neither of us spoke; neither of
us seemed to breathe; it was exactly as if we were held by a spell
entirely without animation. He just stood there looking dreadfully pallid and weary and drained of life. When he started on
up the stairs he moved so languidly, with such a curious lack of
animation, that it did not break the spell at all. I retreated into
the bedroom and leaned against the door.

He was not drunk; I was sure of that. But he looked and
moved as if he were only half-conscious. It was as if his spirit
had gone and only his body moved about in a sort of catalepsy.
What was he doing wandering about in that condition in the
middle of the night when the rest of the house had sunk into
slumber hours ago?

It is perhaps not necessary to say that I got no sleep that
night. Dawn found me still sitting tensely on the edge of the
chaise longue, which I had pulled well out of the revealing path
of light from the bathroom, and my eyes simultaneously on the
door and the window—which, since they were directly opposite

each other, sounds a little involved but was very simple under the circumstances. About three the rain stopped, which was a relief: I was weary with trying to detect any sounds from the balcony through its gently muffling whisper.

By the time the sun came up I had decided two things: one, that Bayard Thatcher had very likely been the victim of a murderous attack and was like to be a completer victim; the other, that I would leave the case at once.

I did not leave the case; I have never left a case, though time was to come when I regretted bitterly that I had not taken to my heels at the first hint of anything unusual.

As the cool dawn crept softly into the room and the sun touched the tops of the elms I rose, flexed my cramped muscles, and went to turn off the bathroom light. As I returned, my patient moved his wounded arm, stirred, and muttered something. I approached the bed, thinking he had called me. He was still asleep. But as I bent over he said very distinctly:

"Damn you, Allen Carick," and then added with difficulty, "Nita's—grave."

I'm sure that's what he said; I've gone over and over it in my mind since then. It's true he spoke as if it was only after a struggle that he got the words out, but it's always that way when people talk in their sleep, and, as I say, the words were very distinct.

Then the words died in a mumble, he stirred again, opened his eyes, and looked at me with a perplexity that was tinged with alarm.

"What—who on earth——" His face cleared. "Oh, you're the nurse, of course. You look like a Valkyrie with your hair streaming about like that. You gave me a sort of shock. I've—been dreaming."

"What were you dreaming?" I moved to get my cap and hairpins.

"Dreaming? Oh, some absurdity. Rained last night, didn't it?"

"Yes. It rained."

At the mirror I put up my hair and pinned on my white cap. Then I went to the balcony window. The rain-drenched garden looked clean and bright and gay, as if it had just had its face washed and liked it; here and there I caught the bright sparkle of drops of rain glittering on the tender green foliage. The lawn was vividly green, a fat robin was digging happily for worms, and somewhere in the trees a blue jay, in an unwontedly tender mood, tinkled its light descending scale of little bells.

Already my night terror was becoming dream-like and uncertain. Uncertain. I glanced at the balcony. The steamer chair had been folded up against the wall. And there were two more inescapable proofs that the watcher on the balcony had been real and material and no fancy of my own imagination. One was a small irregular blotch of mud: it looked as if it might have been a footprint, but was not at all distinct in outline. But the day before, the balcony floor had been spotlessly clean.

The other was a damp white envelope which lay as it seemed to have fallen directly under the slightly projecting window ledge.

Later the thing which was most to interest me was the fact that the steamer chair had been carefully folded up and leaned against the wall. I had left it with its bright canvas exposed, and no one had gone to the balcony from the room since then. As everyone knows, a steamer chair is an extremely awkward thing to fold and is annoyingly whimsical and confusing in its contortions. No ordinary prowler or thief would take the trouble to fold it up and protect it from the rain.

But at the moment I bent and picked up the envelope.

There was no address on it, and it was not sealed. I opened it.

CHAPTER III

"What's that?" asked Bayard sharply. "What's that?"

I had already removed the paper inside the envelope. It was an ordinary piece of writing paper, folded and slipped into the envelope. But the strange thing about it was that it was entirely blank; I might have had some glimmer of understanding if there had been writing on it, but as it was I was entirely baffled.

"Give that to me," ordered Bayard Thatcher curtly. "That's meant for me. What do you mean, opening and reading it?"

"It is not addressed to you or anyone else," I said with spirit. "Here it is. And it's merely a blank piece of paper."

He took it eagerly, examined it with one sharp glance, and then looked angrily at me.

"There was something inside it. You took it."

"I did no such thing!"

Possibly my righteous indignation convinced him; at any rate, he merely frowned at the paper. Then suddenly he smiled, as if he had arrived at some explanation of it.

"Toss it into the waste basket, Miss Keate," he said. "It's only a record of another attempt to best me." And he lay there smiling at the pineapple bedpost. It was just then, I believe, that a thought crossed my mind to the effect that whoever was so determined to expedite Bayard Thatcher's final exit might possibly have a good and sufficient reason for so doing. There was no getting around the fact that there was an occasional look in his yellow-gray eyes that sent a kind of crinkle up my spine. And while a man in fear for his life may be a little nervous, I did not like the way in which he spoke to me.

However, duty is duty.

"See here, Mr. Thatcher," I began. "I've come to the conclusion that you may be right in—what you told me yesterday. Early in the morning. You said, you know, that someone in the house was trying to murder you."

"Not in the house, Miss Keate," he interjected. "I said 'someone in the family,' didn't I? At least, that's what I meant to say."

"Someone in the family, then," I amended. "Though I can't believe it, really. Still—well, if there's any chance of that being the truth of the matter, I think we can take steps to prevent it happening again."

"You can take it for granted that I didn't shoot myself, Miss Keate," he said dryly. "Now, then, why have you changed your mind? What scared you during the night?"

I told him briefly, suppressing my encounter with Dave Thatcher—or at least, with the man I thought to be Dave Thatcher—and leaving out my terror. Thus reduced it was merely a matter of someone having been on the balcony and the doorknob turning and a bedroom door closing. He listened seriously enough, but was not, so far as I could see, particularly frightened.

"And what steps do you suggest taking?" he asked when I had finished.

"Why—tell your family. Tell the doctor. Call the police."

"My family?" he said mockingly. "But they already know it. And the doctor knows it. And there are no police in C——; there's the county sheriff, though. And I believe a constable who got the job when his livery stable passed out. The county sheriff built his house with money borrowed from Hilary's bank."

"A detective from the city."

He laughed at that and did not even reply.

"Well," I said, rather nettled, "if you insist on getting yourself shot, I can't help it. But why don't you leave? I can help you on the train, and you'll be perfectly able to be up and around today if you like. The wound is doing very well, and you aren't exactly helpless."

"No," he said shortly. "No. I can't leave now. But understand this, Miss Keate: it isn't pleasant to know that somebody's out gunning for me. But I happen to have the upper hand. And threats don't mean much. So forget all this, will you? I must have been half out of my head with the stuff the doctor gave me to talk so much. Are you going to stay on the job?"

"I've never yet left a patient," I said with spirit. "But if there's real danger, I think you're a fool to stay on."

"Spoken with decision," he remarked, coldly amused. "Don't be alarmed. I shan't need you more than a day or two."

Later I recalled that I happened to look at my watch as I turned away from him. It was exactly ten minutes after four.

He lapsed again into silence, and I managed to doze a little, waking in time to help him into a dressing gown and slippers and hold the mirror while he shaved with one hand, preparatory to going downstairs to breakfast.

"After all," he said as I remonstrated, fearing the exertion would send his temperature up, "after all, it is my shoulder that's wounded. Not my legs. And I don't expect to turn handsprings down the stairs."

Janice and Adela were already at the table when we arrived at the door of the stately dining room, and Adela started up with a little cry.

"Why, Bayard! I didn't expect you down this morning! Are you sure you are strong enough? Is he strong enough for this, Miss Keate? Florrie, set a place for Mr. Bayard. Sit here, Bayard."

And Janice said, more coolly:

"Good-morning, Bayard. You must be recuperating rapidly."

It was odd, that breakfast, with both women scrupulously polite to Bayard and talking blandly of gardens.

"The gladioluses are doing well."

"It was a good plan to put snapdragons with them. Shall I tell Higby to clip the privet hedge this morning?"

"Yes. Yes, you might."

Not a word of Dave, who again failed to appear. No more of Bayard's wound, although once, when I leaned over to butter his roll, I caught a bleak look in Adela's eyes, and her face was all at once hard as if it had been touched with granite. But she said, prolonging the accented syllables in the curious way she had, which seemed affected and consciously elegant:

"Is there anything you'd especially like, Bayard? I'll tell Emmeline to make some caramel custard. You always like that. Florrie, ask Emmeline to come here, please."

It was her only concession to his invalidism.

It just happened that Emmeline stood directly behind Bayard's chair while Adela made her request for the caramel custard.

"Baked or boiled, ma'am?" she asked harshly, her eyes on the top of Bayard's head, and her hands clutching themselves in such a particularly hungry way that for a startled instant I was in some doubt as to whether she meant the custard.

"Baked," said Adela. "That's all, Emmeline."

Apparently the household followed its normal routine after that; Janice in the garden, Florrie polishing the slender old red mahogany, the upholstery of which had faded to a soft rose beige, Dave not to be seen, the clip of Higby's pruning scissors sounding through the opened windows of the library where my patient had retired, and Adela's voice coming from the telephone in her pleasant little morning room—giving precise grocery orders and running to earth a scandal anent some bottles of cod-liver oil missing from the last hospital bundle of the Benevolent Aid Society. They had, it developed, been diverted by a Mrs. Whiting.

Lunch time came and passed. I remember thinking that Janice might have got overtired working in the sultry heat of the garden, for there wasn't a speck of color in her face; her eyes were rather hollow, with faint black marks under them, and there were soft, moist little curls about her temples.

"I'm going to the farm for butter and eggs this afternoon," she said rather lifelessly. "Shall I get some buttermilk, Adela?"

"Why, yes," said Adela. "Yes, you might. Two quarts. When are you going?"

"About two-thirty, I imagine. I'm going to stop at the garage to get a tire mended, and it's a good half hour's run out to the farm."

"You won't be back in time for the Benevolent Society meeting?"

"No. But I'll stop and bring you home if you like."

"Do. You'll be along about four or four-thirty? You'd better not wait in the car but come right in. There's not much business to see to, but I might be delayed a little, and it's awfully warm after the rain."

It was just then that Dave came into the room.

For it was Dave, that pallid, lifeless young man who had stood on the stair landing in the dead of night and stared at me. Not that there was the faintest cognizance of that encounter in his manner as, at Adela's few words, he nodded briefly at me and slipped into a chair.

"Nothing, Florrie," he said. "Nothing but coffee. Black, please."

"Headache, Dave?" asked my patient a bit too solicitously.

"Rather," said Dave, looking at his plate. He did look ill, pale and tired, with heavy eyelids. On seeing the two men facing each other, I realized that their resemblance was largely a family matter of bone structure and coloring. Dave's face was flabbier than his cousin's, more passive, less hard. His mouth was not thin and predatory, it was indecisive and faintly sullen. He continued: "I promised Allen to go fishing with him this afternoon, and I suppose he'll be along soon."

"Fish aren't biting today," said Bayard. "Too hot."

"They always bite in Thatcher Lake," said Janice. I don't know why I felt that both she and Adela had not expected Dave to appear and that for some reason his presence violently disturbed them. Perhaps it was in the eagerness with which they clutched at conversational openings. "That lake is full of fish. They all but jump at you."

"Here is your coffee, dear," said Adela anxiously. "I don't think you ought to go today. It will be frightfully hot and close there around the lake. It won't do your head any good."

"Nothing will," said Dave.

"So you're going with Allen," said Bayard. He was looking at Janice instead of Dave, whom he apparently addressed. His face wore that sardonic look I was beginning to know. "Well—don't fall in."

Janice's dark eyes dropped, and there was for an instant a kind of pinched look about her mouth. Dave said without much interest:

"Oh, I can swim. Anyway, I shouldn't think it would worry you, Bayard."

"Naturally not," Bayard was beginning, when Adela definitely and firmly interrupted.

"Janice, before you go will you be sure to tell Higby to mow the west lawn this afternoon. Emmeline will be out in the summer kitchen making jelly, and she can keep an eye on him. He's apt to loiter, these warm days, if he isn't watched. You'd better eat some lunch, Dave, if you're going to the lake this afternoon. Allen will be along pretty soon, I imagine. Don't let me forget to ask if Evelyn heard from the boys today. My two nephews," she said to me. "My brother Hilary's sons. Splendid boys—really fine boys. Both away at school now. At some sort of camp. But they are coming home soon for summer holidays. I'm sure they'll enjoy the lake, Dave. Hilary said, by the way, he had bought that old sport roadster of Frank Whiting's for them to use. I was against it; but if they just manage not to break their necks they'll enjoy it, I suppose. Coffee, Miss Keate? Florrie, coffee for Miss Keate, please."

All so bland, all so carefully elegant—curious that her hands, blunt and white below their snowy organdy ruffles, shook a little, and she moved a piece of flat silver beside her plate in a constant pattern. But I daresay she could have kept up that gentle little patter indefinitely while Bayard sat there sipping iced tea and looking at the slice of lemon floating in it and then at Janice with an impenetrable expression in his yellow-gray eyes, and Janice, white as the cloth, avoiding Bayard's eyes and trying to help.

Fortunately lunch was soon over, and shortly after Allen Carick, driving a battered old roadster which I judged to be the one recently purchased for the boys, arrived and presently left again with Dave beside him. Dave's hat was pulled low over his eyes to avoid the glare of the sun, although Allen had no hat at all, his lean brown face exposed as if he liked it, and his sun-bleached hair shining.

At the last moment the dog (whose name, by the way, was Pansy) decided to go along, and waddled fatly down the drive in their wake, her long ears flopping and her tongue lolling, and had to be called back and forcibly restrained by Janice. She was, it seemed, a creature of temperament—the dog, I mean—and as I helped my patient upstairs to his own room for a rest, I could hear her yapping angrily from the library, where Janice had incarcerated her, and scratching pettishly at the closed door in a way which, in a creature less favored, would have brought instant reproof from Adela. I think she relaxed her housekeeping vigilance only for Pansy. And, possibly, for Dave.

"And now," said Bayard Thatcher, when he was once more lying rather wearily on the bed in his own room, "I'm going to take a nap, and I want to be alone."

"But I don't like to leave you," I protested. "It doesn't seem quite—" I hesitated, thinking of the peaceful household, but said—"quite safe."

He laughed.

"Entirely safe, I assure you. Look here. At the east edge of the lawn—you can see it from the window there—is a sort of arbor with some very comfortable chairs. Chairs you can stretch out and sleep in. It's cool, shady, and quiet. Why don't you go down there and get fresh air and rest at the same time?"

Afterward I wondered a little at his solicitude. Even at the time something said faintly in the back of my mind: Is he trying to get you out of the house? Why? But the suggestion was extremely attractive.

"If you are sure——"

"Perfectly sure. Run along, Miss Keate."

Well, I took a book from my bag just in case I couldn't actually sleep, and went, although as a rule I suspect arbors, which are apt to be rather dank places with vines that are too heavy and unexpected spiders dropping on one's head and worms promenading over one's ankles. But this one proved to be merely a shaded place on the lawn's edge, open and pleasant, with gayly cushioned chairs and an unobstructed view of the whole front and east side of the house.

I settled myself drowsily and yielded to the dreamy mood induced by staring lazily across a sun-drenched lawn, listening with half an ear to the sound of the birds and the soothing whir of a lawnmower somewhere out of sight, and digesting an excellent lunch. After all, my terrors of the night might have been mostly imaginative; nothing sinister or dreadful could possibly take place in that tranquil household on that tranquil summer afternoon.

About two-thirty I saw Florrie emerge from the corner back of the house, dressed no doubt in her best for her afternoon out. She walked rapidly down a side path and disappeared toward town. It was very quiet and very warm, with the scent of the flowers in the sun and the mown grass mingling with a faint odor of boiling grapejuice which drifted around the house from the summer kitchen—which, by the way, was built out from the house, entirely separated from it, with a laundry in one end.

I was almost asleep when the front door banged. It was Janice, crisp and dainty in white, with a small white hat over her dark hair. She carried an enormous brown wicker basket over each arm, stopped among the flowers to fill one of the baskets with roses and tall blue Delphiniums, and then walked briskly to the garage. Presently she backed out a small coupé with the most expert precision, turned and drove down the drive and away, the flowers nodding in the seat beside her.

With Janice's departure silence came again, a drowsy, warm silence which was only broken about a quarter of an hour later when the front door banged again. This time it was the dog Pansy, who'd apparently managed to release herself from the library and was bolting across the lawn and into the shrubbery. I was faintly amused to note that she had all the earmarks of a dog who's been recently punished: her tail tucked in, her ears hugging her head, her legs making their best speed. She looked, in fact, as if she'd been kicked, which was absurd, for only Adela and my patient were in the house, and my patient was resting in his own room.

And a few minutes later Adela herself came out on the porch, closing the screened door gently behind her and putting up her parasol before she ventured from the shady porch into the heat of the sun. Idly I watched her dignified progress along the turf path to the road and the sidewalk to town. She looked cool and pleasant in her favorite lavender dotted-swiss, with soft frills about the throat and wrists and her eyeglasses dangling on a ribbon.

It was exactly three o'clock when she turned onto the sidewalk leading to town, and the serenity of complete silence, save for the soft whir of the lawnmower, again lay all about me. The peal of the telephone, which rang about fifteen minutes after Adela left, seemed particularly loud and sharp and demanding against the drowsy stillness. The windows of the house were open, of course, and the sound of the telephone so shrill and imperious that I started to my feet. However, it broke off abruptly in the middle of one of its peals and did not ring again, so I relaxed against my pillows once more. The thought did cross my mind that my patient must have answered it, for Emmeline was deaf, and out in the summer kitchen besides, but if Bayard was up and wandering about the house it couldn't hurt him, and I was too listless to care.

Afterward they asked me if I had slept, even for a few moments, during that quiet sunny afternoon, but I knew I hadn't. I lay there quiet, soaking in the peace and tranquillity that enfolded me, looking lazily at that gracious old house. But I did not sleep. I'm sure of that and always was. It does seem curious that I didn't, when I was so tired from a wakeful night: it's possible that some inner restlessness, some hidden foreboding kept me a little uneasy. But if so it was an entirely unacknowledged premonition. I am a reasonable woman, and my reason told me that the house was quiet and empty save for my sleeping patient. Emmeline was making grape jelly in the summer kitchen, and Higby mowing the lawn steadily around on the west lawn, and all was well.

At four o'clock—I know it was then, for I glanced at my watch and marveled how fast the afternoon was flying—Hilary turned in from the street and walked quickly along the turf path to the house. He looked hot and rather flushed from his walk, and as he stepped up on the porch he took off his hat, passed his handkerchief over his head, and without pausing to ring, opened the door and disappeared in the cool depths of the house. Ten minutes later he emerged, settled his hat on his head, and walked briskly away. I remember thinking that if he'd come to see my patient their interview must have been brief and calm, for there was not, so far as I could see, a shadow of agitation about Hilary's complacent pink face.

He had no more than gone, however, when, coming from the opposite direction in which he had disappeared, the yellow roadster turned smoothly into the drive and stopped at the side of the house. It was Evelyn again at the wheel. She did not see me, but walked directly across the lawn to the porch, her tall figure graceful and handsome in her light summer frock, and her smooth gold head bare. She went at once into the house but emerged in only a moment or two, got into the roadster, and backed with some of Janice's expert exactness out of the drive. I did notice that, once in the road, she drove toward town instead of going in the direction from which she'd come.

Those were the only interruptions during that long, lazy afternoon. After Evelyn's departure the place sank again into its somnolent silence, with Higby's lawnmower still going smoothly and methodically, if a trifle languidly, and the smell of boiling grapejuice growing stronger and more pungent. Once I whistled for the dog, but she seemed to have gone to sleep in some thicket and did not appear.

The shadows were beginning to slant long on the greens of the lawn, and I was thinking of rousing myself and returning to duty when the coupé swung again into the drive, and Janice and Adela got out. Janice carried her two wicker baskets, heavy now, directly into the house, but Adela lingered along the garden, saw me, and approached.

"Did you have a good rest?" she asked pleasantly.

"Very nice indeed. It's been such a lazy, pleasant afternoon."

"I like it under the trees, here. Our home is quite nice in the summer, I think. How good Emmeline's jelly smells! We must have some of it at dinner. Somehow, it always tastes better when it's just made. No, no, don't trouble to come in now. It's a long time till dinner, and I'm sure a nurse needs all the rest she can get."

I watched her walk quietly across the lawn. She had almost reached the step when a scream arose within the house. It rose short and sharp, stabbing the peace like a thin knife. It was followed swiftly by other screams—all of them high and jerky and sharp.

The door flew open. Emmeline ran out, still screaming. Her white apron was dabbled with purple stains. Her arms were bare to the elbow, and she lifted purple hands and waved them jerkily.

"Help!" she screamed. "Murder!"

Adela stopped dead still, as if she'd been struck. The whir of the lawnmower stopped. Every bird hushed, and in the shocked silence the woman shrieked again:

"Murder! Murder! He's shot all to pieces!"

CHAPTER IV

IT WAS BAYARD. WE found him in the library. We stopped our headlong rush at the door. He was lying on the floor near the table. He was on his face, his neck twisted so queerly that you knew at once he was dead. I knew the dressing gown and his hair.

Adela, a granite woman with a gray-white face, walked across the rug, knelt, and turned him over. His face was untouched, his mouth open a little, a lock of hair across his forehead, his yellow eyes closed, his arrogant nose sharper. I knew that there was nothing I could do.

Things wavered and seemed to rock about me. But I was aware that Janice was standing beside me, her fingers digging into my arm, her whole body quivering. And that Higby was in the doorway staring with bulging eyes. And that Adela was trying to speak to me.

"Call Dr. Bouligny," she gasped through blue lips. "Call him. There's a telephone there. In Dave's study." Her eyes were two blank blue stones set in a granite face. I saw them change, lose their blankness, and become aware.

"No, no," she said with a sort of gasp. "I'll telephone. Help me, Emmeline."

Emmeline bent stiffly and laid Bayard back on the rug, and

Adela got clumsily to her feet, as if her muscles were drugged. I followed her, for she looked very near collapse. I reached the door in the end of the long library in time to hear her gasp into the telephone:

"Dr. Bouligny. Yes. Dr. Bouligny. Call him—hurry."

There was a pause. Adela clutched the telephone and looked with unseeing blue eyes out of the window. The room was small, furnished simply with a desk, some chairs, a leather-covered lounge, and a good rug. On the rug at Adela's feet lay a small white something. I suppose I bent, and picked it up, and looked at it merely to give myself something to do. It had looked rather like a tightly folded note, but as I got it into my fingers I found it was only a piece of newspaper wadded up tightly as if to make a sort of wedge.

"Daniel—Daniel, is it you? Yes, yes. Come at once. It's Bayard. He's—been shot. Killed. Hurry, Daniel." I could hear the click of the other telephone. It was quite distinct, and I knew Dr. Bouligny had rung off, but Adela continued: "Burglars. There were burglars," before she put down the telephone.

"Now Hilary," she said in a dazed way. "Now I must call Hilary. No, no—Daniel will stop for him—Hilary must know——"

"Adela." Janice was standing in the doorway, her face strained and tight, without beauty or life. "*Where is Dave?*"

Adela didn't drop into a chair, but she leaned slowly against the desk.

"I don't know. I don't know. Janice, Janice, *what will people say?*"

"But they were fishing. Dave and Allen. Where are they now? Where's Dave?"

Adela made a visible and pathetic effort to pull herself together. That was one of the two occasions when I saw her falter.

Her face was still like gray chalk, but somehow she managed to assume that impenetrable cloak of dignity.

"They are probably still fishing. They'll be back together soon. I must call Hilary. I'm convinced—" and how bravely she said it through her blue lips—"I'm convinced it was burglary."

"Burglary! Why, Adela—do you suppose—I never thought——" Janice's tight face became momentarily animated. "Could it be that?"

"I'm convinced it was burglary. Bayard came upon the burglar and was shot. You read of that happening every day in the papers. That's what happened. The safe's just back of you, Janice. Isn't it open?"

"Why, no—no, it's closed."

"But it must have been burglary. I'll open it. First I'll call Hilary."

There were voices in the library. Janice turned.

"Here is Hilary now. With Dr. Bouligny."

Dr. Bouligny was kneeling. Hilary was at his side looking down, his plump face the color of ashes. In the doorway stood Evelyn, dreadfully pale under her tan. Higby had vanished, but Emmeline remained, twisting her purple hands and watching Dr. Bouligny's mouth.

"Hilary——" said Adela.

"Good God, Adela, this is a terrible thing! How did it happen? Who did it? Who found him? Where is Dave?"

"Dave is fishing with Allen Carick. They aren't back yet. Is there nothing you can do, Daniel?"

Dr. Bouligny got heavily to his feet. He was a fattish, dark man with a good-natured red face and clothes that always bagged. His face now looked mottled.

"There's nothing to be done. He's dead. Who did it?"

"How long has he been dead?" asked Hilary sharply.

"I don't know. I can't tell exactly." The doctor paused thoughtfully and added: "You see, it's so hot this afternoon."

"Oh," gasped Evelyn. She sank into a chair as if her knees refused to hold her and said in a small muffled voice: "*What will people say?*"

Dr. Bouligny glanced quickly at Hilary and then at Adela.

"It's pretty bad. But I was afraid of this——"

"It's a plain case of suicide," interrupted Hilary quickly. His authoritative, slightly pompous manner was returning. "It's a plain case of suicide, and no one can prove it isn't."

"Suicide?" said Dr. Bouligny doubtfully, his large head tipped a little to one side as he studied the tragic huddle at his feet. "Well——"

Evelyn rose suddenly, snatched a scarf from a divan, and laid it swiftly and carefully over Bayard.

"You ought to move him. It isn't decent to just leave him there. Like that. On the floor. After all—it's Bayard."

"Wait. No. We'll have to let the sheriff see him, too, just as we found him," said Dr. Bouligny.

"The sheriff will say suicide," said Hilary confidently. "And you are coroner, Dan."

Dr. Bouligny looked worried.

"I don't like this scandal any more than you, Hilary. It won't hurt me as much, of course—but it's pretty bad for you, everyone knowing there's been bad blood between you and Bayard. Oh, I know—I know—" as Hilary started to protest—"I know you didn't shoot him, but what will people say, do you think? I'll do everything I can to smooth it over—hush it up. But if it's suicide, where's the gun?"

"It's here," said Hilary. "It's here. It's—why, it must be here!"

We were all looking vaguely about on the floor, the tables,

all around the body. I cast my mind back to my first view of the body. There had been no gun close to it, then; I was sure of that.

"But it isn't suicide," said Adela. "It's burglary. It must have been burglary. There's—wait, let me look in the safe. The diamonds are there, you know, Hilary."

We followed her into the small study. The safe, an old-fashioned affair, massive and clumsy, was set in the wall but with no attempt at concealing its dials. We watched her hands fumbling, turning, twisting. And when the heavy door swung outward we watched her search.

And the diamonds *were* gone. Only a stack of empty boxes remained, their yellowed satin linings exposed and gaping as Adela's swift hands opened them one after the other.

"I knew it," she said. "I knew it. See, they're gone. It was burglary. The thief was here, robbing the safe, Bayard heard him and interfered, and the thief shot Bayard and escaped." She was dignified, deliberate. She reached out a hand and touched a red morocco case. "That," she said, "held my mother's sunburst."

It was strange to watch the faces slowly lose their look of terrified apprehension, become slowly more composed; only Janice's face remained cold and rigid. Dr. Bouligny's eyes met Hilary's, and he nodded slowly.

"There you are," he said in a relieved way. "It's happened exactly as Adela says. Everybody's heard of the Thatcher diamonds. And nobody in the county would believe that Bayard Thatcher shot himself."

"But, my God," said Hilary, suddenly bewildered and alarmed again, "the diamonds! It's the family collection. They're worth a small fortune. We've got to get hold of them."

"That's the sheriff's job," said Dr. Bouligny, almost blithely, and at the same moment Adela, her eyes cold and blank, looked strangely at Hilary.

"Don't you think it's worth the price?" she said, coldly.

Hilary looked at her, at Dr. Bouligny, at his wife. He got out a handkerchief, wiped his pale face and said:

"You'll fix things up then, Dan?"

"I'll do what I can with honesty," said Dr. Bouligny. "No more. And there's the sheriff, you know."

"I can fix him," said Hilary easily.

"And there'll have to be an inquest, of course."

After a moment Adela said with difficulty: "*An—inquest!*"

"Why, yes, of course. A violent death. Murder. There's got to be an inquest."

There was another long moment of silence in the little study. The window was closed, and we could not hear a sound from the outside world, and it was as if no one lived or breathed in the small room. And yet that stillness was oddly palpitant, as if unspoken words, unuttered apprehensions, unwelcome thoughts were beating upon our ears. Then Adela stirred, reached out her hand, and closed the gaping door of the safe. It made a heavy, silence-shattering clang.

"An inquest," she repeated. "And what, Daniel, will you ask us at the inquest?"

He ran his fingers worriedly through his thick dark hair.

"It won't be easy," he said unhappily. "There'll be plenty of people just looking for a chance to get at us. To say there's something fishy about it."

Warm though the room was, I saw Adela shiver slightly, and Hilary's plump face all at once looked drawn and haggard.

"Suppose," said Adela, "suppose we go back to the library and talk it over . . . before the sheriff comes." The last words were separated from the rest of her speech in a way which gave them significance.

I followed them back into the large, cool library; I remember feeling as if I were moving about in a nightmare and would presently come to my senses. Everything in the nightmare was, however, extremely clear and vivid. The windows in the long library were open; the shadows on the green lawn were long now and cool looking. It was with a shock that my eyes went to that huddle under the scarf.

"Now, then, Daniel," said Adela. "What will you ask us?"

"Don't put it like that, Adela," he said worriedly. "You make me feel like a conspirator."

Adela's eyebrows slid upward rebukingly. There was a suggestion of outrage in her stiff, desperate dignity.

"My dear Daniel," she said in a remonstrating way.

"He'll want to know when Bayard was last seen alive and who saw him," said Hilary. He rubbed his handkerchief again over his forehead and touched his mouth with it.

"Very well. Janice, you left the house before I did this afternoon, didn't you?"

Janice nodded; her face was still cold and rigid; there was not a trace of beauty in it then, it was a regular, colorless mask.

"Janice, you see, drove out to the farm this afternoon. Dave and Allen Carick went fishing. They aren't back yet. I went to the Benevolent Society, and Janice stopped on her way back and brought me home. Emmeline was in the summer kitchen making jelly. Higby was mowing the lawn. There was no one but Bayard here all afternoon. Bayard and—the thief."

"No. Wait a minute, Adela," protested Hilary miserably. "You are wrong. I was here. About four o'clock."

Adela turned slowly and very stiffly.

"*You! You* were here! You saw Bayard?"

Hilary glanced at his wife, started to speak, but she interrupted him.

"Yes, Hilary was here," said Evelyn directly. "He came in to see how Bayard was getting on. And I was here, too. I was to stop for Hilary in the roadster. Hilary had gone when I arrived, and I left at once and went to Hilary's office."

"Then you——" began Adela in a frozen way.

Dr. Bouligny interrupted.

"Then Bayard was alive then? What time was that?"

"Yes," said Evelyn, and Hilary said: "About four o'clock."

"That limits it, then," said Dr. Bouligny agitatedly. "That limits it. What time did you leave the house, Evelyn?"

"It must have been about twenty minutes after four. I was to meet Hilary at four here. I was a little delayed, and he'd gone. I didn't stay at all, and when I reached his office it was exactly four-thirty by the post-office clock."

"And about what time was it when he was found dead?"

"We'd just returned," said Adela, "Janice and I. Emmeline found him. She met me there on the step of the porch saying——" her voice left her and she finished in an unexpected whisper which was inexpressibly shocking—"saying he—was—shot!"

"Then he was killed sometime after four-twenty. It was after five when you called me—about a quarter after. I take it you telephoned at once? Yes. Where's Emmeline? See here, how did you happen to discover——"

Emmeline advanced, her black back stiff, her stained fingers working.

"Are you talking to me?"

"Yes. About finding Bayard."

"She's deaf, you know, Daniel," reminded Adela.

"Oh, God, yes." Dr. Bouligny rubbed his hands frenziedly over his hair. "About Bayard," he shouted. "When did you find him?"

"What did you say?" asked Emmeline, watching his heavy mouth.

"I said when did you——"

Adela looked troubled. I suppose it did not seem fitting—the doctor shouting in that hushed room above the dead body. It was indecorous. She said gently:

"Let me ask her, Daniel. She understands me. Emmeline, how did you happen to find him? Tell us about it."

"I'd been in the summer kitchen all afternoon," said the woman. "I'd been making grape jelly. I wasn't sure the last batch was ready to jell, and I brought some in on a silver spoon to see what you thought. I knew you'd be back from the Benevolent Society by that time. I looked in here as I went past, and I saw him and looked. There he was—all shot to pieces. I ran out on the porch. And there you were. See, I dropped the spoon there."

I suppose all of us looked at the slender silver spoon on the floor near the table, upside down with a little sticky pool of purple under it.

"Did you see anybody during the afternoon? Did anybody enter the house by the back way?"

"Nary a soul all afternoon. Nobody but Higby was near all afternoon."

"Then the thief didn't come that way," said Hilary. "Emmeline's got eyes like a cat. She never misses anything."

"What time was it, Emmeline?" asked Adela, and as Emmeline hesitated she repeated, "Time—what time was it?"

"Just after five. I had just looked at the clock and thought that Florrie ought to be getting back to help with dinner. She knew I was busy with jelly," added Emmeline resentfully.

"Oh, yes," said Adela to Dr. Bouligny. "I forgot Florrie. But it's her afternoon out."

"Can't you tell exactly what time he died, Dan?" asked Hilary. "I thought you doctors could come pretty close to it in such cases."

"Not as close as that," said Dr. Bouligny with honesty. "We can tell within a few hours. But today I only know that he's not been dead more than a few hours at most, and I can't limit the time by the condition of the body. The heat, you see, has kept the body at near its normal heat and has prevented——"

"*Hush, Daniel!*" It was Adela. "Don't ask such things, Hilary. It's enough if Daniel says so, without going further into the matter. Daniel knows. Now, what else is apt to be covered at the inquest? You know where we all were. What we were doing. Who found the body. The thief must have shot Bayard with—with his own revolver and fled. It's all perfectly clear. We all know exactly what happened. There's only the family here, and Emmeline, who is one of us. We all know why it is——" She stopped abruptly. She was looking at me as if she'd forgotten my existence until that very moment.

Everyone was looking at me.

It was very still. Gradually I became aware of the meaning back of that combined look. It was as if they, all of them, stood definitely opposed to me. It was a look of suspicion, of doubt, of apprehension—it was faintly inimical and tinged with defiance, and all these meanings were veiled in polite, cold stillness. I was the outsider. I was the stranger within the walls. Did I threaten them?

The silence was vastly uncomfortable. I said:

"I was about to say, Miss Thatcher, that since my patient—no longer needs me, I shall return at once to the hospital. Is there anything you want me to do before I leave, Dr. Bouligny?"

"Eh? Oh—no. No. Nothing. Nothing at all."

"Very well, then. I'll go at once."

"Oh, yes. Yes, of course. Yes, certainly, Miss Keate. Miss Thatcher will mail you your check."

"No. Wait, please, Miss Keate," said Adela suddenly. "Won't you stay on with me a few days? This—has been a great shock to me. I should be so grateful for your help. We have liked you very much, haven't we, Janice?—Evelyn? It will be a great favor, really, if you find you can stay with me for a few days. There will be so much to see to—such a strain—I am not in the best of health. Daniel——"

"Certainly, Adela. By all means." Dr. Bouligny answered the half command, half appeal, in her voice very promptly. "Certainly. Miss Thatcher is not at all well, Miss Keate. She will need someone like you for a few days. It would be so much better to have you who already—er—know the circumstances. That is—well, won't you stay on?"

In the end I consented, of course, though I did so reluctantly. I felt, too, somewhat vague as to my prospective duties. Only one thing was clear to me and that was that they wanted me there. In the house.

And I did not dream how desperately I was to regret that decision.

"Now then, Hilary," said Dr. Bouligny. "You'd better call the sheriff. It's been almost an hour since——"

"Sheriff! What's wrong? What's that about the sheriff? What——" Allen Carick came rapidly in from the hall. Tall, lean, brown, his shirt sleeves rolled up, his collar open, his bright hair wavy and wet as if he'd been swimming, his dark blue eyes remarkably like Evelyn's as he looked swiftly around the group. Dave Thatcher followed him closely, and it was Dave who first saw the huddle under the scarf and lunged forward with an incoherent cry and jerked the scarf back before Hilary could stop him.

For a moment he stood there looking; his face became ghastly pale, the hand with which he held the scarf began to tremble. Then he let it fall and dropped into a chair and covered his face with his hands.

He said nothing, but Adela was at his side at once, touching him, talking to him, sending Emmeline for wine, and Hilary was beside him too, telling him over and over that there'd been a robbery, and the burglar had shot Bayard, repeating his words as if to impress them indelibly upon Dave's consciousness. From the study I could hear the doctor's heavy voice telephoning and was subconsciously aware he was calling the sheriff. During the little hubbub I happened to be standing quite near Janice, and I remember Allen Carick stood there, too, and he said in a low voice: "Is that true? Is that what happened?" And I saw the helpless way she turned to him and heard her reply: "I don't know. I don't know. Allen, what should I do?"

"Don't worry. Don't worry," he said, something in his eyes as he looked down at her which I was to remember later. "Dave was fishing with me, remember."

Evelyn touched him on the arm. Her competent brown hand rested there as she spoke.

"The sheriff will be along presently, Janice. I think we ought to get Adela to her room. She can't stand much more of this. Dr. Dan had better call Frank Whiting and have him take care of the body; he'll conduct the funeral, I suppose. I'll tell Emmeline to go ahead with dinner. After all, we have to eat."

"Evelyn," said Hilary from the group by the table, "Dan wants to know if you talked to Bayard when you stopped this afternoon."

I think only I saw that firm brown hand tighten slowly on Allen's arm. Perhaps he felt it.

"No," said Evelyn steadily. "I didn't talk to him. He didn't see me. I just looked into the library, saw Hilary wasn't with him, and left."

"Was Bayard alone, Evelyn?" asked Dr. Bouligny.

"Yes."

"I don't understand how——" Dr. Bouligny interrupted himself and said, "Where were you all this time, Miss Keate?"

"On the lawn." I could not resist adding, "In full view of the house."

"Did you see anyone enter the house?"

"Only Mr. Thatcher and Mrs. Thatcher. No one else. If there was a thief, I didn't see him, and I could see all the front and east side of the house."

Dr. Bouligny was looking thoughtfully at me.

"But—why, you must have heard the shot, Miss Keate. All the windows were open, and it was a quiet afternoon."

"No," I said slowly, "I heard nothing." I had not thought of the fact until his question, and it was with some perplexity that I considered it for a moment while they waited. Even Dave dropped his hands to hear the better what I was going to say. "No," I repeated honestly, "I did not hear the sound of the shot. I can't understand it. It was quiet this afternoon. I heard the front door bang, and from inside the house I heard the telephone ring. I think Bayard must have answered it, for no one else was in the house—I had left him upstairs in his own room, but——"

"He must have come down," interrupted Hilary. "I wonder who talked to him."

"Oh, I called him," said Miss Adela. "I stopped on my way to the Benevolent Society and telephoned from the drug store. I'd forgotten to tell Emmeline that there would be two extra for dinner—you and Evelyn, you know, Hilary—I knew Emmeline wouldn't hear the telephone, but I thought perhaps Miss Keate would reply. But Bayard was down here. He must have been near the telephone."

"I wonder what he was doing down here," said Hilary absently and was about to say more, I think, when there was a long peal at the door bell.

"That's the sheriff," said Dr. Bouligny. "Well, there's one thing. You've all got alibis."

"Why, no, not all," said Evelyn. "I don't seem to have, and I assure you I didn't——" She tried to say, "Shoot him," I suppose, but she looked at the huddle under the scarf and choked.

Allen put his arm around her protectingly, and Hilary cried, "Don't be a perfect idiot, Evelyn, we all know you didn't kill him," and Emmeline appeared at the doorway with the sheriff. Hilary and the doctor and the sheriff all began to talk at once, and Evelyn and Janice were urging Adela toward the door. It was a good time, I thought to myself, to telephone to the hospital for the extra uniforms I would need. I had expected to be on the case only a day or so, and had made my preparations accordingly.

I turned toward the little study at the end of the library. The town boasted automatic telephones, and I had some difficulty in dialing and more difficulty in making the superintendent understand what I wanted. It was very quiet in the little room with the door to the library closed; quiet and tranquil. Impossible to believe that in the next room lay a murdered man, dead on the rug, his eyes closed, his hands—— Wait! His eyes closed!

His eyes closed—*but the eyes of the dead do not close voluntarily*. Someone must close them.

"Hello, hello!" shrilled a voice in my ear.

I gave my message somewhat incoherently and put down the telephone. Full of my discovery, I rose, and in the very act of rising my cap slid off my head and I made another discovery which was almost to push the first from my mind.

I bent to pick up my cap and the pin which had slipped out from it. The cap had fallen on the rug—a handsome affair all in deep red with a touch of blue and gold: I believe it was called a Sarouk.

Strange that it was damp. That the one spot where my cap had fallen was wet to my touch.

I pushed my fingers down against the silky nap and brought them away again.

There was blood on the rug. It had soaked into the thick nap.

But it was the wrong rug.

CHAPTER V

THAT TRAGIC FIGURE LAY on a rug in the library. If he'd been shot here, in the little study, he couldn't possibly have got to the library rug before he fell. I knew that he had died at once. Why, then, was there blood on the Sarouk? And why were his eyes closed? There wasn't any niche for either fact in the story as I had heard it; no conceivable relation to the sequence of events as they'd been rehearsed by the Thatchers and Dr. Bouligny. Yet there was blood on that rug.

The opening of the door and a strange voice—that of the sheriff, I found—saying, "Well, let's have a look at the safe," aroused me. Dr. Bouligny, Hilary, and the sheriff crowded into the small room and around the safe. The sheriff bent to ex-amine it with what seemed to me a rather exaggerated air of professionalism, and I walked quietly back of them and into the library.

My footsteps on the rug were inaudible. Allen Carick did not look up until I stopped abruptly, and he became aware of my presence. He, the only one left in the room with the dead body, was kneeling beside it, going rapidly—feverishly, in fact—through the pockets of the dressing gown and trousers. And the curious thing about it was that even when he felt my astounded gaze and looked up at me he did not stop his search. He only gave me an abstractedly annoyed glance and shot a quick look at the door to the study and shifted the weight of the body a little so he could reach another pocket. Then, frowning and breathing rather quickly, he got to his feet, gave me another annoyed look, as if he didn't like my witnessing his occupation but was too engrossed with far more urgent anxieties to do anything about it, walked swiftly to the door into the hall, and disappeared.

He must have met someone in the hall, for I heard a murmured word or two, and Emmeline appeared at the doorway ushering into the room a fat, ruddy, jolly-looking man who proved to be Frank Whiting, the local undertaker. He lost his color abruptly as he bent over the body.

I did not linger, of course, but went directly upstairs. I did, however, turn for a moment at the doorway to take a last look at Bayard Thatcher. People say a nurse grows callous to death, but it isn't true.

At the top of the stairs I turned at once into Bayard Thatcher's empty room. My instrument kit was in the bathroom, with various bandage scissors and my thermometer scattered about. The room was orderly, the bed smooth save for the outline made by the pressure of Bayard's body on it early in the afternoon. I felt a little sick and dizzy as I looked at that, but even so I was quite certain about the condition of the room. Not a thing was out of place.

I went straight into the bathroom to get together the various articles of mine that lay about. The room was small, and in reaching behind the door for my bag I had closed that door. It may have taken two or three minutes to place the small articles in their respective pockets, and I remember smoothing my hair before the mirror and pinning my cap more securely on my head. I had a drink of water, too, letting it run from the faucet for some time so it would be cold. Perhaps altogether it was five or six minutes before I emerged into the bedroom again—a bedroom which looked exactly as if a hurricane had struck it.

I could not believe my eyes. The bedding was torn from the bed, the pillows out of their linen cases. Even the mattress had been pulled about. The cushions had been jerked off the chairs, every drawer in the old-fashioned dresser was out, the contents flung hurriedly about, even the rugs were flung back, and the pictures crooked on the walls.

And all this had been done in five minutes, and so silently that I, in the very next room, had heard nothing of it.

It frightened me.

There was something ruthless, something incredibly sinister in the swift, silent destruction in that room.

Without warning one of those strange moments of keen perception came upon me; one of those terrifying, chilling moments when you suddenly see yourself in relation to existence and wonder at yourself and what you are and what you desire and why—and that leave you feeling inexpressibly futile and perplexed. It is as if, for the barest moment, veils had dropped from your eyes and you caught a glimpse of reality, and there is always a feeling of apprehension, a need to grasp desperately for your sense of personal identity, as if that, too, might escape you. But this time that subconscious terror had something definite and objective to fasten upon.

All at once the house was a prison to me. I felt I must escape. I would tell Adela Thatcher that I could not stay.

Emmeline appeared on the threshold. If the frightful disorder in the room shocked her, she did not give any evidence of it.

"Miss Adela says will you come to her, please."

I followed Emmeline. Somewhere along the hall the kaleidoscope shifted again, righted itself, and things were nearer normal. I was again Sarah Keate; was inside myself again, intact.

But still frightened.

Adela lay in the middle of an enormous old bed. Janice and Evelyn had got her into a lacy bed jacket; a glass with still a little sherry in it stood on the bedside table. There was a pink spot burning feverishly in each cheek, and her eyes were very bright. Janice sat beside her, still and white, and Evelyn, ever practical, was moving about the room, arranging clothes on delicately scented hangers, and telling Emmeline to send up a tray with dinner for Miss Adela and Miss Keate.

And again, blandly and reasonably, they overrode my protestations and persuaded me to remain. It was done without undue pressure and very deftly. "Just for a few days, Miss Keate, until we can get on our feet again," said Evelyn at last. "This is a terrible shock to us all."

At which Adela sighed and said faintly:

"Terrible. Terrible. I suppose it's all over town by this time. Oh, Evelyn, what will people say?"

"Hilary stands to lose more than any of us," said Evelyn a bit crisply.

"Oh, I can't bear all this," cried Janice. She rose, pushing back her dark hair with both hands in a curiously despairing gesture, and walked to the window. "How can you talk so! Of Hilary. Of what people will say. Of the effect on his bank! Suppose people do talk! What does it matter! We can't help it. You don't say a word of the real horror of it. The real——"

"*Janice!* Janice, darling! You are overwrought. You are hysterical——"

"Janice." Evelyn took both the younger woman's hands in her firm brown clasp and spoke with great earnestness. "You don't know what you are saying, dear. You must try to control yourself. Think of the family name. Think of my boys. Think of——"

"Evelyn, why don't you and Janice go into Janice's room and

try to rest? Or go downstairs and get Dave and Hilary to eat something. Evelyn——" Adela's high-pitched, deliberate voice stopped abruptly, but she could not have said more plainly, "Get Janice out of here—before she says too much."

The room was quiet after they left. Adela lay motionless, staring at the ceiling with blank blue eyes. I remember I moved uneasily about, taking her temperature, feeling for her pulse, from a vague notion that I must be doing something rather than from any particular need on her part for nursing care. Once or twice I caught her watching me silently, a curious look of speculation in her still blue gaze. And I marveled to find myself still in that house and thought how singular it was that I felt rather like a prisoner. Which was absurd. Yet—to be a prisoner in that house where murder had walked would be no pleasant thing.

Emmeline brought two dinner trays to the room. Her hands were still faintly purple from fruit stain, but she'd put on a fresh white apron, and her thin face was immobile. The trays were daintily arranged, and I was a little astonished to find myself eating, and even to see Adela sit up against her laced pillows and touch this and that. She put the tray definitely aside when Hilary entered the room.

"No, don't go, Miss Keate," she said as I rose. "Stay here. Have you discovered anything, Hilary? What did the sheriff say? Had Higby seen anyone about? Sit down. You look dreadful. Did you have any dinner?"

He did look bad; his plump face was pale, and his eyes hollow, and his hands none too steady. He dropped into a chair, rubbed his eyes wearily, and said:

"Do you mind if I smoke, Adela?"

"Not at all. Not at all. What did Higby say?" And as Hilary looked at me and hesitated she added: "Don't mind Miss Keate. Speak freely, Hilary."

"Well," said Hilary in a reluctant way. "Higby said there wasn't anybody near all afternoon. That he mowed the lawn the whole afternoon and that Emmeline was in the summer kitchen, working near the window. That he didn't stop mowing once, and of course, he was on the same side of the house as the windows to the library. He said he didn't hear a sound except the telephone once. We asked him if the sound of the lawnmower so near him might not have muffled the sound of the shot."

"What did he say to that?"

"He said, maybe, but he'd heard the telephone ring distinctly. That it broke off in the middle of one of the peals."

"But he was closer to the house then," said Adela. "He was at the edge of the lawn by late afternoon. I doubt very much if he could have heard the shot above the clatter of the lawnmower. I've been telling him to grease it for the last two weeks. And he's rather stupid. I think it very likely someone could get past into the library windows, or even in the back door, without his seeing them."

Hilary nodded.

"That's what I told Jim Strove. Strove thought so, too. Dan Bouligny didn't think it so likely. But Strove has sent out telephone calls to all the near-by towns. He's doing everything he can to get a line on the thief."

"When will they have the inquest?"

"Tomorrow. Dan said for you not to worry about it."

Adela considered that for a long moment, while Hilary smoked nervously.

Then she said:

"Have many people called?"

Hilary nodded.

"The town's crazy with excitement. A fellow out on Muddy Creek phoned in that there was a suspicious looking man out there, and Strove deputized a bunch of fellows and sent them out. They haven't come back yet. And Mrs. Whiting says she saw a tramp running to catch the five-ten freight; Strove telephoned to Naper to hold him, but when the train got in the bum was gone. If there was one. You know Pearl Whiting. She'll have everybody in town under suspicion by this time tomorrow."

Adela nodded.

"I hope you told Frank Whiting exactly what happened."

"Lord, yes. I've had Emmeline tell everybody that you were ill from shock—had a trained nurse—couldn't see anybody. Dr. Lyman came; brought a cake from his wife. I don't know what in hell she thought we'd want of a cake."

"Hilary, don't speak so. She's your pastor's wife, and she meant it well. Have you sent a telegram to the boys yet?"

"No," he said rather hesitantly. "No, I haven't. I'll let Evelyn do it. She's so—matter-of-fact about things. And I thought we could let the other telegrams go until morning."

"Yes. Yes, that is right. We don't want the house full of relatives for the funeral—I suppose we'd better get it over quite soon."

"Yes. Yes, Adela. That's what I thought."

"Have you had anything to eat? You'd better try to eat. And Hilary—where is Dave?"

Hilary examined his cigarette carefully.

"He's in his room, Adela. Dan gave him something to make him sleep. Quiet his nerves. Dave, you know," he continued, turning in an explanatory way to me, "is a sort of invalid. Has been for years. Not well at all. Anything like this—a shock of any kind—and his nerves go all to pieces."

"Indeed." It occurred to me that Hilary's own nerves were none too good.

He sat in silence for some time after that, and finally left. Just as he reached the door Adela said a peculiar thing.

"Don't let Dave—" she paused, touched me with her eyes and said—"don't let Dave go to the cemetery tomorrow." She stopped again, and then added, "The sun is bad for him."

I couldn't see Hilary's face. He said:

"Very well. I'll be up again with Dan before you go to sleep."

The soft summer night came on slowly. Presently I lighted the shaded lamp on the table. Adela lay without speaking. She had in her hands a long string of turquoise beads, and I remember how she twisted them, pulling them through her fingers, playing with them absently. They made a bright varying patch of blue against the white sheet and her laces. Her eyes looked a little like the beads.

Between nine and ten o'clock Dr. Bouligny and Hilary came again to the room. This time, finding they still had not eaten, Adela asked me to go and tell Emmeline to bring up some coffee and sandwiches. I did so willingly enough.

And it was owing to that that I inadvertently caught a glimpse of that sad and tragic complication which, unsuspected by anyone, played such an important part in the dreadful entanglement of human motives and relationships of which Bayard's murder and the shocking things that followed it were the prolonged climax. I say unsuspected by anyone: I must make an exception there. I've always thought that Evelyn knew of it almost from the beginning, and with her hard common sense recognized it as a factor to be taken into account; she allowed for it, I'm sure, with a sort of mathematical precision, and did not try to brush it aside or propound a fanciful and impractical solution as a more imaginative or even a more sensitive woman might have done. Toward the end, even, she was frankly sympathetic, although she always deplored it; perhaps she permitted herself sympathy because she knew so well that Janice possessed the un-bending loyalty and pride that Evelyn herself possessed.

It was only a glimpse I had that night, but it was a glimpse of something real and touching.

All the lights were blazing through the wide rooms. I had found Emmeline, managed to make my message heard, and left her slicing bread and measuring coffee, and I was returning to the stairway. I felt rather uneasy as I passed the open library door; there was a bare space on the floor near the table, where the rug on which Bayard had lain had been rolled up and tak-en away, probably to be cleaned. I was thinking how strangely empty and lonely all those brightly lighted rooms were when the screen door leading to the dark porch opened and two figures entered the light of the hall. They did not see me; I was at some distance, and they were directly under a light.

They were Janice and Allen Carick. And now that I've come to tell it I find that after all there is very little to tell. The signifi-cance lay entirely in their look, and that was only a kind of still-ness, as if they shared some tremendous and vital understanding. They didn't speak; they just stood there for a moment. Then Al-len put out his arms, and I thought he was going to take Janice into them. He took her hands, however, instead, and looked at them for a moment as if he might never see them again in all the world, and then held them against his eyes. And Janice lifted her face with all its beauty in full flame, and yet so white and spent-looking that I did not see how the man could gently relin-quish her hands and step back. But he did just that, although he too was white under his tan, and he watched her turn and mount the stairs with a look of such sheer agony in his young eyes that I felt indecent witnessing it. Then he was gone; beyond the screen I saw his hand on the latch and then heard his quick steps across the porch.

It had lasted only a moment. And I felt shaken and pitiful, as if I had seen the sacrifice of something living and very lovely.

Which was, I told myself impatiently as I continued on my way, not only sentimental and maudlin, it was entirely without morals on my part. While I have never married and in all likelihood never shall, still I have my views about matrimony. I have always felt that flirtatiousness in a married woman is due to a sort of compound of vanity, idleness, and not enough spankings as a child.

But that moment in the hall had been real. And I suppose people do fall in love sometimes whether they want to or not. And how can they know it until it's happened?

This untimely reflection threatened my own self-respect, and it was with further chagrin that I found I had brought up at the door of the room which had been Bayard Thatcher's with my hand on the doorknob.

I drew it away sharply. The hall was long and empty and but dimly lighted. Was it only last night that I'd stood there watching in that mirror the reflection of a door closing? Since then murder had been at large in the silent house. Had ravaged the peace of a summer day; had charged the tranquil dignity of the house with fear and violence.

Where there's been murder there will be murder.

As if by physical motion I could remove myself from that unwelcome thought, I stirred and walked hurriedly to Adela's door, knocked, and at her word entered.

It was not more than an hour later that I came upon the letter.

Dr. Bouligny, in leaving, had ordered me to give Adela a rather heavy opiate to insure her rest during the long hours of the night, and I was fumbling in my instrument bag for the case which held a hypodermic needle when my fingers encountered an envelope, tucked well out of sight. It was not addressed. I opened it and took out the sheet of paper it held.

It was part of a letter. I never knew exactly why it was in my bag, although I was to surmise with, I think, a fair degree of accuracy. I did not realize what it was until I'd read a portion of it, and then I could not stop. Not that I'm making apology for what I did; still, it was quite evidently a letter meant for only one pair of eyes. The first of it was gone; the written words leaped to my gaze:

"... *freedom and taking love when it comes and living your own life. But it's all wrong. It doesn't take into account—well, just integrity. One's measures of honesty and pride. I can't leave Dave. Though God knows I've reason to, poor Dave.*

"*You must go. I can't bear seeing you. It's terrible to write that and to know that my moments of living are those moments when I can see you, expect you, hear you speak. Such a few moments out of all the years and years, so brief—all the rest such a dreadful waste.*

"*I'm growing hysterical; I must stop. I'll put this in a pocket of your coat. You left it on the porch. I loathe myself for doing it in such a way. But I must make you understand, and I can't say all this—not while you're near me. Believe me, there isn't a way out of it; not any way we can take.*

"*After all, we'll forget. People do. That's worse than anything. But it's true. Janice.*"

For a moment I stood there holding that sheet of paper under the light. Then deliberately I read it again.

It was without doubt a compromising letter; I was torn with disapproval and a kind of reluctant pity. After all, she had tried to be honest; it was a bit hysterical, but emotion is apt to sound like that. And it was sincere and direct and entirely lacked that theatrical quality of artificial romance with which women so often invest their letters, as if they were seeing themselves in some romantic rôle.

Somehow I assumed that the letter was meant for Allen, and I was feeling sorry for them all, Dave and Janice and Allen, caught in such a tragic mesh. But was it Allen? Could it have been Bayard Thatcher—Bayard, dead now, his harsh smile gone? He had had access to my instrument bag, not Allen. Bayard also she might conceivably have begged to go. Perhaps Dave had discovered it. He seemed to be a neurotic type: a man who would act first and reason afterward. But Dave and Allen had been fishing together all the afternoon. And I had seen Janice with Allen there at the foot of the stairs. No, the man she loved was Allen. But Janice herself—*Janice herself had been in the house alone with Bayard for fully five minutes before the murder was discovered!* Until that very moment I had forgotten it. Upon their return she and Adela had got out of the car together, but she had gone directly into the house, while Adela lingered among the flowers and talked to me. It could have been only five minutes at the longest, possibly less than that, but it does not take long to send a bullet speeding to its target. It was incredible—but who else was there?

There was a light knock on the door of the adjoining bedroom. I heard Adela speak and then scream. It was a sharp, sucking sound, that scream; like taffeta when it tears.

Then I was in the bedroom, too.

Adela was sitting upright in bed. Her eyes were blank and hard, and her mouth tight. You'd never have guessed she had just screamed.

Emmeline stood near the bed. In one hand she carried the brown wicker egg basket. There were still some eggs in it.

In her other hand she held a revolver.

"I found——" she said, and saw me and stopped.

CHAPTER VI

AFTERWARDS IT SEEMED STRANGE to me and a little sad that the curious understanding which had existed probably for so many years between mistress and maid should have failed at that crucial moment. For Adela opened her lips and said in a hoarse kind of whisper:

"Take it away."

And I'm sure Emmeline thought she asked where she'd found the revolver, for the woman said:

"It was in the egg basket, in the refrigerator. It's Mr. Dave's. There's two shots out of it." She held the revolver almost at arm's length, looked at it reflectively, and added, "You ought to feel how cold it is, being in the icebox."

Adela closed her eyes.

"Put it on the table, here," she said. "That's all, Emmeline."

After the maid had stalked away again, bearing her basket of eggs, Adela lay there for a moment, marshaling her forces, and then opened her eyes and said wearily:

"It's strange that Dave's revolver should turn up in the egg basket. But it means nothing. Nothing. The revolver was likely in the coupé when Janice took it out this afternoon, and she dropped it into the egg basket, intending to take it into the house and put it away, and then she forgot about it. Yes, that's what happened. You can see for yourself, Miss Keate, that it couldn't have been the revolver with which——" a small spasm contorted her mouth as she said stiffly—"with which Bayard was shot. But I'm going to ask you to say nothing of this, please. Dr. Bouligny is a good man, and he means well, but he's a bit stupid. He might think—— Well, it's best, I think, not to confuse things."

"A ballistics expert would soon know whether that was the revolver that killed Bayard, if that's what you mean," I said crisply. The variety of experience which falls to a nurse's lot has given me some slight acquaintance with crime. Besides, I read the newspapers.

My comment did not please Adela. She looked coldly at me.

"Surely you don't think a burglar would not only use Dave's revolver, but would hide it in the egg basket in the kitchen refrigerator," she said frigidly. "Besides, he wouldn't have had time. If you'll give me the medicine Dr. Bouligny ordered, I'll go to sleep."

And when I stood beside the bed a few moments later with the hypodermic needle ready in my hand, I glanced at the table. The revolver was gone; I knew she must have placed it in some drawer in the room, and I could certainly have found it—could find it later on, if I felt it my duty to bring the matter to the coroner's attention.

She went to sleep almost immediately. I was adjusting the window preparatory to leaving her when Pansy scratched and whined at the door. I let her in; she waddled breathlessly over to the bed, gave Adela's hand which lay on the edge an abstracted lick and retreated to a cushion in the corner. She was still nervous and watched me suspiciously and with not too flattering attention as I moved about the room.

It was with a touch of uneasiness that I entered the room next door, which I was to have, and snapped on the light. I remember I glanced rather quickly about, under the bed and into the old wardrobe and back of the screen, before I closed and locked the door. Yet I can't say there was any definite thing that I feared. It was something impalpable; quite intangible. Murder as a word is only a word; but murder as an actuality, dragged into the calm circumference of one's own living, is a violent and cyclonic experience.

The Thatchers were what we call nice people. They were temperate, self-controlled, proud. They did not lack courage, they scorned dishonesty, and their emotions were orderly. People of that sort do not breed murderers. But Bayard Thatcher had been murdered. Even that night, before I had time or inclination to try to arrive at any conclusion as to who had murdered him— even then, I felt instinctively that it was one of the Thatchers. Otherwise it would not, perhaps, have been so terrible and so profoundly exciting an experience. It is true it seemed entirely incredible to think that under that placid, calm, well ordered surface strange and turbulent and violent emotions were seething. Emotions which must have had their roots far, far beyond the somewhat paradoxical but rigidly ordered state of affairs we call civilization and which excludes murder.

Contrary to my expectations I fell at once into a heavy, dreamless sleep; I was, of course, desperately weary. The night— clear and moonlit—was, so far as I know, entirely peaceful. I do not believe there were, even, any tears for Bayard.

It was morning when I awoke with a start and a conviction that I had heard the continued barking of a dog somewhere near. It had ceased, however, by the time I was thoroughly awake, and I did not hear it again. It was a warm, placid summer morning, too warm even at that hour, but pleasant and quiet. The horror of the thing that had happened swept back into my consciousness with a kind of incredulous shock.

I hurried a little about dressing. My fears of the night seemed unreal as I unlocked and opened the door on a peaceful sunlit hall. Adela's door was closed, and she did not respond to my knock, so I went quietly away; it would be a good thing to let her sleep as late as possible. Not a soul was about upstairs, though I met Florrie in the lower hall. Her green chambray was fresh and clean as always, but her cap was crooked, and she gave me a rather sullen good-morning. I stopped for a moment in the doorway, I remember, to glance out across the porch and the lovely sunny lawns. When I turned she had arrested herself in the very act of dusting a table and was looking fixedly over her shoulder at me. She dropped her eyes at once and began to wield the duster vigorously, and when I said, "A pleasant morning," she muttered something unintelligible and turned into the library.

I walked on down the hall. As I reached the dining-room door something made me turn. The girl was standing half in, half out the library door watching me. She bobbed out of sight, but not before I had caught a strangely sullen look in her plain face. It vaguely disturbed me; it was as if she were accusing me of something.

Evelyn was sitting behind the tall silver coffee service. Apparently she had not gone home for the night, for she still wore the light summer gown, a flowered chiffon, which she had worn the previous afternoon. It looked gay and out of place, especially when Janice, who followed my entrance by a moment or two, appeared in a crisp white linen morning frock.

"Good-morning, Miss Keate," said Evelyn as I entered. "No one else is down yet, but we may as well tell Emmeline to serve our breakfast. There's no need to wait. Hilary and I stayed here last night, you know." Matter-of-fact, calm, practical. You would never have dreamed from Evelyn's manner that anything at all unusual had happened. Her gold hair was smooth and neat, her shoulders erect, her dark blue eyes steady and cool, and only the dark pockets around them showed that it had been, as it must have been, a night of anxiety. Her poise compelled my admiration, although I think it was not due so much to courage as it was to a certain lack of temperament; a faculty for seeing only the practical, material aspects of a problem. She would never harass herself with doubts or regrets or fears. She concerned herself only with expediency.

Her brown hand was very steady as it touched the bell, and her voice clear as she asked Emmeline to serve breakfast. She was pouring my coffee when Janice entered.

"Oh, my dear, I didn't expect you down so early. Here, sit here in this place. I didn't mean to usurp your place behind the coffee."

"No, no, don't move." Janice sat wearily in her customary place. "Good-morning, Miss Keate. Isn't Adela coming down to breakfast, Evelyn?"

"She seems to be sleeping late," replied Evelyn, handing me my cup. "It's just as well. She looked bad last night. Adela's not as young as we are."

"Thanks." Janice took her own cup, drank some of the coffee, and began to look a little less drained of life. Except for its look of terrible burned-out fatigue, her face was rather cold and rigid and as immaculate of feeling as her white frock. I could detect nothing of the passion that had written itself into her letter; of the extremely sentient and aware look that had lit her face with so spent and tragic a beauty only the night before, when she'd left Allen standing there in the hall looking as if his heart and his every hope went with her up those stairs. She was not beautiful that morning; I think she was controlling her every thought.

"Did you sleep?" asked Evelyn.

"No," said Janice briefly. "Where's Hilary?"

"He went home to shave and get fresh clothes. He ought to be back in a few moments. Allen is coming with him. I thought we might as well have breakfast here together. Dr. Bouligny said he would stop in to tell us about the inquest—when it's to be, and all. Dave is sleeping late, too."

"Yes."

Rapid footsteps along the hall preluded Hilary's appearance at the door. He was, as usual, immaculate; his thin hair carefully brushed so as to make the most of what there was, his tie neatly knotted, his light suit looking as if it had just come from the tailor's, his face freshly shaved and powdered. But the night had not been kind to him; his eyes were puffy and red from lack of sleep, and there were heavy pouches under them; his whole face seemed to have sagged and lost its pinkness, and his hands were not steady as he pulled out a chair and picked up his napkin and took the cup of coffee Evelyn handed him.

"Good-morning, Janice. Miss Keate. There's some mail on the hall table for you, Evelyn. Thank you. No cream."

"Where's Allen?" asked Evelyn.

"He's coming. Rode over with me. He stopped to speak to Strove."

"Strove? So early!"

Hilary nodded rather grimly.

"He was on the lawn—looking below the library windows. I don't know what he expects to find. Footprints, perhaps. Here's Allen, now. I'll take another cup of coffee, Evelyn."

Allen showed the effects of the last twenty-four hours less than any of us. But even he looked taut and weary, as if he hadn't slept. He sat in the chair next to Evelyn and refrained from looking at Janice after he'd included us all in a quiet good-morning.

"What'd Strove have to say?" asked Hilary.

Allen shrugged.

"Nothing. But what do you think he had? A magnifying glass."

Hilary laughed shortly.

"He won't get very far with that. It's a damn good thing you and Dave were fishing together all yesterday afternoon, Allen. Can you think of anyone who saw you? It would help clinch matters. Dan and I aren't going to have too easy a time over this inquest."

There was a rather tight look about Allen's mouth. But he added sugar to his grapefruit with a steady hand—nice hands, he had, lean and firm with long sensitive fingers—and said at once:

"I don't just think of anyone. And after all, Hilary, no one will dare come out and say things openly."

"They'll say plenty afterward. We've got to be mighty careful about the inquest."

"You understand, Miss Keate," said Evelyn hurriedly. "We are a bit worried about the unpleasant comment this affair may cause."

If her intention was to warn Hilary that there was an outsider present, she succeeded. He gave me an annoyed look and said nothing further. The conversation lapsed until Dr. Bouligny arrived a few minutes later. Dr. Bouligny, too, looked haggard and took the coffee Evelyn offered him with eagerness.

"My housekeeper can't make coffee," he complained. "I wish Emmeline would show her how. Adela still asleep?"

The inquest was to be that morning, it developed, and Dr. Bouligny thought it would be wise to arrange for the funeral the following day.

"Better get it over and forgotten as soon as possible," he said bluntly, and Hilary agreed.

"Will you get the telegrams off this morning, Evelyn?"

"How about the boys, Hilary?" said Evelyn slowly. There was

an anxious note in her voice. I felt sure she did not want the boys to come home for the funeral.

"I—don't know," replied Hilary. "I—what do you think, Evelyn?"

"Well—I don't know that there's any need for their coming. They knew Bayard, of course. But they are such children. There's really no need for them to come. And it would interrupt their work at camp. The swimming competition takes place in a few days." It was not like Evelyn to seek excuses.

Allen gave her a quick look and said:

"I shouldn't consider sending for them. Wire them what's happened, for they'll see something, likely, in the papers. At any rate, they'll have to know sooner or later, and it won't do to let them wonder why they were not told of it. But tell them not to come. They won't want to, anyway. And by the time they do come home——" He checked himself with a glance at me. But Evelyn, always literal, finished.

"By the time they do come home, the whole thing will have blown over. I think Allen is right, Hilary. Do you?"

"Yes," agreed Hilary in a relieved way. "That's exactly right. I leave it to you, Evelyn. Now, then, Dan, if you have finished your coffee—I've got a thousand things to see to this morning. Suppose you go to the office with me. I'll ride in your car. They'll need mine here, likely. Did you say the inquest is at ten? It's nine now. Allen, you bring the girls, will you? And Dave, of course. And how about Emmeline and the nurse, Dan? Had they better come too?"

"Why, yes," said Dr. Bouligny. "You don't mind, do you, Miss Keate?"

"Oh, not at all," I said promptly. A little too promptly, perhaps, for I caught Allen smiling at his plate.

"I will probably have only a few questions to ask you, if any," added Dr. Bouligny. "Since the cause of death is so—er—clear, we'll make the inquest as brief as possible. Tell Adela, Evelyn, not to be alarmed or nervous."

"Don't worry about Adela," said Hilary. "She'll be cooler than any of us. You can always count on Adela."

"At ten," repeated Janice thoughtfully. "That doesn't give us much time. I'd better get the grocery order off. You and Hilary and Allen will eat here today, won't you, Evelyn? We'll want to be together in case——" She did not finish the sentence and rose.

Hilary turned at the door.

"I may not see you again before the inquest," he said. "But I'll meet you there at the courthouse. I'll go now with Dan, and we'll fix up the—the line of inquiry. Just answer what you are asked. Don't—" he warned, his eyes on Janice—"volunteer anything. Be careful what you say."

"If you mean that for me, Hilary," said Janice—she spoke gravely and not at all sharply as her words might imply—"you can trust me. I'll not let you down. In public, anyhow."

"There, there, now, Janice," said Hilary fussily. "I didn't mean that, at all. I only meant not to tell anything that might—that is, not to make any indiscreet—not to——"

"You're making things worse, Hilary," said Allen coolly. "Do go along. We'll be all right. Come on out in the garden, Janice. It will do you good. You too, Evelyn," he added as a polite afterthought. But Janice would not. She had, she said, to see to the grocery order.

"Heaven only knows what's in the refrigerator for lunch," she said. "Emmeline has her own notions, and I've got to be sure you'll have something to eat."

"I don't imagine any of us will be exactly hungry," said Allen, rising.

I rose too. Hilary and the doctor had, of course, gone; Allen and Evelyn strolled toward the hall, and Janice disappeared toward the kitchen. I think it was the word refrigerator that, without my knowing it, impelled me to follow Janice, for when I turned to go into the kitchen I'm sure that only the thought of arranging a dainty breakfast tray for Adela was in my mind.

Back of the dining room was a generous butler's pantry, and beyond this and through a swinging door a large, clean kitchen with starched white curtains and shining floor. It was a big old room, only fairly modern in its appointments, but obviously meant for cooking, for the preparation of generous meals, and the storing of bounteous supplies. It was as vital and essential a part of the life the house had known as was its library with its worn books. Show me a woman's kitchen, her books, and her dressing table, and I can tell you much of the woman.

But I gave the room only a brief glance, for Janice was standing at its far end; her back was turned toward me, and she had not heard my entrance. Emmeline was not to be seen.

Janice was standing directly before the large refrigerator. Its heavy door was open. The girl's head was bent over a large brown wicker basket, and I could see that she was exploring its depths with her hand. It was, I had no doubt, the egg basket in which Emmeline had found the revolver.

There was a noise at the side door, and Emmeline entered. At the sound Janice's head went up with a jerk and turned, and I could see how paper-white her face was, as if the frightened racing of her heart had drawn every drop of blood from it.

Emmeline stopped still when she saw Janice.

"Oh, it's you," she said harshly. "What do you want?"

"Emmeline," said Janice breathlessly. "Who has been in the kitchen? Has Jim Strove been here?"

"What's that?" said Emmeline. "Talk a little louder."

Janice gave her a hopeless look, became conscious again, it seemed, of the egg basket, and turned and replaced it carefully in the refrigerator.

"Better put those eggs in a pan," she said loudly and closed the door of the icebox with a muffled bang and turned and saw me.

It gave me a sort of pang to witness the stark terror in her white face, the sudden flaring of it in her wide dark eyes, the way her hand groped backward as if for support. I advanced at once.

"I came to get a breakfast tray for Miss Adela," I said. "Perhaps you would better ask Emmeline for it. She is not accustomed to my voice, and I have difficulty making her understand. I think your sister will want something hot to drink as soon as she wakes."

It gave her time for recovery. She needed only a few seconds. She repeated my request to Emmeline.

"Oh," said Emmeline. "Then Miss Adela's got back."

CHAPTER VII

SHE WALKED STIFFLY TOWARD a cupboard and took down a tray. "I'll fix it right away," she continued. "She'll be tired."

I found my voice.

"Got back? Why, what do you mean? Did she go some place? I thought she was in her room. I thought she was sleeping."

Apparently Emmeline did not hear me, though she gave me a sharp and comprehensive glance. Janice, too, looked surprised and alarmed.

"What do you mean, Emmeline?" she said quickly. "Isn't Miss Adela in her room? She said nothing to me of any errand. Tell me at once what you mean. Where did she go?"

But Emmeline was very deaf indeed. She said:

"The grocery list is there on the table, if you want to order, Miss Janice. I thought the family would all be together likely for meals today. What would you think of pressed chicken with cucumber salad for lunch? And maybe a lemon cream pie."

Janice turned rather helplessly to me.

"Will you see if Adela is in her room, Miss Keate? I can't imagine what Emmeline means." She took up the grocery list, absent-mindedly scanning it, and I went to the door. It was entirely by accident that I caught my skirt in the swinging door and was obliged to linger a moment to release it. And I heard Janice say clearly:

"Tell me at once where Miss Adela went."

And Emmeline replied hoarsely:

"Cemetery. What about the lemon cream pie?"

"What do you—no, not pie. Hilary can't eat it. His blood pressure, you know."

Emmeline probably did not understand her, for Janice shouted, "Blood pressure. Hilary," and I went reluctantly away.

The cemetery. Well, that was a peaceful enough errand. But it did occur to me that the Thatchers took an unusual and peculiar interest in cemeteries. Although, in view of the fact that there was about to be an addition to the family burial plot, Adela's interest was perhaps not incomprehensible.

Thinking that Emmeline might be mistaken, I went to Adela's room and knocked. When she did not reply I opened the door cautiously and then more boldly. The bed was empty, Adela was certainly gone. The dog, Pansy, got up wearily from her corner and waddled over to me, sniffing suspiciously and puffing as if she had asthma. A dog's barking had awakened me; it must have been Pansy, left alone. Adela, then, had been gone for some time.

It was an hour or so yet before the inquest. I went downstairs again and out to the wide porch. There were chairs out there, and it was pleasant and cool out of the sun, although the morning gave promise of an unusually hot and stifling day.

Higby was not to be seen, and the lawn was deserted save for the birds bathing and drinking and fluttering their wings under the gentle spray of the lawn sprinkler which someone had turned on. Death and murder might visit that house, but its routine was unchanging.

Back of me, from the depths of the house I could hear an

occasional murmur of voices and the frequent ringing of the telephone; several cars drove slowly past with their occupants craning their necks to stare at me and at the house, although no one stopped—I suppose Adela had never encouraged the informality of early morning calls—and presently Allen came out with a sheaf of telegraph blanks in one hand. He did not see me, and strode briskly along the turf path, his crisp light hair shining in the sun, his tall body lean and lithe and young.

Sitting there, I had my first opportunity to weigh and sift, so to speak, the evidence I possessed.

There is also this about murder: I discovered it during the Thatcher case: every man becomes a hunter. I could not have helped making every effort to discover the identity of the person who killed Bayard Thatcher—who had deliberately taken the life of a fellow man. It is not a mere matter of vulgar prying into other people's affairs. Not in the least. It is exactly as if a tiger had escaped and were preying upon human life. It is a matter of self-preservation: the tiger must be discovered and captured.

On reflection it seemed to me there were three major considerations. There was first the problem of whether or not all of them—Adela and Hilary and Evelyn and Emmeline and Janice—yes, and even Higby—were telling the truth. If they were telling the truth, Evelyn had left Bayard alive, Emmeline had found him dead, and only Janice and Emmeline had been inside the house in that short interval. Besides, of course, the highly problematic burglar.

Second, if they were not telling the truth, the problem of the identity of the murderer was still limited to the immediate family circle of Adela, Hilary, Evelyn, Janice, and Emmeline. And, of course, Higby. There had been no one else about.

Unless, and here was my third consideration, unless Higby and Emmeline were both lying to the same purpose and someone had entered the house at the back, unknown to me. I knew that Emmeline, Higby, and I between us commanded a view of the entire house, and that one of us could scarcely have failed to see any intruder coming or going. Much, it seemed to me, hinged upon the truth of their testimony.

There was, too, ever in my consciousness the fact of Bayard's having been wounded by a revolver shot only a day or so before he'd been killed. He had known that first attack for what it was, and I reproached myself for having been so loath to credit his statement. Still, I had urged him to protect himself, to leave. And that very afternoon he had been killed.

The family knew, in all likelihood, who had fired that first shot that wounded Bayard's shoulder. It was not probable that there were two people intent upon doing away with Bayard Thatcher. If I could discover who made that first attack—— But they wouldn't tell. None of the Thatchers would tell.

And there were other things that seemed to me highly significant. Why did I hear—that calm afternoon—no sound of the shot? Why were Bayard's eyes closed? Who had tried to enter his room that first night? Why was there blood on the wrong rug?

And was there a possibility that it was a burglar after all? If not, what had happened to the diamonds?

Then there was the problem of Janice and the revolver and the egg basket. Janice and her presence in the house alone with Bayard for the ten minutes or so immediately preceding the discovery of his death. Janice and the mysterious letter. Had the letter any possible bearing upon the situation? I must find some way to return the letter to her.

It seems unbelievable now to think that, from the very beginning, I had the key to the puzzle in my own hands. And didn't know it. Did not recognize it for what it was. It was all so simple, so dreadfully simple once I recognized that clue, and it was a mere matter of recognition.

When I finally returned to Adela's room I was a little astonished to find her sitting calmly, talking to Janice. She was dressed in plain white and looked weary but cold and a little severe, with her gold-rimmed eyeglasses and her white gloves and delicate handkerchief at hand. As I asked her if she felt well, she replied in the coolest affirmative and told me it was time for me to prepare to go with them to the inquest.

"Did Evelyn go home?" she asked Janice.

"Just to change her dress. She'll be back soon."

"Well, you'd better get ready at once, Miss Keate. Allen will take us all in the big car. We'll meet Hilary at the courthouse, I suppose. We are all rather anxious to get it over. Not a pleasant affair."

How well I remember Adela's deliberately elegant voice calling it "not a pleasant affair." It was odd, that inquest. Odd, but after all not much happened. Not much, perhaps, with Dr. Bouligny presiding, could happen. It all lasted barely half an hour.

It was held in the old courthouse, C—— being, as perhaps I have indicated, the county seat. The main street of the town, as we drove through it a few moments before ten, looked like a market day, it was so full of automobiles belonging to the farmers who had driven in to talk of the news and to attend the inquest. I daresay they felt a little cheated at the brevity of the proceedings in the packed courtroom. But I doubt if those old walls ever held a half hour so crowded with secret drama. It was not, however, until much later that I knew the true significance of those careful questions, and those cautious, guarded replies.

I sat, of course, with the family. It was something to witness their determined calm, their dignity of bearing; to note the manner with which they met the nods and looks and subdued greet-

ings of their neighbors and acquaintances. There was no con-
descension in the Thatcher manner, no patronage; at the same
time, there was something which said: "This dreadful thing has
happened to us, it's true. We admit it openly. But we are still
Thatchers."

An analyst would have said their very manner admitted the
thing they were so determined to keep hidden. But I am not an
analyst, and it was only later that I received that.

Inwardly I was shocked at the cut-and-dried way in which
Dr. Bouligny and Hilary between them managed to hurry the
inquest along. It was done so deftly and so adroitly that it almost convinced me—would have quite convinced me had I not
known what I knew—and the jury did not even leave the room
to make its decision that Bayard Thatcher met his death at the
hands of an unknown person. Much was made, and in a most
effective way, of the loss of the Thatcher diamonds, of which everyone in the room seemed to know.

Only once did anything threaten to break through that carefully built up fabric of supposition. That was when one of the
jurors, a farmer with a weatherbeaten face and shrewd gray eyes,
asked rather hesitantly if it wasn't true that Bayard Thatcher had
been shot in the shoulder just a day or so before he was killed.

"The question," said Dr. Bouligny in a stately way, "is irrele-
vant. However," he added quickly, as the farmer appeared about
to speak again, "he was. It is no secret. He was cleaning a revolver, and it went off accidentally, wounding him slightly. I myself
was the attending physician. I know exactly how it happened. It
has nothing at all to do with a burglar shooting him yesterday.
Higby, we'll have your testimony now."

And Higby's testimony, under Dr. Bouligny's inquiries, em-
phasized the fact that the lawnmower had been a noisy one, that
he'd been at some distance from the house during the late after-

noon, and that in traversing the lawn back and forth all that long afternoon there had been many times when his back was turned to the library windows.

"But not long enough for anybody to cross the lawn and get the screen off a window and get into the house without I saw him," muttered Higby stubbornly. His meaning was clearer than his syntax, and Dr. Bouligny wound him up rather hurriedly and sent him back to his seat. And Adela, beside me, touched her blue lips with a delicately laced handkerchief.

My own testimony was equally brief, and when, after asking me only a very obvious question or two, Dr. Bouligny dismissed me with thanks I caught Hilary giving Dr. Bouligny a relieved and distinctly congratulatory glance.

As I say, the decision was very prompt. Riding home in the sedan at the side of Adela, I reflected that at least no one had come out openly to accuse any of the Thatcher family of murder. There would undoubtedly be talk; I could see it even then in the glances, the bent heads, the whispers, the way the groups on the sidewalks stopped talking and watched us pass, but at least the inquest was safely over. And I thought of Adela's despairing cry, "What will people say?"

The sheriff followed us home, and I sat and listened while Adela gave a description of the vanished diamonds. I can still hear her deliberate voice:

"One ring, set with a carat diamond, a blue Jaegar, and two pearls."

And Jim Strove scratching away in a notebook: "How do you spell Jaegar?"

"Two carat Wesseltons set in a ring with a design of clasped hands. One necklace, eleven diamonds. One sunburst, twenty-six—oh, but you would know my mother's sunburst anywhere, Mr. Strove. You've seen her wear it hundreds of times."

"Oh, sure, Miss Adela. But I've got to telegraph this all over the country. You'll have to give me a more detailed description of the stones. Don't you have a written record? A jeweler's——"

"Yes. Yes. Very well. One sunburst——"

On and on it went, emblematic of a time when a family was scarcely a family until it had collected a certain amount of land, silver, and diamonds. The collection was not enormous, and none of the pieces was very valuable; still, all put together it was nothing to be sneezed at.

I left them presently and went to my own room to change from the street gown I had worn at the inquest. I found Florrie there, her stolidity shaken and her hair a bit wild. She was changing the bed, flourishing the sheets widely. She gave a little gasp when I entered.

"Do you mind, ma'am," she said, "if I finish the room while you are here?" And as I said no, she continued, "I'm late about things this morning. Seems like I'm kind of nervous. Keep feeling like something's coming at me from behind."

"Nonsense. Not in broad daylight."

She gave me a slow look.

"It happened yesterday in broad daylight," she said, shaking out a pillow case.

Well, of course that was true.

"And—" she added, holding the pillow by one corner between her teeth and speaking through them—her teeth, I mean—so that her words had a sort of hissing ferocity—"it can happen again."

"Nonsense," I repeated. And because I rather agreed with her than otherwise I said briskly, "Nothing is going to happen. You're a little nervous, that's all."

"And who wouldn't be nervous?" she asked fiercely. "A man shot all to pieces in the very house. Mark my words, ma'am, it ain't going to end there. You see," she added, releasing the pillow and speaking with greater clearness, "I'm a seventh daughter."

"A seventh daughter! Do you mean a Native daughter? Or a Daughter of the Revolution? Or a—— By the way, hasn't Miss Thatcher told you not to hold pillows between your teeth like that?"

"Yes," she admitted. "But when I get excited I sort of forget. It's lots easier. The seventh daughter of a seventh daughter."

It began to sound like a lodge. She picked up the other pillow, caught it expertly between her teeth, and hissed, "I see things!"

"You see things! What on earth——"

She took the pillow out of her mouth and said, "I mean I see things. I've got second sight. That is, sometimes I have second sight. And I've got it right now. I see trouble."

Her earnestness was rather convincing. I was a little taken aback and vaguely uneasy in the face of such certainty.

"Why, you can't!" I cried. "That's all nonsense."

She gave me a strange look; her plain face was still, almost trance-like.

"Can't I?" she said in a low voice. "Then why do I feel death in this house? Why did my mother know it yesterday? Before we had heard what happened here. Why did she say to me, 'Florrie, don't you go back to that Thatcher house. There's been trouble there.'"

The girl took a step or two in my direction, and I found myself retreating a little.

"And there was trouble, wasn't there? When I got back last night. There'd been murder. And I see—" she was motionless now, her eyes fixed in a vacant way—"I see more trouble. I see death."

I had reached the window. I pressed against the ledge, took a deep breath, and said crisply, though a bit jerkily:

"Now, Florrie, stop talking like that. I shall be obliged to tell Miss Thatcher, if you keep this up. You are hysterical. You are letting your imagination run away with you. Stop it at once and get back to your work."

She was not at all affected. Her face did not alter its still look, but she went back to the bed.

"It's coming," she said, pulling a sheet straight. "You'll see. And I'm afraid. I'm afraid where murder is going to strike next."

"That's enough," I said sharply.

"Very well, ma'am. But my mother's always warned me. She sees clearer than I do. She's had more experience. And she says I've got to guard against being murdered in my sleep."

"M-murdered——"

The girl nodded.

"In my sleep. It's got to be a full moon and something out of a box. I always lock my door when it's a full moon. But there's never till now been the third thing."

"The—third thing——"

"Yes. Mother says when all three things are there I've got to protect myself. Or I'll be murdered in my sleep. The trouble is to come from the third thing, and that is—" she tucked the counterpane deftly over the pillows—"a red-headed woman. Your hair's red, ain't it, ma'am?"

"Florrie! You are out of your senses. What do you mean! Do you think I'm going to murder you?"

"I didn't say that," she said. "But your hair's red, ain't it?"

"It is auburn. And if you keep on talking like this, my girl——"

"It looks red to me. And I'm just telling you. I suppose it

sounds silly to you. Maybe it is. But Mother's never yet been wrong. What kind of soap do you want, ma'am?"

"Your mother likely knew from what you'd said that Mr. Bayard had been wounded by a revolver shot and that I'd come to nurse him," I said, although I couldn't have told why I chose to explain the absurd affair. "Of course, she would say there was trouble coming."

"H'mm," said Florrie. She gave me a long and singularly discerning look. "H'mm. So you knew it was no accident, too."

CHAPTER VIII

AFTER A MOMENT I said:

"What do you mean?"

"What do I mean?" she repeated with a sort of scorn. "I mean, I've got eyes in my head. And ears. If you'd heard what I heard——"

She glanced nervously at the door and leaned toward me.

"I heard them quarreling, Bayard and Allen Carick. They was right outside the kitchen window, there on the path. I was wiping dishes. I heard Allen Carick say, 'I'll kill you for this.' And Bayard laughed. And that very night he was shot. Accidentally! Accidentally on purpose, I say."

"But—did Allen Carick shoot him?"

She frowned suspiciously at me, as if I were trying to trap her. She had colorless eyebrows over light greenish eyes, and a broad, clean-looking face; her absurdly primitive superstitions went badly with her prim green uniform.

"I don't know," she said. "But I don't know who else would. And didn't I hear him threaten to? Bayard and Dave was thick as thieves. That is, most of the time they was. But they had their quarrels. The Thatchers are like that. To look at them you'd think there never was such a loving family. It's different when you know them like I know them."

"You must not talk like this, Florrie."

"You won't tell," said the girl easily. "And I'm kind of nervous. Seems like I can't settle down. It's your hair, ma'am, that's got me upset. Right after the murder, too. To think of me being in the house where there's been a murder." Her green eyes looked strange and trancelike again, and she said, "I think things would be better, ma'am, if you was to leave."

I thought so myself. But not for the same reason.

"Why don't you leave if you're afraid of—more trouble?"

She shrugged her thick shoulders.

"It's a good job," she said. "And I'll keep my door locked nights."

I did not like the way she looked at me.

I said, "My box from the hospital hasn't come yet. I think I'll telephone again," and walked toward the door.

"There's a telephone in Miss Adela's morning room. You'll use that, I suppose, ma'am?"

"Why—yes. Or the telephone in the study off the library."

"Oh, don't use that one, ma'am. That's in Dave's room. Mr. Dave's room, I mean. You see, we all went to grade school together, and I can't remember to say Mr. Dave, like Miss Adela says to."

"But why shouldn't I use that telephone?" I asked. "There's nothing wrong with it, is there?"

"Oh, we never go into Mr. Dave's room. It's his study, you know. He writes. Poetry or something. At least, everyone says he writes. I've never seen a scrap of it, myself. But nobody goes near that room. He keeps it locked most of the time."

"It wasn't locked yesterday afternoon."

"Oh, wasn't it! Well, it usually is. I suppose he forgot. Miss Adela says we mustn't ever bother him. Not even to dust. She says some day we'll be proud of him. I don't think so myself. I think it's silly. Look at all the books there are already. What do they want more books for?

"But there's one good thing," she continued rather resentfully. "Since he's got that soundproof stuff in the walls and door she doesn't go around shushing everybody for fear we'll bother——"

I was at her side, seizing her by the shoulders.

"What did you say? What do you mean?"

She backed away, writhing out of my clasp, her eyes glaring like a frightened cat's.

"Don't you touch me," she cried. "You keep away from me. I can protect myself, I can. You stay away."

"Oh, for heaven's sake! I'm not going to hurt you. Don't be such an idiot. Tell me what you mean. Where is there sound-proofing? Is it in Dave's study? When you're in that room, can you hear anything that goes on outside—in another room? Is the study really soundproof?"

My eager questions confused and frightened her. She backed steadily toward the door.

"I mean he—Dave—fixed it so when the door is closed and you are in the study you might as well be a hundred miles away from the rest of the house so far as hearing anything's concerned. You can't hear a sound. But don't you go grabbing me like that again, ma'am. I don't like it. Not in anybody with hair like yours. Not after what my mother told me. You let me alone."

"You are an out-and-out fool," I snapped. "Get out of my sight before I do something to you!"

It was an unfortunate choice of words. She turned a faint green, scooped up the stack of linen, and vanished, all but slamming the door behind her, and leaving me in a turmoil of conflicting emotions. I longed to shake the girl until her silly teeth rattled. I felt uneasy and very unhappy in that suddenly quiet room, and more than anything I was excited by my discovery. A soundproof room. That would explain why I had heard no sound of the revolver shot that killed Bayard. And it would explain the blood on the rug in the study. Bayard Thatcher had actually been killed in that little study. I was morally certain of it.

But the wound was such that he could not possibly have walked from the study to the library in which he was found. And the door to that little study was as a rule locked. And no one entered it but Dave. It was definitely Dave's room. Why had Bayard been moved to the library after his death? Who had moved him? Who had closed his eyes?

Dave was fishing, though, all the afternoon of the murder, with Allen Carick.

With Allen Carick. Why had Allen Carick and Bayard quarreled so bitterly that Allen had threatened to kill Bayard? Had Allen actually attempted to do so? Was that the explanation of that first attack upon Bayard?

And there was Janice—Janice of the still face and the unfathomable dark eyes. Had she shot Bayard Thatcher in the quiet little study—opened the door, then, and dragged that shattered, dying body across the library?

The thought chilled me. I could see her slender body bending to the effort, her white hands avoiding stain. I stirred impatiently, trying to escape the ugly thought. Her letter: I must find some way to return it. The letter being what it was, I could scarcely walk up to her and say, "Here's your letter. I found it and read it, and here it is."

Lunch that day was a strange meal which, in spite of the grave and dreadful circumstances, assumed an almost festive air, owing to the guests—for Dr. Bouligny was present, also, besides Hilary and Evelyn and Allen Carick—and the arrival of numerous telegrams which began to flow in as Evelyn's messages of the morning reached their various destinations and were answered.

Adela presided. She looked unutterably weary, but she was serene, less cold and severe now that the danger of the inquest was passed; her gray hair was smooth, her eyeglasses shining, and she had taken the pains, even, to change into a soft gray chiffon gown with flowing sleeves, and was wearing her amethysts.

Janice and Evelyn, thoroughbreds too, played up to Adela.

It was more difficult for the men. Dr. Bouligny was frankly nervous and unable, apparently, to get his mind off the inquest. He was, I think, a little trying to Adela. At any rate, she gave him a very cold look after he'd said something to the effect that he was glad it was safely over, and pointedly turned the conversation to the weather. Hilary didn't speak at all, but looked very pink and worried, and once, when he looked up from his salad suddenly and caught me watching him—I was thinking, as a matter of fact, that it wouldn't hurt him to diet—he flushed angrily and returned my look with one of positive malevolence.

Already I had grown accustomed to Dave's silence. He had never a good appetite, and how well I remember him sitting morosely beside Evelyn and unheeding Adela's continual looks. Allen, of course, was there too; also quiet and having difficulty keeping his eyes from Janice. And Emmeline and Florrie in the background. Along toward dessert I caught Florrie's eyes and was a little disturbed by the look in them, and she served me in such a wary and distant manner that I was quite obliged to snatch for what I wanted.

It seems to me, looking back, that I recall those meals with particular clarity; perhaps it is because at those times the whole family was present, seated around that long gracious table with its ever sparkling crystal and gleaming silver and lovely old china. There were always flowers from the gardens, heavy crimson roses or tall gladioluses. And there was always excellent food, well served.

But the significant thing, the thing that caught my imagination, was the presence of the Thatchers. Adela, determined, poised, resolute; Hilary, frightened; Evelyn, cool and practical; Dave, always a puzzle, and Janice and Allen deep in their own urgent problem—and all of them, even Dr. Bouligny and Emmeline and Florrie, contributing in some measure to that tragic mystery.

It is a rather curious tribute to the Thatchers that I could not—I simply could not feel that I was sitting at the same table with a murderer. One who is forever cut off from his fellow man by reason of that dark and dreadful experience he has had.

At the thought I began to feel a little faint and sick, and I put down my fork. But just then Emmeline brought another telegram, and Adela opened it in a leisurely way, adjusted her eyeglasses, read it slowly to herself, and then deliberately and blandly, as if she were reading a newspaper, read it aloud.

"It's from Cousin Helen," she said. "She says, 'Received telegram shocked and grieved Tommy down with measles love.'" Carefully Adela folded up the telegram and replaced it in its envelope. "Exactly ten words," she remarked blandly. "Helen Thatcher was never one to waste money."

"She's not coming to the funeral, then," said Evelyn. "I doubt if anyone comes. She is the nearest. There isn't quite time enough for anyone else to get here."

"You told everyone what time it would be?" asked Adela.

"Oh, yes. I said in my telegrams nine o'clock tomorrow morning."

"That's right. Oh, by the way, Hilary, you might ask Dr. Lyman to call this afternoon to make arrangements about the services."

"You are going to hold it here? In the house?" asked Dr. Bouligny.

Again that touch of granite was in Adela's face. But she said calmly:

"Why, yes. I think that's best. Don't you, Hilary?"

"I don't care where it is," said Hilary, pink and agitated. "Only, for God's sake, get it over as soon as you can——"

Evelyn interrupted hurriedly.

"So Tommy's got measles. Actually that child has everything."

And Janice continued at once:

"This time he's got something twice. He had measles last winter, too."

"Probably," said Adela, "it's just a rash. Children are so apt to get a rash in the summer time. Hilary, now, always broke out after he'd had strawberries."

By that time I had returned to my lunch and was eating quite heartily.

The afternoon was long and warm and, save for the coming and going of various callers and messengers, quiet. Adela rested for some time, although she came downstairs when Dr. Lyman called about four, and I sat in the little morning room with Evelyn and Janice, helping them write notes, receive telephone calls and telegrams, and dispose of a number of tremulous female visitors.

Around six a Mrs. Whiting arrived; she, I had no doubt, of the cod-liver-oil notoriety, an indomitable woman with a chin. She had all the air of an intimate of the household and talked steadily and with not a great amount of tact. I think it was when she said she had just been in her husband's place of business and that Bayard was going to look very well that Janice gave a little gasp and rose, looking rather white, and asked me somewhat incoherently if I didn't want a walk.

I followed her at once. Behind us I heard Mrs. Whiting

boom, "Janice looks bad, Evelyn. She doesn't look well at all. She hasn't looked well all summer. She isn't worried about anything, is she? How is Dave?"

We didn't hear the reply.

"She is a dreadful woman," said Janice in a low voice. "I feel guilty leaving poor Evelyn to her, but I—I simply can't stay there and listen to her. Let's slip out to the garden for a moment. It will be such a rest after this terrible day. Oh—" she caught her breath—"oh, I didn't see you, Allen."

Allen rose from a chair and crossed the porch.

"I'll go along, if you don't mind," he said.

Janice slipped her hand under my arm. Her fingers were rather tight upon it. It was almost as if she'd said, "Stay with me." But she actually said:

"Why, of course, Allen." And the three of us walked across that smooth green lawn to where the flowers spread their masses of gorgeous summer color amid green paths.

It was a lovely place; a serene and happy place and a beautiful one. But I looked up and saw the vine-twined balcony that led to what had been Bayard Thatcher's room, and recalled the mid-night visitor on that balcony, and things were not so lovely or so peaceful.

I was conscious, too, of the effort Janice and Allen were making to talk in an easy and natural way for my ears. I felt a sort of pity as I watched the two—Janice so lovely, now, her whole face animate with beauty, and Allen so carefully restrained, so determinedly quiet, his firm mouth rather tight, but his blue eyes vivid and almost vehement as he watched Janice.

Yet, as if it had been a living thing, I was aware of the feeling that existed between them. I think that even if I had not known what I knew—and what they did not dream of my knowing—I should have been aware of the thing that bound them to each other whether they liked or not; the thing that was like a current flowing through them and drawing them irresistibly together. But only once was there any outward evidence of it.

That was when we reached the rose garden, which was just below the balcony I knew so well and rioted in beauty and extravagant color and fragrance. Janice stopped before one of the bushes, looked at the flowers for a moment, and then bent, graceful and lovely in her soft green gown, and picked one of the heavy crimson roses and held it against her soft cheek. I don't think she knew exactly what she was doing or how the sweetness of that little caress must affect the man who watched her. I'm sure she did not know how beautiful she looked with the slanting sunlight gently warm on her hair, her body slim and yet round under her thin frock, whose delicate green was outlined against the deeper greens of the foliage, and her white arm lifted with that deep crimson rose against her face. And her face all flamed into beauty.

We had paused to wait for her. I suppose we both stared at her, marveling—Allen until he could bear it no longer. I heard him take a quick breath, and he stepped suddenly to her side and took the hand with the rose in it and looked down at her face, and then as abruptly released her hand and turned away, rather white, and said a little breathlessly:

"Beautiful roses. Fragrant. Those roses below the balcony. They are nice."

"Yes," said Janice. "Yes, they are lovely things. Did you ever see such heavy clusters as we have this year?"

"Those roses below the balcony"—"Those roses below the balcony." I did not enjoy the rest of the walk; my mind was too busy with the fragrance of the roses when drenched with summer rain. And the memory of a shadow on that balcony. What had Florrie said about Allen quarreling with Bayard?—but I could recall all too clearly her every word.

It was a chance remark of Janice's that aroused me.

". . . must get Aunt Ella's address so as to get her letter off in tonight's post. Her address is in my desk upstairs, and if I go through the hall Pearl Whiting will clutch me. Do you suppose the woman intends to stay forever? Poor Evelyn—I shouldn't have run away."

"Oh, Evelyn can take care of herself," said her brother carelessly.

And then I remembered the letter. I would be able to slip into Janice's room and leave the thing on her desk where she could not fail to find it. She would have to get the address almost immediately if she wanted to catch the evening post, and that being the case, I ran little risk of the letter being found by someone else.

Ignoring Janice's clasp on my arm and the unconscious appeal in her dark eyes, I left the two in the garden, crossed the quiet green lawn where the shadows were growing longer as sunset approached, and entered the cool polished hall. From the little morning room I caught the steady boom of Mrs. Whiting's voice, and as I went to the stairway Hilary came out of the library, saw me, gave me what I thought was an unreasonably annoyed look—after all, I could scarcely help being some place, and the stairway was certainly an inoffensive spot—and backed into the library again.

No one was about upstairs. The letter was still where I had replaced it, tucked carefully out of sight in my instrument bag. I slipped it into my pocket and went into the hall again. Down toward the back, Florrie, formal now in her afternoon black, whisked out of a door with a stack of towels over one arm. I approached her, disregarding the far from flattering gesture with which she flung the arm with the towels on it in front of her like a shield.

"Where," I said with dignity, "is Miss Janice's room?"

Florrie stepped sidewise into a convenient doorway.

"East side front. Second door from the windows," she said with brevity, and vanished, closing the door firmly behind her.

East side front. Second door from the windows.

After a moment during which I rather felt that Florrie was listening from the other side of the door for my retreating foot-steps, I walked slowly and thoughtfully toward the front of the hall—past my former patient's door, past the stair well, past the long mirror. It had been Janice, then—Janice who had watched me, Janice who must have tried to enter Bayard's room that strange night.

Well, I would return the letter.

Cautiously, feeling guilty in spite of my honorable errand, I reached the door, opened it, and entered. I glanced backward down the hall as I did so and was a little disconcerted to see a white cap flash out of sight around a doorway, but continued.

I did not stop to look about me, though one brief glance gave me a picture of the pleasant room, wide and cool and somehow, in its lack of over-adornment, a bit austere and the more beautiful thereby. I went directly to the desk. On its darkly gleaming surface was a vase, some kind of gray-white pottery it was, filled with an enormous cluster of the deep crimson roses I had seen Janice caress there in the garden. I lifted the vase a bit and slipped the letter barely under its edge; it could not be blown off the desk by any stray current of air and it was very prominent against the dark wood. Then I left.

The whole thing had taken scarcely a moment.

Once in my own room I left the door ajar so I could see Janice pass on her way to her room. When I had seen her enter her room I should feel that the letter was safe in her hands again.

But in a moment or two Florrie went past. Vaguely uneasy, I started toward the door. If she entered the room—if she found and looked at Janice's letter—— I was on the very point of returning to Janice's room, if need be to rescue the letter, when there were light footsteps along the hall, and Janice at last passed. I caught just a glimpse of her light green frock and her dark hair.

I stepped into the hall in time to see her enter her room. If Florrie had not preceded her all would be well.

But Florrie had. There were voices, not loud but audible in the quiet of the hall. I walked slowly along the hall. And I heard Janice say distinctly:

"Put that down at once. You will regret this, Florrie."

And Florrie said, "I didn't read a word. I didn't know—it was here—I was tidying up the—I thought——"

"You may go."

To escape Florrie I retired somewhat hastily to Adela's room, the door of which stood conveniently open behind me. Unfortunately Florrie followed me into the room, and I was obliged further to retreat to the bathroom, where I sat on the edge of the tub and listened to the girl moving about the adjoining room. I became so lost in thought of Janice that I did not note her departure. It was with a decided shock that I was suddenly aware that with her exit someone else had entered Adela's room. That the door to the hall was closed with decision. And that someone was saying:

". . . and get him away before someone finds out he shot Bayard."

CHAPTER IX

IT WAS EVELYN'S VOICE.

I sat down again on the bathtub.

No one answered her for a moment. There was a sound of motion, as if someone sat down on a chair, and I heard a window shade being pulled. Then a man—it was Hilary—spoke.

"What do you think, Adela?"

Adela and Evelyn and Hilary. A confidential family conference, and I was sitting on the bathtub hearing every word of it. I started to make my presence known. And Adela said:

"It's the nurse. She's our danger."

"That's right. If we can silence her—— We ought never to have got her here, in the first place."

"I know it now," said Adela. "But at the time I thought it was the best thing to do. After what happened. I thought she would stand between them, in a sense. Bayard refused to leave; I couldn't send him away sick—after that."

"But I don't like her," said Hilary in a peevish way. "She makes me nervous. Always about where you don't expect her."

There was a short pause during which I wondered what Hilary would do if he knew where I was at that moment; then he continued, still rather fretfully:

"Why didn't you let her leave right away after he was killed?

102

I don't understand you, Adela. She's right here among us, seeing our every move. How long do you think we can keep her thinking it was a burglar shot him?"

"But it *was* a burglar who shot him," said Adela stubbornly. "And think, Hilary, how mad it would have been to send her away unconvinced. I can see doubt in her eyes. I could see it yesterday afternoon, there in the library. We've got to keep her here. Where we can watch her."

"Indefinitely?" asked Hilary unpleasantly.

"Don't talk that way, Hilary," said Evelyn sharply. "Adela's quite right about it. You can manage the sheriff, and Adela can manage Dan Bouligny, and all of us together can face down the talk in the county. It's that nurse who is our problem. It's she who threatens us. But I don't know what we are going to do about it. Of course, we can't keep her here forever. She keeps saying she must go; I think she suspects. You'll have to think up things for her to do, Adela, to keep her busy."

"Don't you see, Hilary," said Adela. "If we can convince her that it was done by a burglar somebody— *anybody* but one of the family, we will have nothing further to fear. If we can keep her here somehow and manage to prove to her that no one in the family had—had anything to do with Bayard's death, we have, practically speaking, convinced the world."

"It won't be easy," said Hilary. "She's got the sharpest eyes I ever saw. But you may be right. I didn't exactly like the way she looked at me this morning. Do you realize that if she hadn't been sitting in that confounded arbor all yesterday afternoon we wouldn't have a thing to worry about? Nobody else knew I was here; nobody would have known Evelyn was here; a burglar could have entered by the front door. Oh, it's that damn nurse that's got everything in a snarl." He paused and after a moment added, "As it is, I expect any moment to hear somebody's been saying I killed him. Everybody knows we never liked each other."

There was another pause, and then Adela said in a still way:

"Hilary—you and Bayard hadn't had any particular trouble about anything, had you?"

"No," he said explosively. "Good God, no! What do you mean, Adela?"

"I don't mean anything, Hilary. I only want to be sure you had had no trouble. You see, even if everyone does know you were not friendly, still, they can have nothing definite to say. No definite cause, I mean, for you—for you——"

"For me to have shot him, I suppose you mean, Adela," blurted Hilary disagreeably. Evelyn murmured warningly: "Now, Hilary—now, be careful," and Hilary went on, "Well, get this into your head, Adela. I didn't shoot him. I always hated him, and you know why. And he hated me. But I didn't shoot him."

"Look out, Hilary," said Adela coolly. "Your face is terribly red. Remember your blood pressure."

"Blood pressure, hell," said Hilary. "Do you think I'm going to sit here and let even you accuse me of murdering a man? There are limits, Adela——"

"Hilary!" said Evelyn sharply. "You are forgetting yourself. Adela's the best friend you've got, and you know it. And anyway—maybe there was a burglar. There are the diamonds, you know."

"The diamonds!" cried Hilary. "Yes, and where are they? That's another thing I don't understand about this. Dave says he knows nothing of them. They undoubtedly were gone from the safe when Adela opened it there right after the murder. Those diamonds are worth a lot. We've got to get hold of them."

"To my notion," said Evelyn bluntly, "the disappearance of

the diamonds is the only hopeful aspect of the whole situation. I don't want to know what's happened to them. And the nurse was there and saw with her own eyes that they were actually gone. I think, like Adela, that it's worth the price."

"You women," said Hilary hopelessly, "are crazy. Sometimes I think I'm crazy too. You insist that there was a burglar and that he stole the diamonds and that you're glad of it. In the next breath you practically accuse me of killing Bayard, and then you——"

"Hilary." It was Adela, her voice lower than usual and very quiet, and so stripped of its usual affectation that it seemed indecently bare and significant. "Hilary, what did you and Bayard talk of when you came here yesterday afternoon?"

"Why, I—that is, we—we talked of—I don't know exactly." He stopped, floundering, cleared his throat, and said, "Why do you want to know, Adela?"

"Because," said Adela slowly, "that's what people will want to know. Are you quite sure, Hilary, that you—" she paused, and it was very silent before she continued—"that you talked to him at all?"

I could hear him spring to his feet and his quick footsteps on the floor.

"What do you mean by that, Adela? I swear I didn't shoot him. I didn't kill him. I had no reason to kill him. You—you are driving me mad!" His voice was shaking with rage and a kind of fright.

"Are you sure," said Adela, "that you had no reason?"

"Adela, you are driving me out of my senses. You make it sound as if I'd sneaked into the house and shot him dead before he could call for help or defend himself. And I didn't. I tell you, I didn't!" His voice had lifted as if he were approaching hysteria.

"Now then, Hilary, you must learn to control yourself." It was Evelyn, speaking with the infuriating coolness of a long-married wife. "You'll have a stroke if you keep on like this. Look at your face there in the mirror. For heaven's sake, cool down a little. Adela hasn't accused you of anything. She only asked you to tell her what you talked about. That ought to be easy."

"What did he say over the phone to you, Adela?" asked Hilary.

"Scarcely a word," said Adela. "Just 'yes' and 'all right.' You didn't even speak to him, Evelyn, when you stopped for Hilary?"

"Not a word," said Evelyn steadily.

"Didn't he even hear you come to the door?"

"No," said Evelyn. "No. He didn't hear me. I saw Hilary had gone, so I didn't linger."

"Oh, Evelyn," cried Adela, suddenly losing her customary deliberation of manner and speaking with a sort of burst, "why don't you tell me the truth? There is something you and Hilary are keeping from me. I know it. I feel it. You must tell me. We can only save ourselves by knowing everything. If you saw any-thing—know anything——"

"Nothing, Adela. Nothing," said Evelyn. "You are nervous. You——"

"Nervous, nothing!" cried Adela with a sharp fury of which I shouldn't have believed her capable. "You treat me like an old woman. And it's my house. And my family. And I've got to know."

"Get her a drink of water, Evelyn," said Hilary. "Now—now, Adela——"

I lost the rest of his admonition. "Get her a drink of water." Evelyn would be at the bathroom door in another moment. A purely primitive terror gripped me. They had said I was a danger.

They were implacable. What would they do to me if they discovered I had heard every damning word they'd said!

Then common sense returned, and I realized they couldn't do anything. And yet—couldn't they? There was Bayard.

My eyes were going frantically about the small room and discovering that a flea would have had difficulty hiding for long in the glittering expanse of porcelain and white walls, let alone a woman of not inconsiderable height and a weight that—well, never mind my weight. Even the shower was caged in shining glass. And the door began to open.

It opened several inches. I cannot describe my feeling as I watched it.

And in the very nick of time Hilary, from the bedroom, said:

"No, Evelyn, here's some sherry. That will be better. Here, Adela, drink this. You ought not to overtax your heart like that."

Evelyn moved away from the door; I could feel rather than hear her withdrawal. And the door, left to itself, swung gently and slowly to its original position. But my heart was pounding so heavily that for a moment or two I actually could not hear what they were saying in the next room.

". . . all nervous and upset, and no wonder," Hilary was saying when I regained my senses. "We know damn well that somebody in the family killed him. And it's not a nice thing to know. Ours is not a big family. But all this talk's doing no good. We've got to get Dave away from here. Before the nurse gets onto things."

"What's your plan about the nurse?" asked Evelyn. "You do feel better, don't you, Adela?"

"I don't feel ill at all," said Adela crisply. "And I don't want Dave to leave just now. He's not well, and I think he's terribly depressed over Bayard's death. But about the nurse. I think I can manage her. You see, if I can prove to her that it must have been the burglar—as, of course, it was," she interpolated hurriedly—"that no one of the family killed him, then we'll be safe. No troublesome witness to bob up later against us. And I think I can."

"It won't be easy," said Hilary thoughtfully. "I wonder if Bayard told her anything before he died. Do you suppose he did? I wonder—" he paused and went on finally—"I wonder if she knows who shot him."

"I've wondered that, too," said Evelyn. "It seems to me she's got a sort of knowing look. You weren't too careful what you said at breakfast about the inquest."

"But we didn't mention him."

"I wasn't there," said Adela. "What was it?"

"Nothing at all," said Hilary in a blustering way, as if he had been called to account and felt guilty.

"Only enough to let her know that you were managing the inquest to suit yourself. The veriest child would have known you were trying to hide something. You and Dr. Dan. Where were you this morning, Adela? I thought you were asleep until I came up here after breakfast, and you had gone. Poor old Pansy looked like she'd lost her last friend."

"I had just gone for a little walk," said Adela blandly. "I needed some fresh air. I woke up feeling stuffy. What about Dave, now? I don't really like him to leave just now."

"He's got to leave," said Hilary. "He'll give himself away."

"Hilary!" said Adela sharply. "*You don't think Dave killed Bayard?*"

There was a long silence. Then Hilary said with difficulty:

"No, Adela. No. But we all know he tried to kill him the other night. It wasn't his fault Bayard dodged and the bullet caught him in the shoulder. Dave would have shot again and killed him then and there if you hadn't interfered. It's lucky you heard and got there in time to grab Dave's hand. Talk him out of it. I think Dave must have been out of his senses."

"But he didn't kill him that night," said Adela. She spoke with accentuated care and slowness, as if her mouth were stiff. "And yesterday, when Bayard was actually killed, Dave and Allen were together all afternoon. That proves it wasn't Dave, Hilary. That proves it. You dare not call your own brother a murderer. And I won't have him sent away."

There was a knock at the door, and without waiting for answer someone opened it.

"There are ways," Evelyn was saying. "People have been silenced——" when her voice broke off sharply. I could feel the sudden silence and restraint in the room beyond. Then someone moved and Adela said with a sort of relief in her voice:

"Oh, it's you, Emmeline. What is it?"

"Some newspaper men from the city, ma'am. They want to take some pictures and ask you some questions."

"Send them away at once. Tell them I can't see them."

"Wait, Adela. You are making a mistake. We can't afford to antagonize the press," said Hilary heavily. "Tell the gentlemen, Emmeline, that we'll see them. Can you bear it, Adela?"

"You are quite right, Hilary," said Adela. "Just let me look at myself in the mirror. Do you want some powder, Evelyn? Your eyes are rather red. Better touch them with water."

"Hurry up," said Hilary impatiently. "But, for heaven's sake, be careful what you say. Better let me do the talking."

"My dear Hilary," said Adela somewhat waspishly. "Nothing would suit me better. Come, Evelyn."

I heard them leave. I heard the diminishing murmur of voices, the rustle of footsteps on rugs and of Adela's skirts.

Even then it was a moment or two before I dared peer through the crack of the door. The room was empty.

I rose and did not draw a free breath until I was safe in my own room.

So it was Dave.

Dave.

It had been in Dave's study that Bayard was killed. I felt certain of that. The blood on the rug in the study and no sound of the revolver shot—yes, I was sure Bayard had been killed in Dave's study. Dave's revolver with its two shots gone. Dave himself, silent, languid, morose—entirely perplexing.

And Dave had made that first attempt to murder Bayard. He would have shot again, they said, if Adela had not stopped him. I had been convinced all along that when I knew who had shot Bayard that first time, when only his shoulder was wounded, I would know who had finally murdered him.

But Dave had been with Allen all that long afternoon. Allen had quarreled bitterly with Bayard. Dave had taken a revolver and shot Bayard. But both the men had alibis for that interval of time during which Bayard was actually murdered.

Who, then, could have killed him? It was curious that, as I thought of the Thatcher family, the only member of it who seemed psychologically capable of cold-blooded murder was Evelyn. Evelyn with her firm brown hands and her bluntness and her matter-of-fact way of looking at things. If, for some good reason, she had made up her mind that Bayard should be got out of the way she would kill him with as little compunction as she would step on a spider. After it was over she would not harass herself with fears or doubts or regrets; she would act exactly as she had acted—write her notes, send her telegrams, meet and calmly dispose of callers, help with household matters. The only signs of weakness she had displayed about the whole ugly business were when she had said, there over Bayard's dead body in the library, "What will people say?" And that was not exactly a sign of weakness. The other was more significant: that was her reluctance to let her sons come home—come home to that grim and sordid tragedy of murder. Even an unimaginative woman would not want her sons entangled in the murder she had done.

And so far as material evidence went—which after all is rather conclusive, for there's no getting around it, if a man's killed with a bullet that bullet's got to come out of a gun, and guns don't fire themselves—so far as material evidence went she—or Janice—was the last one known to have seen Bayard alive.

Well, it had been a strange conversation I had heard; it seemed to me that the omissions were quite as significant as the hints and warnings and open admissions. There were many things they had quite definitely failed to talk of. Dave's reason for trying to kill Bayard, for instance. Or why Hilary so hated the dead man.

Evelyn or Janice had certainly been the last person to see Bayard alive. I could not believe that Janice with her loveliness and her youth and her charm had killed Bayard. And Evelyn would have had to have a very urgent motive for murdering him; it would have had to be a motive that even her gift for expediency and her extremely practical intelligence could discover no other possible way to satisfy. And while it's true that a woman like Janice, passionately and hopelessly in love, may be impelled to do extraordinary things—still I don't know that she need take to manslaughter as a relief for her feelings.

But there was the time and opportunity Janice had had— there was the egg basket and the revolver and that compromising episode in the kitchen the very next morning following the murder. There was no escaping the deduction that she'd known the revolver was in that basket and that she'd gone to the refrigerator either to be sure it was still undetected or to remove it to a safer place.

A dozen pictures of Janice returned to me: the frightened, beautiful girl in soft yellow chiffon, bravely holding her fright in leash and showing me into Bayard Thatcher's room; the slim child in green dimity working among the flowers, herself lovelier than any of them; the tortured woman with the spent white face leaving her love and her lover without surrender there at the foot of the stairs, with the still summer night and the moonlight and shadows and the scent of the roses outside. And there was her letter with its pride and pain and honesty. And there was the girl of the afternoon, happy and warm in spite of herself because Allen was there beside her, and holding that dark red rose to her cheek as if that were the one thing she might caress.

No, it couldn't be Janice.

Yet Bayard Thatcher had certainly been murdered. I always came back to that.

Twilight was coming on when I went downstairs. That night dinner was a silent and a rather dreadful meal. Those desperate efforts to keep up appearances had flagged from very weariness with the long and trying day, and I daresay everyone dreaded tomorrow's ordeal. Tomorrow, when they would lay Bayard's body away with those other Thatchers, and would know, every one of them, that in their small circle was that one who had murdered him. No, it was no pleasant thing to anticipate, and there was no escaping it. There were, even, no more telegrams to be opened and read and discussed with a determined pretense of the ordinary and the commonplace. Flowers, however, had begun to come with the arrival of the evening train; they had been stored in tubs of cold water in the summer kitchen, but among them were lilies whose cloying fragrance had filled the house before the sheaf was removed, and which now clung to everything, a ghostly notice of the ordeal to come.

To my surprise Janice was white and tired and failed to catch the occasional effort Evelyn made to introduce some safe topic of conversation. The meal was half over before I discovered why; somehow, I had expected her to be greatly relieved from alarm and anxiety by the return of her letter and to show it in her face and bearing. But, possibly from not having had an overwhelming amount of experience in such matters, I am rather clumsy. I had not perceived that her distress and anxiety as to who had read her letter would be greater than her relief at getting it into her own hands once again. After all, it might have been kinder to tell her.

After dinner we sat out on the porch in the quiet, deepening summer night. There was very little said. The greens of the lawn lost themselves in shadow; the cigarettes became small red spots of light; the street lights away down at the corner made the trees loom huge and black and far away, with leaves edged in light silver where the light touched them. The moon came up finally; the dusk was lost, and the shrubs and trees stood out black against the white lawn, and white strip of road. The moon, I thought idly, was at its full.

After a long time Evelyn murmured something about going home, and Adela stirred to say, out of the darkness beside me, that she'd like them to stay there again for the night. There was no appeal in her deliberate voice, but I felt she wanted Hilary and Evelyn near her. Evelyn agreed at once.

"Allen won't mind staying over at the house alone," she said. "But I'll want a few things from home. Allen, will you take the car over and ask Julia to pack my overnight bag. Tell her to put in that new white silk. The crêpe with the long sleeves; she'll know the gown I mean. And the white hat that goes with it. And gloves. Tell her to fold the silk carefully, I don't want to have to press it. We'd better wear white tomorrow, Janice. Adela will wear black with her long crêpe veil, but I think plain white summer dresses with white hats would be better for us to wear. People will like it. Do you mind, Allen?"

"I hope I get the right things," said Allen, rising from the step. Against the moonlit lawn his tall figure looked strong and full of life and vitality. His cigarette was a small red comet across the lawn, and he said:

"Better come along, Janice. The drive will do you good."

"Oh, no. No," said Janice. There was a hint of panic in her voice. Of what had she been thinking, I wondered, as she sat there so quiet in the shadow of the clematis vine and watched Allen in the moonlight, and felt the soft summer night and wanted, perhaps, the touch of his hands and his arms and his mouth. Poor Janice, who knew so well what love could be. But perhaps Allen suffered more when he thought of Dave. Dave! With some chagrin I reminded myself that my morals were tottering—morals which had served me well for longer than it's necessary to mention. There was Dave, too, to be pitied; Dave whose wife no longer loved him; Dave whose friend was treacherous. Dave, who, by all rights, ought to be pitied more than any of them. But for the life of me I could not feel particularly sorry for Dave; perhaps it was owing to his curious detachment, his enigmatic lack of interest in his lovely wife, his morose silences, his somber, withdrawn look.

Wearily I found myself again in that hopeless circle of speculation and resolved to leave it at least for the night. But I was not permitted to do so; one of the strangest things about the Thatcher case was the inexorable destiny which dragged me into every phase of it.

Evelyn, too, may have caught some meaning note in Janice's voice, for she rose.

"Perhaps I'd better go along after all," she said firmly. "We'll be awfully hurried tomorrow morning, and I'd better be sure I have everything. I'll bring your things, too, Hilary. I think I know what you'll want."

The sound of the car shook the still night. Janice had shrunk back into the shadow of the vine. "Such a few moments," she had said, "out of all the years. All the rest such a dreadful waste."

Adela stood.

"I'll say good-night," she said. "As Evelyn says, we'll be hurried in the morning." She sighed. "I only hope no one says anything about our hurrying the funeral so. It doesn't seem fitting not to wait—but tomorrow's Sunday—perhaps they'll think——" She checked herself and said in a more collected way, "Will you come with me, please, Miss Keate? I am very tired."

I went with her, of course. She did look dreadfully weary. I was giving her a back massage when someone knocked at the door. At Adela's word Florrie entered.

"Well, Florrie, what is it?" asked Adela.

"I'm sorry to trouble you, Miss Adela," said Florrie. "But I thought you might have some aspirin. I've got one of my bad headaches. And I don't want to be sick for tomorrow, ma'am. There'll be a lot to do."

"Why, certainly, Florrie. There ought to be some in the medicine chest, there in my bathroom. Go and look."

But there wasn't, it developed, and Adela sent Florrie to Janice's room.

"I'm sure she has some. Just look in the medicine chest in her dressing room. She always keeps it on hand for Mr. Dave's headaches."

Florrie went away. It was perhaps five minutes later that she returned. At first sight of her eyes, shining a little, and that odd look of malice in her usually stolid face, I straightened up and looked at the thing she held in her hands. It was a small white felt hat. Adela looked, too, and became an old, old woman before my very eyes.

"I thought I ought to bring this to you, ma'am," said Florrie, her voice shrill with a kind of ugly triumph. "I saw it accidentally. It was stuffed back of the radiator in Miss Janice's dressing room, ma'am. Right there below the medicine cabinet."

I have never before or since admired Adela as I did at that moment. She said:

"Give it to me, Florrie. Miss Keate, haven't you some aspirin for her?"

I did have: a large boxful of tablets. A pasteboard box into which I had tumbled the tablets for convenience and which I had labeled. It was in my small instrument bag, and I got it at once and thrust box and all into Florrie's hand and told her not to take too many of them.

"You may go now, Florrie," said Adela. Her bluish lips looked stiff, and her eyes like ice. The girl went; she looked frightened.

Adela did not try to dissemble before me. I suppose she knew it was no use. I looked at the small hat.

It was the hat Janice had worn the previous afternoon; I knew it at once. And I remembered with frightful clarity that she had worn it when she entered the house alone, not more than ten minutes before Bayard was found murdered. And that when, at the alarm, she had appeared in the library beside us all she had worn no hat.

But on the white brim of that small felt hat were four red-brown smudges. I have seen dried blood too often not to recognize it immediately.

Adela said stiffly:

"Take it. Nurse——"

And at that very instant there was a knock on the door, and without waiting for a reply it was pushed open.

Janice stood on the threshold.

Her dark eyes went to me and then to Adela and then fastened upon the hat. It was not nice to see the loveliness leave her face; to see it become a stiff, strained white mask, hiding terror.

CHAPTER X

MANY TIMES DURING MY stay in the Thatcher home I was astonished at the Thatcher capacity for utter silence. Utter and complete silence at times when an ordinary person would have burst into frenzied explanations. But I was never more taken aback by that baffling trait than when Janice merely looked at that bloodstained little hat, that dreadful witness against her, for a long moment, and then said:

"What are you doing with my hat?" Her voice was quite steady, but then I had seen something of her powers of self-control. And her face was still white and drained of life.

"Your—hat," said Adela with difficulty. It was not exactly a question or a statement; it was just the utterance of words in a curiously tentative way. She offered, I thought, a chance for Janice to deny the hat.

But Janice said, "Why, certainly. You know it's my hat. What are you doing with it?"

"It was—found," said Adela. She looked shrunken and terribly old. "It was found and brought to me."

"Who found it?"

"Florrie."

"Oh," said Janice. "Oh. Florrie. Florrie seems to be taking quite an interest in my affairs lately. Well, if you are quite through with it, I'll take it."

She walked swiftly to the bed and picked up the hat. I noted that her slender fingers seemed to avoid touching the brim; that brim that showed where four fingers had touched it and had left so ugly a mark of their pressure. To complete my bewilderment she bent over Adela, kissed her cheek lightly, said, "Have a good night, darling. Don't worry about tomorrow," and turned away. At the door she remembered my presence and said over her shoulder, "Good-night, Miss Keate."

She said it coolly, her dark eyes unfathomable, her slender figure erect, her chin up, and the tell-tale little hat crushed in her hand. Then she closed the door firmly behind her, and Adela sighed.

"You see, Miss Keate, we were wrong. We both leaped to an unjust and horrible conclusion. Or not so much a conclusion as a very dreadful suspicion. It only goes to show how one's nerves may trick one. We are both unstrung by the dreadful and shocking circumstances of Bayard's death. He was killed by a burglar, and we know it. And yet merely the sight of—the sight of——" She could not say the word and substituted, "merely the stain on Janice's hat made us both fear——" Deep waters here, Adela. And she realized it. For she checked her words to cough delicately, to hunt for a handkerchief, to ask me for a drink of water. And finally to resume:

"Absurd of us. When there are so many ways that could happen. Of course. I know my own family. I know none of them are capable of—that Janice is not—that she could not——" She stuck again. Poor Adela, she could not bring herself to voice her thought.

As for me, I should have been much happier if Janice had

said something—anything—to explain that hat. Her silence was almost as damning as the bloody fingerprints; more so, in fact, for I felt if there'd been an innocent explanation she would have given it.

And the grim little incident brought rather forcibly to my mind the danger in which I stood. I, the stranger; I, the outsider. I said quietly:

"By the way, Miss Thatcher, you won't need me past tomorrow. I can return to the hospital after the funeral."

Even if I did not know what I knew, I would have guessed something of it from the sudden bleakness of her blue eyes, the way her face set itself again.

"Oh, certainly, Miss Keate," she said. "Certainly. I didn't realize that I was keeping you here when there was something else you were anxious to do. Is there a case waiting for you?"

"No," I said honestly. "But I must—go."

"Oh, then," she said affably, "if there's no case waiting for you, you won't mind staying with me a few days longer. Surely you don't feel that we expect too much of you? I haven't had a chance, really, to tell you how grateful we all are for the way you've helped us. I don't know what we should have done without you. But I'm sorry we have worked you too hard."

"Oh, no," I said helplessly. "Not too hard. But you don't need my nursing care, you know, and——"

"My dear, you are too conscientious," said Adela pleasantly. "I see what's wrong. You like to be busy, and you feel you aren't doing enough. Well, then, I must tell you that we—we depend upon you. Of course, if you don't like it with us, I will not try to keep you. But I—I'm not in very good health, as you surely have seen. And you can't possibly realize what a help you've been to me. But don't let me persuade you. I can probably get along. It's only that it's been such a shock. Such a dreadful shock——" Her voice broke. That much was true, and I knew it; I even wondered how long she could endure the dreadful strain put upon her.

Afterward I reflected that she had very cleverly used the only weapon that would touch me; opposition I could have resisted, defencelessness weakened my resolution. And at the time I felt no definite, physical fear of any one member of the Thatcher family; it was only a kind of grim uneasiness, a feeling of uncertainty that clutched rather coldly at my heart now and then and was immediately dispelled at the sound of Adela's calm, deliberately elegant voice.

"Never mind, now," I said. "You must get some sleep. I'll not leave for a day or two, at any rate. Now then, I'll just give you something Dr. Bouligny left to make you sleep. You must have a good night's rest."

Wisely she left the matter of my departure rest. Adela was always wise. But she refused the sedative.

"I don't like drugs," she said sharply. "I never feel well the morning after I take a sedative. And besides, I—well, I don't like them. I hate drugs. Dr. Bouligny is too free with them. I'll do better not to take any tonight, Miss Keate. Just hand me those turquoise beads, will you? I like to—Thank you. I've had these many years. It always calms me a little to feel them in my hands. But you might read aloud to me a little, if you will, Miss Keate. Reading aloud is very soothing, I think. There are some books on that shelf back of you. Choose what you like."

There wasn't much choice: from a history of the Thatcher Family, a volume of Drummond's sermons, and *The Last of the Mohicans*, I chose the latter as being livelier and reflected inwardly that whoever of the Thatchers had collected that splendid library downstairs it was not, in all probability, Adela.

But the green and savage forest failed to charm, and though I read steadily and stubbornly onward I found my thoughts holding to the Thatcher problem to such a degree that once I read Janice instead of Alice and another time found I had skipped an entire page—and an important page, which left Cora at the river's brim in very equivocal circumstances indeed. But Adela did not note my slight lapses; she lay there staring at the ceiling, pulling her turquoise beads through her fingers, thinking, I felt, rather desperately while I tried to retrieve my errors by reading with increased expression and feeling.

Finally she said to me:

"I've been thinking about Florrie, Miss Keate. You may stop reading; yes, thank you, that was very nice, I'm sure. Very soothing," she said with a politeness which, I must say, left me a bit dashed; I have always felt that I read aloud rather well—particularly the more dramatic portions. "You see, there's no telling what Florrie is apt to think about—about that hat. Janice's hat, you know. And Florrie is a very stupid girl and a talkative one. If she gets some silly notion in her head, it will go straight to her mother, and the whole town will know it in half a day. I think I'd better speak to Florrie at once. Tell her—something; anything to hold her tongue. I shall rest better when I've done so. Would you call her, Miss Keate? I daresay everyone else has gone to bed. It's been very quiet in the house for some time. Florrie is probably asleep by this time. But I think you'd better wake her."

"Very well." I replaced the book on the shelf. It had grown very quiet as I read; the moonlight was white and still on the lawns outside the windows and the great trees hushed and black.

"Where is her room?"

"On the third floor. At the back of the hall is a stairway leading to the third floor. Her room is on the east side of the third-floor hall; the gable room. You can find it without any difficulty. Don't be long, Miss Keate. I feel—a little nervous, somehow, uneasy. I'm sure I'll feel better after I've talked to Florrie."

The wide hall was quiet, deserted. The night light only faintly illuminated its dim length. The rest of the household had apparently gone to sleep, for there was no sound of voices or motion in the whole house. The silence was so deep that, when I passed the stair well, I could actually hear the great clock ticking slowly and deliberately downstairs. I walked rather quickly down the hall, past all those closed doors. Sure enough, at its end, running up a few steps to a sharp landing at right angles to the hall, I found the stairway leading to the third floor. At the same angle were other stairs leading down to, presumably, the back part of the house; at the time the house was built a back stairway was almost of itself an evidence of gentility.

Something about the sleeping house and the quiet shadowy hall made me, too, feel uneasy. And an unkind trick of memory brought to me suddenly a mental vision of Bayard Thatcher— Bayard Thatcher, shattered and dead on the library rug. The silent house knew and held the secret of his death.

I settled my cap and went up the stairs, feeling my way along by clinging to the railing until I emerged upon a narrow passage at the top along which white fingers of moonlight stretched ghostly.

I had no difficulty following Adela's directions. The door that must be Florrie's was closed, and I knocked and knocked again.

There was no answer. The moonlight was white on the floor. The whole place was silent. There was not a breath of sound anywhere.

I knocked once more; louder this time, and wishing myself back in Adela's softly lit room. Or, better, my own room, with the door locked. With the door locked! Hadn't Florrie said she always locked her door? She'd said other things, too. Silly things. Absurd things.

"Florrie," I called. My voice was not too steady. I said more clearly, "Florrie. Miss Thatcher wants you."

There was still no reply.

I think it was the complete deathlike silence that frightened me, rather than the memory of her stolid, foolish voice saying, "murdered in my sleep—murdered in my sleep." But whatever it was I was suddenly in a panic. She ought to answer. She ought to come to open the door. My last knock resounded in the still passage.

All at once I was trembling. My hands were shaking as I tried the door, pushed against it, and rattled the doorknob. It was locked, and there was still no sound from the girl inside.

Then, quite as if my body were acting of itself, involuntarily, without my consent or council, I was flying down that narrow stairway, groping for the railing, stumbling, whirling around the turn and down the long hall. I'm sure I didn't cry out, but perhaps my footsteps roused the uneasy house. From some desire to save Adela I found myself at Janice's door rather than at Adela's, knocking and sobbing out something.

She flung open the door, her face as white as her nightdress.

"What is it? Miss Keate——"

"The keys," I said. "Florrie. Something's wrong. We'll need the key to her room."

She did not stop to question me. She snatched a negligee from a chair.

"Adela's got the keys. I'll go——"

We were in Adela's room, meeting her shocked eyes, grasping the keys. We were running along the hall again. Hilary, in purple-striped pajamas, bounced out of a door as we passed, panted something I didn't hear, and followed. I was vaguely conscious that Evelyn was there, too, for I remember her long yellow braids swinging beside me as Janice fitted the key in the lock. We had some trouble getting it to turn. Florrie's key had been left in the other side, and it was Hilary who finally managed it. By that time Emmeline was in the hall, too: a bizarre figure in a bright Japanese crêpe kimono and her hair in curlers.

But we did get the door unlocked. I was the first one through it.

The moonlight streamed whitely into the room. It was so radiant and bright that the figure of the girl on the bed was very clear.

There was a sort of hush back of me. Then Hilary said in a high, squeaky voice:

"Oh, my God! Oh, my God! The girl's dead!"

Well, she wasn't dead.

She was and is still, so far as I know, alive. But she was as near death as are few people in this world who yet live. She was already in that vast shadowy borderland whence there are so few returns.

We were barely in time.

I did not, intentionally, play a heroic part in bringing Florrie back to life. But I was trained. I knew what to do. I knew what, after hunting for that feeble flicker that was her pulse, to look for. And I found it on the table beside her. The box of aspirin tablets I had given her stood there. It was open. But the tablets were not aspirin. I looked, tasted.

"Make some strong black coffee as quick as you can. Call the doctor. Help me get her out of bed. On her feet. The girl's nearly dead with veronal."

How we worked, Evelyn and Janice and I, with Hilary hurrying to the telephone, and Emmeline to the kitchen for coffee, and Adela panting upstairs to get us cold towels and watch us with blank blue eyes while we walked that inert burden up and down, up and down, holding her sliding weight somehow between us. Hilary was back soon, puffing from the climb, telling us to do what we were already doing and that Dr. Bouligny was on the way. And I remember how haggard and old he looked, huddled in a shabby old dressing gown, his hair rumpled and untidy; Hilary, whose finical tidiness often reminded me of a sleek cat.

We worked furiously; well-nigh frantically. The night was warm and our faces glistened. It took supreme physical exertion to keep the girl moving. It was dreadfully difficult to force the coffee down her throat, and for a long time after that the aroma of strong black coffee made me feel ill and faint. I was only barely conscious of Dr. Bouligny's arrival, and of the hidden horror back of Adela's bleak blue eyes when she told him as far as she could what had happened.

But we did save the girl. Although I suppose only I and the doctor knew how narrowly we had saved her.

It was approaching dawn when Dr. Bouligny said, "She'll do now," and sent Janice and Evelyn away to get some rest. Adela he had sent back to bed long ago, and Hilary had dropped dully into a chair in the corner of the room from which he watched us with weary, troubled eyes.

"Miss Keate has worked harder than anybody," said Janice. "I'm not tired. Let her go and get some sleep, and I'll stay with Florrie."

"You'll have to go to the funeral," said Dr. Bouligny brusquely. "Miss Keate can rest later in the day. Go along, child, and try to sleep some. You look as if you're about to drop. Now then, Miss Keate—you'd better stay a moment, Hilary—how did you happen to give this girl veronal?"

"But I didn't," I said. "I didn't have any veronal."

"This is the box you gave Florrie, isn't it? Adela said it was. And it's your handwriting on the label. It says aspirin, but——"

"Oh, that's the box I gave her," I said sharply. "Of course it is. I always carry aspirin in a flat box like that. And there was aspirin in the box. I could not make such a mistake. There are a hundred ways I can prove it."

"But there are veronal tablets in it now," persisted Dr. Bouligny. "Come, Miss Keate. If you made a mistake, I know it was an accident, and no one regrets it more than you. I also know that you don't as a rule—in fact, I feel confident that you almost never make a mistake. And since we have saved the girl, there's no irreparable harm done."

"But I tell you I did not put veronal tablets in that box!"

"Now, Miss Keate," said Hilary anxiously, "don't get all upset about this. Nobody's blaming you. But don't you see the tablets—the veronal tablets, I mean—are in it now? When did you last open that pill box?"

"The day before I came here. I filled it with aspirin tablets, labeled it and put it in my instrument bag. Nobody could ever confuse aspirin tablets and veronal tablets. And I didn't touch it again until Florrie asked for aspirin last night and I took the box out and handed it to her. If veronal is there now instead of aspirin, as it is, somebody in this house put it there."

"Nonsense, Miss Keate! Why should anyone do that? I hope you aren't suggesting that someone tried to—to kill Florrie. That isn't reasonable. Aside from the fact that no one in the house— oh, it's quite absurd even to consider it!—had any reason to kill Florrie, nobody could have known ahead of time that she would have a headache and wouldn't be able to find as common a thing as aspirin anywhere in the house and would finally come to you for it and get the veronal instead. And that she would take

enough of it to kill her. Really, Miss Keate, that's going too far!"
He ended with a sort of explosion, his face very pink and his eyes
ugly.

"Keep your temper, Hilary," said Dr. Bouligny quickly.
"Don't get excited like that. Miss Keate doesn't think anyone
tried to kill Florrie with veronal. That would be altogether
too far-fetched. But, Miss Keate, who has had access to your
instrument bag?"

"Everyone in the house, I imagine. I left it in the bathroom
off Bayard Thatcher's room until I was asked to care for Miss
Thatcher, immediately after his death. Then I went into his
room and got the bag and left it in the bathroom adjoining Miss
Thatcher's room."

"Was that entirely safe?" asked Hilary unpleasantly.

"Safe! I don't see why not! There's nothing in it but dressings,
bandage scissors, thermometers, a bottle of alcohol, a rubber
sheet——"

"There, there, now, Miss Keate. Mr. Thatcher isn't accusing
you of carelessness. Your own accusation that someone in this
house removed the harmless aspirin in that box and substituted
veronal is far more serious. Have you any real reason to suspect
your instrument bag has been tampered with?"

"Yes."

"What's that? What do you mean?" cried Hilary.

"I—it was—well, I know someone—tampered with it."

"Who? How do you know?"

"I found something in it. Something—unimportant. I re-
stored it to its owner."

Hilary was leaning forward; his face faintly purple.

"You'll have to explain yourself, Miss Keate. You have said
too much not to say more."

"I'll do no such thing. That had nothing to do with the veronal. As a matter of fact, every single one of you had access to it. And your own sister suggested that I give Florrie aspirin."

"My sister! Janice?"

"No."

"Adela! Good God, Miss Keate, you are out of your senses." Hilary had leaped to his feet, a bizarre fat figure in agitated purple stripes. "Do you hear her, Dan? She's out of her senses. She's a dangerous woman. She ought to be removed. Put where she can't do any damage. Adela! She says Adela gave Florrie veronal."

"I said nothing of the kind," I cried, shocked. "I meant nothing of the kind. I said she suggested I give Florrie veronal—I mean, aspirin—and I did. I wanted you to understand that I didn't offer it to her voluntarily. I had nothing at all to do with it. Somebody here put veronal in that box. I didn't. And I'll not be accused of it."

"There now, Miss Keate," said Dr. Bouligny heavily. "Do cool down, Hilary. You ought not permit yourself to get in such rages."

"Not permit myself," spluttered Hilary, quite beside himself. "When she sits and looks at me like that. I'll not—" said Hilary—"be looked at."

"Well, I don't see how you are going to help it," said Dr. Bouligny rather wearily. "What was it you found in your instrument bag, Miss Keate? To whom did you return it?"

That took the wind out of my sails; it is very difficult for a nurse of many years' experience to refuse to answer a doctor's question.

I looked past the narrow bed where Florrie lay, her face more natural, her breath coming and going heavily, out through the gable window. Dawn was touching the treetops with gold, and I thought of the other two dawns I had seen in that house. A cool breath of morning air billowed the ruffled curtain and touched my hot, tired face. It had been a dreadful night, a night to sap one's energies, to test one's stamina, to try one's courage to the utmost.

Dr. Bouligny was watching me anxiously, his heavy hand rubbing his dark, unshaven chin. Hilary was breathing heavily, his face still flushed, and his eyes narrow and wary.

"Come, Miss Keate," urged Dr. Bouligny. "Who was it?"

"What does it matter?" I said wearily. "We've saved the girl. That's the main thing."

"What was it you found in your bag? Tell us at once." Hilary's voice was sharply commanding. It annoyed me.

"I prefer," I said loftily, "not to tell. It was nothing that could have any connection at all with this. I returned it to the owner, and even the owner does not know I saw—found it. I'm sorry I spoke of it. I only did so to prove that my instrument bag was quite accessible to other people besides myself. I refuse to say any more. If I were questioned in a court of law, of course——"

Hilary's face flushed darker.

"You'd tell, then, I don't doubt," he said nastily. "Well, this isn't going to get to a court of law. Not this trouble with Florrie. And as for anything else you may know about our family affairs, nurse, you aren't going to have a chance to tell that in a court of law either. You can be sure of that."

"Hilary," said Dr. Bouligny in some exasperation, "I'll swear you go out of your way to be a plain damn fool. Your temper and your tongue are going to get you into bad trouble some day, if they haven't already. Can't you see that you are alienating——"

I didn't see that Dr. Bouligny was making matters any better. Perhaps it was fortunate that Janice interrupted just when she did. She said, "Hilary," and we all turned and saw her in the doorway. I wondered how long she'd been standing there. I could tell nothing from her steady dark eyes and her white face.

"Adela wants you," she went on. "You, too, Dr. Dan. I'm afraid she'll collapse if we don't get her to sleep. She's determined to go through with the funeral. It's morning. You'd better go to her at once."

The two men pulled themselves to their feet. Dr. Bouligny murmured a direction or two about Florrie and said he'd be back later in the day, and not to let her get pneumonia. He did have the grace to add a sort of apology about overworking me and that it was fortunate I was there and had known what to do for the girl. Hilary said nothing. I could hear the muffled sound of their voices as they went down the narrow stairway, and I caught the words "dangerous enemy" in Hilary's voice. I had no doubt he referred to me.

Janice had walked to the window and was standing there, her back to me. There was a long moment of silence with the sound of the descending footsteps of the men growing fainter. It was a peaceful silence, with the cool summer dawn filling the room, dispelling the horror of the dreadful, hot night. Janice's voice, when it came, was calm too, but it was the calm of great weariness and of final surrender. She said:

"So you knew about the letter. My letter."

CHAPTER XI

THE UNCONSCIOUS GIRL ON the bed moaned stupidly, and I went to her.

Presently I said:

"Yes."

"And you returned it to me? Placed it there on my desk?"

"Yes."

"It was—you found it there in your instrument bag?"

"Yes."

"And—read it?" There was pain in the reluctant question, pain and pride. Janice could always face things. She was standing quiet; her dark hair hung down her back like a child's—it was not long and it ended in a soft, dark confusion of loose curls. The dressing gown she wore, the pale yellow chiffon in which I had first seen her, fell softly about her slender young figure. I longed to say I had not read the letter.

"Yes I read it."

"But you didn't tell. You didn't tell."

"No. I've never felt that duty demands a free tongue."

"Then you don't think—you don't think I'm——" She stopped. It was a moment before I realized she was trying to keep back sobs. The night we had had was enough to break even Janice's steel-like self-control; I did not think the less of her.

"No," I said. "No, I don't think anything, you poor child!"

She turned then, very slowly, tears in her dark eyes and on her soft cheeks.

I squirmed. I don't like tears, and besides, there was a lump in my throat that hurt. I said:

"We are both exhausted after such a night. Sit down and we'll talk quietly. I've had enough of emotions for one night."

She gave me a long look.

"No," she said. "I've said enough. One reaches a point where one must talk. It was good of you not to tell. I'm trying, you see, to do what I think is right. But I'd better tell you. You see, I had written that letter to explain to Allen how I felt. It was so difficult to tell him. And Bayard found the letter. Took the letter, rather; saw me place it in the pocket of Allen's coat and deliberately took it. Somehow, though, he had managed to get only the second sheet of it—but that was enough. And Bayard—I wonder what you know of Bayard, Miss Keate. He was—he was——"

"Predatory," I said out of my memory. She looked at me with surprise.

"I don't know how you knew that," she said, "but it is true. Terribly true. You see, Bayard—it's hard to tell it, Miss Keate."

"Blackmailed you, I suppose. Or tried to."

"Yes," she said faintly. "Yes. He threatened to tell Dave. Adela. Evelyn and Hilary. By that time everyone would have known it. Oh—I can't tell you how awful it would have been." She covered her face with her hands.

"I can imagine it would have been very bad," I said.

"It would have broken Adela's heart."

"Then I suppose Bayard put that letter in my bag?"

"I suppose so." She looked at me with wide eyes. "We wouldn't give him what he wanted. I couldn't. I have no money of my own. Allen wouldn't. He said Bayard had been bleeding this family for years. He told me not to worry. That he'd find a way out of it. That he wasn't afraid of Bayard. But—it's been terrible, Miss Keate. Bayard goaded us. Hinted at things. I was always conscious of it. He wouldn't let me forget for a moment. He— it's horrible to say it but—" her voice sank to a whisper—"I'm glad he's dead. I am. I'm glad he's dead."

So that was why Allen had searched the dead man's pockets so feverishly. But did Janice realize what she was telling me? That she and Allen both had the strongest of motives for wishing Bayard Thatcher out of the way? But Allen had an alibi; he had been with Dave the entire afternoon.

"Yes," she said thoughtfully. "I suppose Bayard hid the letter in your bag. He'd have thought there was no danger of its being found. He knew, of course, that Allen and I would do our utmost to recover it. He must have been afraid Allen would search his things while he was ill."

"My dear," I said gently. "Why did Dave shoot Bayard?"

She shrank back against the window.

"Shoot Bayard! Then you knew?"

"Yes. And that the bullet wounded Bayard's shoulder and that Adela heard and got there in time to keep Dave from shooting again."

The color came slowly back to her lips.

"I don't know," she said soberly. "I'm not sure. But it had nothing to do with my letter; I'm sure of that. Dave would have told me; confronted me with it. Dave's been terribly depressed since Bayard's death—and before that. He isn't like himself at all since he's been sick so much."

"Janice." It was Evelyn from the doorway. "Oh, there you are. Emmeline has made some coffee for us. You'd better come down and drink some and then try to rest. We've got so much to do today. Miss Keate, I'll send some coffee up here to you."

"No," I said hurriedly. "Let me have a glass of warm milk. I don't want coffee." I shuddered as I glanced at Florrie's pale face on the pillow—her loose mouth.

"Of course," said Evelyn, blissfully matter-of-fact. "Come, Janice. You look dreadfully tired."

At the door Janice hesitated, and as Evelyn preceded her into the passage she came back, paused beside me, and said, "Thank you," in a low voice and was gone. I knew she was not thanking me for concealing the matter of the letter.

But the sound of their light footsteps had not more than died away before I was in a very turmoil of conflicting emotions and desires again. Why had I not asked her about all those things which gave such hideous witness against her? Why had I not at least asked her about the bloodstained hat?

Florrie moved, and I went to take her pulse. Feeling for the throb, I thought impatiently that after all I could have done no more than I did. It is extraordinarily difficult—indeed, it is quite impossible to approach a lovely young woman and say to her, "My dear young lady, this is all very well, but did you murder the man?"

No, I couldn't have done that. But I felt rather sick as I thought of the accumulating evidence against her.

And then there was the inexplicable matter of the veronal tablets. The box was still there on the table, and I looked at it, considering. The whole affair seemed an extraordinarily purposeless thing. It was against reason to think that Florrie had been the victim of a real and intentionally murderous attack; as Hilary had pointed out, no one could have known in advance that she would have a headache, want aspirin, and be unable to secure any of it anywhere else in the house and would come to me. I believe I felt from the first that the veronal had been placed in that box for quite another purpose—what it was I couldn't guess—and that Florrie's taking it and coming so near death was only an unlucky and nearly fatal accident. The significant thing was the fact of the veronal having been brought to the house by someone and that curious matter of the substitution. I know now that it should have given me a clue to the whole situation, and I suppose it did, after a fashion. But aftersight is always better than foresight.

Veronal, I might add, is not from a nurse's viewpoint exactly a dangerous drug. It may, of course, be taken to excess, when it is promptly fatal. It is a hypnotic, used a great deal for insomnia. It is true that once in a while some poor soul becomes an addict to the drug, takes it as a habit, becomes firmly and terribly attached to it, but even this may be taken in time and cured. In many states the sale of veronal except by doctor's prescription is prohibited, and this being the case in our own state increased the complexity of the matter. Someone in that house evidently had access to fairly large quantities of the drug.

It is needless to say that I revolved the matter at length in my mind, and that by noon I had, I daresay, a hundred explanations, none of which satisfied me.

It was a long, quiet day, that Sunday, with the slow, melodious sound of church bells coming clearly and frequently to my ears. C—— is not a large town, but it has five churches. Sunday, I learned, is a favorite day for funerals, owing to the farmers and shopkeepers being at leisure; not, in other words, having anything else to do and rather welcoming the diversion. Thus burying Bayard on that day was considered in all quarters the proper and fitting thing to do and did not in the least savor of unseemly and suspicious haste.

I spent most of the day in the small room with Florrie, the open gable window letting in the soft summer air and sunlight and sound of church bells and the girl slowly recovering. I saw

little of the funeral, for which I was not sorry. Only a few subdued sounds of people arriving and the heavy scents of flowers
and the murmur of a hymn or two reached us there on the third
floor.

And when I slipped downstairs about eleven o'clock I found
they were already back from the cemetery, and the only remind-
ers of what had taken place were the stacks of chairs folded on
the porch and waiting to be taken away, the heavy, cloying odor
of flowers, and the heap of cards from the flowers with their
white ribbons still clinging to them which was on Adela's desk.
Janice and Evelyn were rearranging furniture which had been
pushed out of place in the wide drawing rooms, and Adela was
conferring with Emmeline in the morning room.

It always rather pleased me, somehow, to note how competent all the Thatcher women were about managing a house. They
seemed to know certain things by instinct and the machinery ran
smoothly and unobtrusively. There were always generosity and
solid plenty, but never lavishness and waste. After all, there is a
certain dignity about thrift and the caring for things, of which
we see too little, and there is an extremely pleasant and fine dignity about a well cared for house.

There were even, I learned, certain traditions: several times I
heard echoes of "Evelyn's fudge cake" or "Adela's quince pickles,"
and it appeared that only Adela could mend lace or table linen
and that Janice could make flowers grow. "Roses," I have heard
Adela say in her bland, assured way, "either grow for you or don't
grow. But they grow for Janice. She has a magic touch with flowers."

All graces of which one hears very little now; still, they are
lovely and serene.

To my disappointment my box of fresh uniforms had still
not arrived, and I was obliged to continue wearing the limp and

wrinkled white dress which had seen me through that hot night. I wrote a hurried note to the hospital, sealed and stamped it, and left it with some other outgoing mail on the hall table.

At lunch I caught a glimpse of the family, although it was an unusually hurried meal, with Hilary arriving with the city newspapers—which, since nothing had happened that summer but a drought, were inclined to play up the story of the burglar and the missing diamonds and the death of Bayard Thatcher—"of the Thatcher County Thatchers," said the newspaper I saw, "the prominent pioneer family of a name which has long been of importance in the state"—and Jim Strove, the sheriff, and Dr. Bouligny arriving before the meal was quite over. Strove came to say apologetically that he had three suspects in the county jail and would Hilary come down and question them; he asked Adela to forgive him for troubling them on Sunday, seemed a little discouraged and doubtful, but did not have the air of a conspirator; from which I judged that Hilary had dealt with him rather adroitly. And Dr. Bouligny came to see how our patient was progressing.

I accompanied him, of course, to Florrie's room. As we passed the hall table, something about my note, which lay face downward on top, caught my eye. I don't yet know exactly what it was, but I picked up the note and looked sharply at it. I have good eyes and a good nose; it took only a moment to discover that the envelope had been opened and then pasted down again with library paste.

It chilled me. There was nothing in the note that anyone might not read, but it was difficult to associate letter-opening with the Thatchers.

Looking back, I can see that with Florrie's unlucky accident the net of suave surveillance to which I was subjected became really definite and tight. But it was drawn so deftly that it actually

seemed that the Thatcher family had only become very gracious-
ly and cordially disposed toward me. If I had a letter to post,
someone offered to post it for me; if I had an errand to town,
someone offered to do it for me; if I went for a walk, someone
either offered to go along or turned up somewhere along my way.
They were friendly, bland, and unrelenting.

Florrie was much better; her recovery was only a matter of
time and care in order to avoid veronal pneumonia. That day she
was well enough to permit me to nap on a small day bed which
Emmeline, gaunt and uncommunicative, and Hilary, red and
puffing and reluctant, carried up the narrow stairway and placed
in Florrie's room for me. I think Hilary would as soon I'd have
gone without that small attention.

But the day was quiet. I suppose the Thatchers thought I was
quite safe.

Evelyn came up about five to say she would stay with Florrie
while I got some fresh air. It was like Evelyn to think of that,
even in the midst of her grave anxiety, and I accepted her offer
readily. She looked tired, of course, with the strain of the ghastly night and trying day—tired and anxious. Her color was bad,
sallow and dark, and there were brown hollows around her eyes.
She would lie on the day bed and rest, she said, and told me not
to hurry.

As I left I glanced at the table to see that everything was
there that Florrie might need. I'm sure the box which held the
veronal tablets was on the table then, for the thought flashed
through my mind that Dr. Bouligny ought to have taken them
away with him, and that I must remind him the next call he
made. The thought of the tablets' being a danger did not, I'm
sure, after all that had happened, occur to me; if it had, I would
have taken them in my own charge.

It was accident, as much as anything, that took me to the

family cemetery. I'm sure it was accident that permitted me to leave the house unobserved and unaccompanied; perhaps Evelyn had not told the others that she intended to relieve me.

I walked first through the garden, then along a path back of the house and past a large vegetable garden. This was enclosed at the back by a high lattice fence, painted green, with a door through which I walked and found a well defined path leading across a meadow, over a small bridge, up and across a low, rolling hill, plentifully wooded with old oak trees, and thence, before I knew it, to the cemetery itself.

It was, of course, the family burial plot which had existed earlier, I imagine, than the town itself, and where, by some manipulating probably of property lines and county politics, the Thatchers were still buried. It was not a large place, with its old iron fence and gate, its black cedars, its small old headstones and neatly tended graves. I wandered about for some time looking at the quaint epitaphs on some of the older stones, and finally brought up back of a thick cluster of cedars at the new grave. I was standing there, staring at the wilting wreaths of flowers and thinking of Bayard's death and feeling, I must admit, extremely depressed and uneasy, when I heard the click of the gate. I looked through the thick cedar boughs, not realizing that, even in my white dress, I was likely quite invisible to the person entering the gate.

The person was Dave.

Dave in a light suit that made him look thin, and his hat pulled low over his eyes. He fastened the latch of the gate and walked slowly and with a curiously uncertain gait, as if his muscles did not coördinate perfectly, toward me. Or rather toward the cedars behind which I stood.

Was he coming to mourn at the grave of the man he had so nearly killed?

I don't know exactly what impulse impelled me rather hurriedly away from those wilting flowers and toward another grave, an old one just opposite. But I went, and in another moment met Dave face to face.

And he looked startled and frightened as he rounded the clump of cedars and saw me.

"Why—it's you, Miss Keate!" His voice was not very steady. He took off his hat and passed his hand across his forehead and said, "I didn't see you at first—your white dress—you gave me rather a shock. I've been having a little trouble with my eyes. Silly of me——"

"I was walking," I said. "And I happened to walk this way. What an interesting old place this is! It's very old, isn't it?"

"I believe so. Did you read some of the epitaphs? The Thatchers all seemed very sure of going to their rewards. The family has always kept the place up. It's one of the spots of historical interest in the state. At least, frenzied females with notebooks and cameras come every so often to look at it. Adela gives them tea and shows them the family portraits and thoroughly enjoys herself."

"Indeed," I said, and found myself reading the words on the headstone beside us. "Nita Thatcher" was distinctly carved on the old stone.

Nita Thatcher. In a fraction of an instant I had traced its familiarity. Bayard had said in his sleep, "Nita's grave."

The thought flashed through my mind that here at last I might have stumbled on the solution to the puzzle. I was sure Bayard had said, "Nita's grave." Was there here some buried story, buried but not well enough; some not forgotten tragedy? Lost loves, revenge, even contested wills surged swiftly and rather wildly through my mind, and I bent forward to look at the stone. Below the name were dates, and they were rather conclusive:

1839-1881. She had died, had Nita Thatcher, long before Bayard or Dave was born. In some bewilderment I drew back. And became aware of the sudden dark suspicion in Dave's face.

"What are you doing here?" he demanded in such sudden and sullen fury that I was struck quite dumb with astonishment. "Why have you come here? See here, Nurse—you'll be wise not to interfere with things that are no concern of yours. Remember that."

He turned and walked away and was out the gate and disappearing over the brow of the hill before I struggled out of the fog of a bewilderment induced as much by his sudden and irrational rage as by that singular matter of Nita Thatcher's grave. For it had certainly been Nita's grave Bayard had mentioned, and Dave had certainly walked directly to that grave as if it were his destination and purpose in coming to the cemetery.

I went very thoughtfully back to the house.

Evelyn inquired politely about my walk, made a few obvious comments about the weather and about Florrie, and left. It did not improve my spirits to discover that she had taken the box of remaining veronal tablets away with her. At least, when I went to hand Florrie a glass of water from the table, the box was indisputably gone. Florrie, on being questioned, said she'd been drowsy but was sure only Miss Evelyn had been in the room during my absence. Well, if the veronal was safe anywhere it was safe with Evelyn, I told myself, but a nagging little worry persisted in the back of my mind, and it began to seem to me that I'd been criminally careless about the tablets. And yet—veronal is not like poison or some really dangerous drug.

About nine o'clock that night Adela came up, looking very weary but still faintly bland, and panting a little from the climb up two flights of stairs.

"How is your patient, Miss Keate?" she asked. "Better, I hope. You are better, aren't you, Florrie? You gave us quite a fright."

"I'm all right," said Florrie rather weakly. "Miss Evelyn told me all about what happened. I don't suppose anybody meant to give me the wrong stuff." She glanced at me rather doubtfully but continued: "Miss Evelyn said I owed my life to the nurse. I suppose I do. But I ought to have known not to take the pills. A red-haired woman and the moon at its full and something out of a——"

Adela thought she was still only half-conscious. She bent over the bed.

"There now, Florrie. Try to get some rest and natural sleep. Dr. Bouligny says you are going to be all right. Isn't it fine that Miss Keate was here and knew just what to do for you?"

Florrie looked at me again; it was a curious look in which suspicion and gratitude were oddly blended.

"Oh, yes," she said. "But I ought to have known better than to take them. But I guess she didn't mean to do it."

"Why, of course she didn't mean to do it. It was a very terrible accident, but you are going to be all right now. Miss Keate will stay here and take care of you and——"

"I think I'd be better off alone, ma'am, if you don't mind."

"Alone! Oh, no, Florrie, Dr. Bouligny says it's best for Miss Keate to stay with you, and I think she's very kind to do it."

"Yes," muttered Florrie. "But there's a full moon tonight."

Adela looked perplexed.

"Florrie, you aren't yourself yet. But don't worry: you'll be all right if you do just as the doctor says. Will you be comfortable, Miss Keate? Is there anything you need? I can't tell you how grateful we are to you. If you hadn't been here last night——" Her face was hard all at once, touched with granite. She went on:

"Don't hesitate to ask Emmeline to help you or get anything you want. Goodnight."

Her silk skirts swished delicately on the stairs. Florrie sighed.

"I don't think you really meant to give me those tablets, Miss Keate," she said forgivingly. "You've been awful good to me today. I guess you didn't mean to. Miss Evelyn said I'd have died sure if you hadn't known what to do for me."

I could see no good purpose in telling Florrie anything of the mystery of the veronal tablets. I said:

"That's good. Now I'll just fluff up your pillows, and you try to sleep."

"Say, Miss Keate, did they have the funeral today?"

"Yes."

"Was it a big one?"

"I don't know; there were lots of flowers."

"There would be. Likely the whole town was here. Say, Miss Keate, have they caught the burglar yet?"

"No."

She brooded on that for some time. Then she said with a slow sort of smile:

"They won't catch him, either. Those diamonds—" she laughed outright—"those diamonds. Say, Miss Keate, nobody stole those diamonds. I know exactly where they are."

CHAPTER XII

AFTER A MOMENT I realized that I had known it all along; had known there was something faulty, something too pat, about the missing diamonds; had known there was something conspiratorial about that supposed theft of which so much had been made. But with my own eyes I had seen Adela open that safe and discover the loss of the jewels. Who, then, had arranged their disappearance at so apt a moment?

"Where? How do you know? Why didn't you tell?"

It was difficult to persuade Florrie to talk.

"The only way to be safe in this house is to mind your own business," she said.

It was only when I combined a delicate threat to tell Miss Thatcher with a sort of provisional promise to keep what she had told me a secret unless I found it absolutely necessary to tell it that she resumed her communicative mood.

The diamonds, she said, were in the tall jar of green bath salts in the bathroom adjoining Janice's bedroom. She had seen them there the morning following Bayard's murder. She had been cleaning the room rather hurriedly, and had picked up the jar to wipe the shelf under it and had caught the glimmer of one of the jewels which had somehow slipped through the concealing layers of crystals and next the glass. She had explored then and there, and while she didn't remember exactly the entire collection of diamonds, she thought they were all there. Or most of them.

"It was a good place to hide them," she said ruminatively. "The bath salts are sort of shiny; it was just the light catching one of the diamonds that made me look. But I didn't say anything to anybody. I wanted to keep out of it. And I knew they were safe there because Miss Janice hates bath salts and never uses them. She says she just keeps the jar there for the color scheme. Did you ever see her bathroom, Miss Keate? She's got water lilies painted all around the walls. And little green frogs. Heathenish, I say."

"Are they still there?"

"Oh, sure. They're painted."

"The diamonds, I mean."

She looked evasive.

"The last time I looked they were," she said. "Say, Nurse, do you suppose Miss Janice managed so I got those tablets—veronal? Is that what you call them?"

"I don't know how it happened, Florrie. Why did you think she might have—managed it?"

"She don't like me," said Florrie, still evasive. "She threatened me just yesterday."

"Threatened you!"

"Well, she said I'd regret something I did. And I got those tablets right afterward and nearly died."

I suppressed a smile at the thought of the salutary effect of Janice's rebuke. Whatever Florrie's conclusion regarding the veronal tablets came to be, I thought it highly unlikely she would ever do any more prowling among Janice's things. Then another thought struck me:

"Florrie, think now and answer carefully. Did you leave that box of tablets anywhere in the house before you took them? Did you put it down on a table? Or anywhere? Was the box out of your possession even for a moment?"

"No," said Florrie at once. "I'm sure of that, Miss Keate. I took the box from you and came straight up here to my room and took the first two tablets before I even undressed. Then my head was no better, so I kept on taking them."

"How many did you take altogether?" I asked, and when she told me I shuddered.

"But didn't you see they were not aspirin? They are much larger, for one thing."

"Why, no," she said. "Coming from a hospital, I expected them to be a little different from regular aspirin. Hospitals are such queer places. Do you know what people are saying about who killed Bayard?"

"No. You'd better go to sleep, Florrie."

"I don't know either. But they'll say Hilary killed him. You see if I'm not right. Hilary and Bayard never liked each other."

"Florrie, do you know anything about a Nita Thatcher? Have you ever heard any of the family mention Nita's grave?"

"No," she said after a thoughtful moment. "There's a grave up at the Thatcher cemetery marked Nita Thatcher, but I never heard anything about it. The Thatchers are funny about that cemetery," she went on, pondering. "Dave is always going up there. And Miss Adela. And even Bayard used to go up there once in awhile."

"Was she—Nita—any connection to Bayard?"

Florrie wrinkled her colorless eyebrows.

"I don't know, Miss Keate, but I don't think so. I never heard anything at all about her. And if there'd been anything," added Florrie not at all enigmatically, "I'd have known it."

I very nearly said, "You and everybody in C——."

For three whole days I nursed Florrie. They were to all outward aspects quiet days, chiefly characterized by a determined and outwardly successful effort on the part of the Thatchers to ignore the matter of Bayard's dreadful death and to present an unruffled countenance to the world. The only visible evidences that things were not as they appeared lay in the fact that Hilary and Evelyn stayed on, instead of returning to their own household, and that instead of getting a new housemaid during Florrie's illness, Janice and Evelyn between them took over her duties. This was, I had no doubt, to prevent letting a girl from town into the house and its intimate workings, a girl who would talk, would relate every scrap of gossip she could garner to all too willing ears. I knew that, so far, they had managed to keep Florrie's illness a secret, although once Adela went to see Florrie's mother, and I suppose she told her of it. I never knew what measures she took to insure the woman's silence.

Almost frantically they resumed that orderly daily routine and clung to it as a man may cling to a straw to save himself from drowning. During those days I saw them together mostly at meals when they were bland, gracious, preoccupied with the housekeeping and gardens and affairs of the town. At the same time I could hardly help knowing in a general way what went on in the house. Once I ventured into Bayard's room and found it prim and orderly with drawn shades and Bayard's possessions— for I looked to make sure—removed and I suppose packed away. I wondered fleetingly what had become of the gin.

Bayard was never mentioned. Every so often Strove would come to the house and talk apologetically of the diamonds and the burglar, and I would wonder anew just where my duty lay concerning those diamonds—and more urgently concerning my accumulating evidence that Bayard Thatcher had been murdered not by a marauding burglar but by one of his own family. If the county authorities chose to ignore it, as they did, to whom ought I to appeal? Or ought I to appeal at all? I think I had some faint notion that if any stranger actually was made a victim of, and the thing came to his arrest, I should step forward with what I knew. But in my heart I felt, I am sure, that it would not come to that. That things would somehow work out. For a feeling of something impending was everywhere: in the air we breathed and the food we ate and in our eyes meeting and glancing quickly away.

A climax was coming. We all knew it. It was in Janice's set white face as she went about the cool, polished spaces of the house doing Florrie's dusting, or working in her garden and later appearing fresh and beautiful at the dinner table, ready to take her role in that tragi-comedy of manners that went on every night—avoiding me and avoiding Allen, her dark eyes somber above quiet lips.

It was in Adela's bleak eyes and her blunt white fingers as they worked ceaselessly with her long turquoise beads or with the flat silver beside her plate, and in her bland observations which saved us so frequently from a conversational trap and which yet were apt to break off in the middle as if she'd completely forgotten what she had been saying.

Even Emmeline grew nervous; she twisted her fingers constantly and took to having neuralgia and wafting a smell of vehement winter-green salve which did not add to our combined peace of mind.

Allen Carick looked taut and spent, as if he'd been sleeping badly. And Evelyn decided to have the boys kept on at camp for a while after the summer session was over.

"It's as well not to let them come home just now," she said, and later I heard her sending a carefully worded telegram over the telephone to the head of the school.

I grew restless under that prevailing sense of strain and expectation, under the goading pressure of my many unanswered questions and unproved theories, and—more definitely—that unrelenting chaperonage. Every one of those three days I left the house for a time, and never, after Sunday, alone. Evelyn volunteered once to go for a walk with me, and I could scarcely refuse. Another time Hilary turned up about four with the sedan and took Adela and me for a long and silent country ride—reluctantly, I think, and with a very red neck, which was all I could see of him from the tonneau. And another time, by leaving from the back door, I got away from the house unobserved, only to meet Allen a quarter of a mile away, rather breathless, as if he'd run across country. He stuck to me like a burr, but was lost in his own not too pleasant thoughts, for he tramped along steadily with his hands in his pockets and his blue eyes frowning at the path, and only spoke twice during the whole walk, which I somewhat unkindly prolonged, taking him through some thickets where there were opening milkweed pods whose soft silks clung stubbornly to his trousers and resisted his savage efforts to brush them off. He swore a little under his breath and brushed with his hands and looked up at me and surprisingly laughed. He was very nice when he laughed: his sullen frown gave place to a sort of bright blue twinkle, and he had a direct and very charming way of smiling exactly into your eyes.

"You win, Nurse," he said, admitting his espionage almost in words. But he stayed with me until he saw me safe and incommunicado, so to speak, inside the door of the Thatcher house.

The whole thing was an admission, I suppose, that something was to come. That there must be some change, some development, some climax of those hidden forces. But I think none of us guessed the dreadful turn that development was to take.

My nerves were on edge, and I slept poorly at night. There

were times when I suspected every member of that family of having murdered Bayard.

My only desire during those days was to get away. And Dr. Bouligny insisted on prolonging my stay. Florrie needed my care, he said. And the semblance of the ordinary, everyday state of affairs which they had built up was so real in its outward aspects that I could not refuse. I could not say openly that I wanted to leave, because—well, because Adela looked worried, harassed, and old—or Evelyn dark and ill—or Hilary frightened. That I wanted to leave because a man had been killed in that house. That I was afraid.

And I scarcely dared say that I wanted to leave because I was convinced that one of them had murdered a man.

Nothing, however, happened during those three days; it seems incredible as I write it, but it's true. Florrie had got over her communicativeness; Dave stayed out of sight, and when Dr. Bouligny asked what I had done with the remaining veronal tablets and I told him Evelyn had them he seemed quite satisfied and said no more about it.

It was when Florrie was sitting up in a chair and an amazing dressing gown which only Florrie could have thought anything but poisonous, and was obviously about to get up and stay up, that Adela undertook her campaign. I wonder how often she had rehearsed it, gone over every step of it, testing its weak points, before she sent for me the afternoon of the fourth day of Florrie's illness.

She was in the library. The high-backed chair she had chosen added to her little air of stateliness. Her bleak blue eyes looked colder, back of her polished eyeglasses. Her lavender silk gown fell in delicate folds, and there were her favorite snowy ruffles about her throat and wrists.

She asked me a few questions about Florrie, said she hoped

I would be with them a few days longer, gave me no opportunity to voice my own somewhat urgent views of the matter, and began:

"Miss Keate," she said, "I have liked you very much. I feel you to be a woman of common sense and sanity. I want your help."

"My help?"

"Yes. You see—" her bleak blue eyes went to the open window for a moment to linger on the green stretches of sunlit lawn and the cool shadows of the shrubbery at its edge—"Bayard's death has been a great shock. You know that. So far, we have not succeeded in discovering the man who did it. The man who stole the diamonds. Mr. Strove doesn't seem to think we shall ever find him. Now then, first I want you to understand that I myself am convinced—entirely convinced—that Bayard met his death at the hands of a wicked thief. At the same time it happened here—in my house—the Thatcher home for generations. There will be people who will say things. Anything. People are always ready to talk of a family which—" she hesitated here and then continued with quiet simplicity—"which has been more or less prominent and which has never lacked—worldly goods. I could never be more completely convinced than I am now that the members of my family are innocent of this thing. Even the thought is absurd. But for their own protection I intend to prove it."

There was silence in the long old room: a silence so complete it was as if the books and the portraits and the old walls themselves were repeating her words: "I intend to prove it."

Even with the memory of that conversation which I had overheard when she had told Hilary and Evelyn that she would convince me I could not quite credit my ears.

All those damaging things I knew swarmed into my thoughts. How could she prove their innocence when I knew there was no burglar? When I knew that the diamonds had never been stolen? When I knew about the revolver and about poor little Janice's bloodstained hat? When I knew so many things—and yet not enough.

Janice said Bayard had been "bleeding the family for years."

Silence in that long room with the bare space almost at my feet where there had been the rug on which we found Bayard, dead. And the door to the little study where I knew he'd actually been killed securely closed. I don't know why I felt so sure that Dave was at that very moment in his soundproof study unless it was because I so seldom saw him and I knew that was his retreat.

"I intend," said Adela, slowly and deliberately in her elegant voice, "to prove it. And you can help me, Miss Keate, if you will be so good. I want you to hear every thing I ask, every inquiry I make and its answer. And if you feel that, in any case, I have not fully and thoroughly covered the ground, I want you to say so. To ask, in fact, anything that occurs to you."

Gradually I grasped the thing she proposed to do, which was apparently to conduct her own inquiry. To question in my hearing those who might be thought to have had some connection with the death of Bayard Thatcher. I wondered that she dared. It would take the wisdom of a serpent, the wiliness of a diplomat, the guarded care with which one walks on the edge of a precipice. She continued:

"I have asked Emmeline to come first. I intend to question her, Miss Keate. And I want you to listen carefully. And if you are not entirely satis—" she checked herself on the very verge of giving herself and her motives away—" I mean if you think I have overlooked any—anything, don't hesitate to speak."

"You mean," I said, "that you really want me to ask any questions that occur to me? To make any inquiry I wish to make?"

She looked relieved; I suppose because that was exactly what she did want. That was the only way in which I could be convinced.

"That is exactly it, Miss Keate," she said. "Please don't hesitate at all. Don't feel that any inquiry is at all——" She floundered a little and then adroitly skirted the dangerous ground. "You see, you have so much clearer a viewpoint than I. You are so much more apt to think of the obvious.—Oh, there you are, Emmeline. Come in, please. You may sit down. Emmeline," as the gaunt woman sat stiffly and uncomfortably on the edge of a chair, glanced with distrust at me, and then back to Adela's mouth, "Emmeline, I want to ask you a few questions about—about the afternoon of the robbery, and I want you to answer freely. Do you understand?"

"Yes, ma'am," said Emmeline hoarsely, with another side glance at me, and her hands working in her white-aproned lap.

There was a brief pause while Adela formulated her questions, and I remember wondering that Adela dared undertake such a dangerous campaign. Was she really convinced that her family—every member of it—was innocent? Or could it be that she knew who had murdered Bayard? Knew and counted on her powers to protect him?

"You were making jelly in the back kitchen that afternoon. Did you see anybody at all besides Higby all that afternoon?"

"No, ma'am, not a soul."

"But of course you were not at the window of the kitchen all that time?"

"Why, yes, ma'am, I was."

"But, Emmeline, you couldn't have been at the window every moment." Adela's face was granite again, her blue eyes like two stones. How she must have longed to beat down Emmeline's testimony; yet she had not asked the woman to lie.

"Why, yes, ma'am," said Emmeline. "I was. Higby gets lazy when the weather gets warm. And Miss Janice had told me you would all be gone that afternoon and I'd better keep an eye on him. So I just brought all the sugar and glasses and strainers and everything I would need to the long table below the window. I had the little stove right there too—you know how wide the windows are, Miss Adela—so there was no need for me to leave at all. And I kept an eye on him all the time like I said I would. He knew it, too. And worked right along."

"You can see the back door from there?"

"Why, of course. You know that, Miss Adela. You can't help seeing the back door. It's right square in front of the window. No, ma'am, nobody went in that back door. There was nobody at all around the back of the house that whole afternoon, ma'am. I'm sure of it."

Adela's face looked gray and old and tired. But she was still stately and unmoved.

"Can you see the library windows from the back kitchen?"

Emmeline looked scornful.

"You know I can't, ma'am."

"Then anybody could have entered the library windows without your seeing him?"

Emmeline did not understand her immediately, and the question had to be repeated. It was just at that moment, I believe, that Pansy waddled across the room, looked at me suspiciously like a cranky little old woman, and settled with a tired puff at Adela's feet.

"Why, yes, Miss Adela, I suppose so. But Higby was out there on the lawn all afternoon. I know that. I can see most of the lawn, you know, and nobody could have crossed it without my seeing him. Unless he came from the front, and then Higby——"

"We'll let Higby speak for himself," said Adela rather sharply. "That is all, Emmeline—unless—Miss Keate?"

"When she came in through the house and found Bayard dead here in the library, did she see anybody? Was the house quite deserted?"

Adela looked approving; she put my question to Emmeline at once.

"No," said Emmeline. "There was nobody about. I'd have seen him if there was. I have to let my eyes make up for my ears."

"Did you look through the rooms downstairs? Or upstairs?"

"Why, of course not. You know what I did. When I passed the library door and looked in and saw him—right there where you are sitting, Miss Keate, ma'am—I ran in to look at him. Right there on the floor he was. Dead as a doornail. I dropped my spoonful of jelly and ran outdoors, and there you was on the steps. I've told you all that."

"You see, Miss Keate, someone could have been hiding here without Emmeline's knowing it. Although I really think the burglar made his escape immediately. Is there anything else you think of?"

"Not just now," I said slowly, thinking how difficult it was going to be to ask the things I really wanted to know without bringing somewhat dangerous suspicion on my own head. What would they do, what would they say, when they discovered all those things I knew!

"Very well, Emmeline. That is all. Higby is on the east lawn. Will you send him here, please."

We were silent while we waited; Adela stared out on the lawn with unseeing blue eyes. I could not know what she thought of Emmeline's stubborn refusal to admit the possibility of the fictitious burglar having got past her sharp eyes. It was one of the ironies of life that so short a time was to elapse before Adela was to be so frantically glad for that stubborn refusal. But she couldn't know that, then, and I wondered what her thoughts were as we sat there waiting for Higby.

Higby was easier to confuse. Probably Adela's bland stateliness awed him. He began by saying that not a fly could have got into the library windows without his, Higby's, seeing it, and ended by admitting that there were many times when his back was of necessity turned to those windows.

"But there's no shrubbery near the house, Miss Adela, except there in front. And my back would be turned only for a moment or two at a time."

"Much can happen in a moment," said Adela. "Don't you agree with me, Miss Keate, that the burglar could have made his entrance into the house without Higby's seeing him?"

"I don't think anybody could——" began Higby helplessly, and stopped on encountering Adela's cold blue gaze.

"There's only this," I said slowly. "A thief would have had to approach the windows from the back or front of the house. Since there are no side doors, he couldn't have entered that way. And Emmeline is positive no one was at the back of the house. And I am equally positive no one came from the front of the house. Between the three of us the whole circuit of the house was under observation."

Adela always knew when to agree.

"That's quite true, Miss Keate. But don't you think it possible for an intruder to have somehow managed to approach the house from the west?"

"No, ma'am," said Higby, sticking to his guns for a rather brief moment. "I know nobody did."

"But you were mowing the lawn continuously," reminded Adela affably.

"Yes, ma'am," said Higby, looking uncomfortable and shifting about on his feet.

"And in pushing the lawnmower up and down the stretches of lawn your back was often turned to the windows and to the lawn itself at different angles. And you were paying attention to your work."

"Oh, yes, ma'am," said Higby looking further discomfited.

"You see, Miss Keate," said Adela blandly, "he was watching his work all the time. Probably paid little attention to anything else. It seems very clear to me that someone could have run across the lawn back of him, watched his chance, likely, to do so, and then slipped into the house. These screens, you see, can be unhooked and opened quite readily. And closed as readily. Thieves are very adept at that sort of thing. Do you think of anything you'd like to ask? Do you feel quite convinced?"

"Were the screens, then, closed when they examined the house after Bayard's—death?"

"Why, really," said Adela politely, "I don't know. I don't believe anyone thought to look. They can be opened and closed so readily." Her bland voice trailed away into space as if my question had not been of much interest.

"But, ma'am," said Higby, lingering, "I don't think—I'm sure nobody—it ain't possible for anybody to cross that wide strip of open lawn——"

"But you've already said it was possible, Higby," said Adela pleasantly. "I'm afraid we can't depend upon your testimony at all, if you change about like this. You may go now," she concluded loftily. And added, "Thank you," in a way that sent Higby, crushed, out of the room. He stopped in the doorway to say again, in the manner of one who fires his last shot but knows in his heart it will have no effect, "But nobody did——" and Adela murmured, "That is all." He disappeared, vanquished, and she smiled at me.

"I'm afraid poor Higby isn't too certain of anything. That type seldom is. He and his family would have starved long ago if we hadn't found something for him to do. But he doesn't like to work. Has to be watched and directed every moment."

Emmeline stood in the doorway and approached.

"Mrs. Steadway calling, ma'am."

I think Adela was glad for the respite. She said affably: "Ask her to come in here, Emmeline. It's the wife of the man who manages the east farm," she said in an explanatory way to me. "Very worthy people, they are. We've never had better on that farm. Oh, good afternoon, Mrs. Steadway. Come in. It's good of you to come."

"I'd have come long ago, Miss Adela, but I've been busy with the canning. We are so sorry to hear about the trouble you've had."

She was a fresh-faced woman, large and neat and capable looking, but a little uncomfortable under Adela's eyeglasses and graciousness.

"Do sit down, Mrs. Steadway. This is my nurse, Miss Keate. Yes, it's been a great shock to me. To us all."

"That's what I told my husband. Miss Janice was out to the farm that very afternoon for butter and eggs. I guess she didn't dream what was happening here."

"No. No. Dear Janice. Such a shock."

Adela sat erect and stately in the high-backed chair regarding her caller through her eyeglasses. There was a short silence. Mrs. Steadway's faint look of discomfort became more acute. She moved uneasily in her chair, glanced at me, glanced at Adela, hunted for something to say.

"Yes, that's what I told my husband. I said, she didn't dream what was happening here while she stopped her car there on the hill above the farm and talked to young Mr. Carick."

CHAPTER XIII

IN ALL PROBABILITY MRS. Steadway has never known the fateful part she played in the Thatcher case. Indeed, it was imperative from Adela's viewpoint that she should not know. This was apparent even in that first moment of shocked astonishment following the unexpected revelation, while I watched Adela's face lose its careful graciousness and become stiffly blank. The swift, anxious drawing together of her reserves to meet this new development was so visible to me that I marveled that our caller could sit there, still with that air of timid politeness, entirely unaware of the crushing blow she had dealt.

"You mean Allen Carick?" said Adela stiffly. "He is visiting my brother Mr. Thatcher and his wife. He is Evelyn's brother, you know. We are all very fond of Allen," she said deliberately, and then, because she had to know, she added, "Dave—my brother Dave—was with him."

"Oh, no," said Mrs. Steadway, only too glad to relieve her awkward discomfort with conversation. "No, he wasn't there. There was just Mr. Carick. He was driving Frank Whiting's old roadster, and when I saw the car stop there beside the coupé Miss Janice was driving I thought it must be Frank Whiting, and I wondered if somebody had died out our way. Then I saw Mr. Carick get out; he went and leaned against the door of the coupé, and they talked for quite a while. But young Mr. Thatcher wasn't with him."

"Yes. Yes. We are all so fond of Allen," repeated Adela with blue lips. "Hilary bought the old roadster of Mr. Whiting for the boys to use. They will soon be home for the rest of the summer. How did you get along with your canning? Things are early this year, aren't they?"

And she sat there, fumbling with her blue beads, looking at her caller with bleak blue eyes, still stately, still gracious, somehow asking questions of the farm and listening to their replies and finally permitting the conversation to lapse suggestively. Mrs. Steadway's skirt had scarcely vanished into the hall before Adela rose with a soft rustling of lavender silk, gave me a blank look that might have meant anything, and walked slowly to the door of Dave's study.

She knocked, listened for a moment, and returned slowly to her chair.

"I don't like to disturb him," she said to me. "He hasn't been well lately. But of course I must ask him—— I thought they were together all afternoon. Fishing. He and Allen. But Emmeline said no one came—— Oh, Janice. It's you. Come in, my dear."

Janice hesitated for a moment, sensing, I think, something in the atmosphere, for she looked swiftly from Adela to me and back again and said:

"Is anything wrong?"

"No. No. Only, Janice—Mrs. Steadway was here just now, and she happened to mention that Allen met you on the hill above the farm the afternoon Bayard was killed. And that Dave—Dave was not with him. Is that true?"

Janice walked slowly toward us, her plain white dress, rather severely tailored, showing the graceful lines of her young body.

Her face had for an instant flamed into beauty, as if the recollection of those few moments was so sweet that their loveliness could not be denied even at such an anxious moment. Then the beauty was gone, and she looked tired and a little frightened. She sat down, her hands going out to clasp the arms of the chair. The light from the west windows was on her face and showed rather cruelly the purple marks under her eyes, and caught a high light from her slender wedding ring.

"Yes," she said.

Adela looked bewildered, frightened, and hard.

"But you didn't mention it before. We all thought Dave and Allen were together the entire afternoon."

"No, I didn't mention it. We, Allen and I, thought it better not to. And Dave said nothing. Under the circumstances, we thought it as well to let people suppose what you all assumed was true. That Allen and Dave had been together all afternoon. It was only to prevent unpleasant comment or—questions."

"Then, Janice, where was Dave?"

"I don't know." The girl glanced doubtfully at me.

Adela closed her eyes for a moment as if to summon strength.

"Speak freely before Miss Keate, Janice. I know that none of my family is in any way connected with—with Bayard's death. I know it so well that I am undertaking to prove it. I want Miss Keate to hear everything. I am convinced that she can hear everything."

"I don't know where Dave was," said Janice slowly. "And he's not been feeling well lately—I didn't like to ask him. Allen said when I met him there above the farm that Dave had found it pretty warm fishing and said he'd take a walk. That it would help his head. So Allen took the roadster, drove out toward the farm, met me just leaving. We talked a while, and then he drove back to the lake and met Dave. Dave said his headache was gone and they both fished until—well, until they came back to the house. And found us all—here in the library."

"Dave took a walk?" said Adela. "Where did he go?"

The eyes of the two women met.

"I don't know," said Janice. "But—of course, he didn't come back to the house. Emmeline would have seen him. Or Higby. Or Miss Keate."

"That's true," said Adela at once. "That's quite true. He couldn't have walked in this direction. I'll ask him, though. I should have known this long ago; yet you and Allen were right not to speak of it. It was quite unnecessary to mention. Janice, dear, do you mind answering a few questions?"

"Not at all, Adela. You mean questions about——"

"About Bayard, my dear."

"Oh. About Bayard." Janice's white fingers seemed to clutch the arms of her chair. There was no beauty now in her face. But there was a certain comprehension, as if she guessed Adela's purpose. And there was also a guarded look I did not like to see. "Very well, Adela."

But Adela, resolute though she was with her bleak eyes and the granite in her face, found her inquiries difficult. She sat there, drawing the blank blue beads through her blunt fingers. Presently she said:

"Janice, the afternoon Bayard was killed, when we—you and I—returned home late in the afternoon, I walked down among the flowers, and you took the baskets and went directly to the house. What did you do?"

Very white was Janice now, her slender fingers taut.

"I took the baskets to the kitchen and went up the back stairs."

"Where did you leave the baskets?"

"I put the egg basket in the refrigerator. The basket with

the butter and buttermilk I left on the table for Emmeline to empty."

"When you went past the door of the library—this door— did you—— Oh, Janice, my dear, I can't question you like this. Won't you tell me the truth? Wasn't Bayard dead—here on the rug—then?"

Janice rose, walked to the door of Dave's study, listened for a moment, then walked slowly back, her dark head bent. She looked grave and yet steady.

"Is Dave in his study?" she asked Adela.

"Yes, I believe so. I haven't seen the poor boy since breakfast. I'm afraid he's got one of his headaches, but I don't like to disturb him. He may be asleep. He sleeps so wretchedly. I shouldn't like to wake him if he's actually getting any rest." Something about protesting too much went vaguely through my head, though I couldn't have told why.

Janice had stopped beside a chair, her hands moving over its high carved back.

"He's not been at all well," she said thoughtfully. "I'm afraid he's taken Bayard's death badly. None of us blames him for it. Yes, Adela, Bayard was dead when I came through the hall."

Some of the hard lines disappeared from Adela's face as if she had fought a battle and won.

"And you came in and bent to look at him?"

"Yes."

"And you had on—forgive me, dear, but I must ask it—you had on your white felt hat? And you bent and—and touched him to be sure he was dead? And your fingers—that's how the stain was on your hat?"

Janice was looking somberly out the window; her eyes were large and dark in her white face, and it seemed to me I caught a flicker of horror in their depths.

"Yes. That's how it happened."

"And you were shocked. So shocked you didn't know what you were doing. And frightened—as any sensitive girl would be frightened. You ran upstairs. Took off your hat. Heard Emmeline's screams and came down again. And then in the excitement and hurry and commotion there was no occasion for you to tell that your own discovery had preceded Emmeline's by a moment or two."

"No occasion," said Janice in a stifled sort of way, still looking out onto the green summer lawn.

"You see, Miss Keate? And then, Janice, you didn't purposely hide your hat. I mean you didn't hide it because of the—the stains on it. Did you?"

"Not exactly hide it, Adela. But I—didn't like the stains on it. I intended to clean it. In cold water, you know. But I didn't have time. And of course, I didn't want anyone to see it. But Florrie found it." There was no apology, no suggestion of explanation in Janice's voice. It was rather detached and remote, as if she were stating quite impersonal facts about something that was of very little interest to her. "That hat, you know, was the least of it."

"Then there is—the matter of the revolver, Janice darling. You see, Emmeline found it. Brought it to me. Miss Keate was with me at the time. We—you—you didn't——"

Suddenly the detached manner left Janice. Her face became full of life and she turned swiftly toward Adela.

"Don't ask me about the revolver, Adela," she said almost fiercely. "Don't ask me that. You see, I don't lie very well."

Adela stood, stately, a little severe in her lavender silk with her eyeglasses catching the light.

"I'm not asking you to lie, Janice," she said. "I only want you to tell me the truth. The truth is the only thing that can save us."

The two women faced each other for a long moment. Each

so resolute, each so proudly unbent; Janice's swift steel matched against Adela's sturdy, rocklike determination.

Finally Janice said:

"You don't know—you can't know what you are asking."

I believe, just for the moment, they had forgotten me.

"But I do know. I know. Why don't you tell me the truth? None of you will tell me. I feel you are all keeping something back. You and Hilary and Evelyn—all of you. As if I were a helpless old woman. And I'm not. It's my house. It's my family. I must know." Adela's blunt white hands were shaking. It was the only time I saw her drop that impregnable shield of dignity with which she faced her family and the world.

Her appeal touched Janice. I could see the girl's face soften; I felt she was about to speak. It was curiously tantalizing, like a play, that Evelyn should appear in the doorway at exactly that moment and enter.

Both Adela and Janice turned at the sound of her footsteps. Evelyn's dark blue eyes went rapidly from one to the other. She said, as Janice had said:

"Is anything wrong?"

"No," said Janice.

"Yes," said Adela. "Why will none of you help me? I can't do this alone."

Evelyn did not ask what. With her swift common sense she grasped the situation at once, I think. Perhaps Adela's amazing moment of weakness shocked her as it did me.

"We'll do anything we can to help you, Adela," she said calmly. "Good heavens, it's warm this afternoon! Can't Emmeline make us some iced tea? Never mind, Adela, I'll speak to her."

It was very still in the library while Evelyn walked with her customary long, graceful strides to the door. Emmeline must have been near, for we could clearly hear Evelyn's concise directions. Adela turned away from Janice and sat down again in her high-backed chair and resumed at once her beads and her dignity.

And Janice, white and still, stood by the table, touching and arranging the roses in the big green bowl, with hands that trembled a little. Her eyes were still dark and wide and touched with horror, and I think she did not quite know what she was doing. Then Evelyn was back in the room, tossing her hat onto a chair and sitting down with a sigh.

"Now, then," she said, coolly matter-of-fact, "what is it you want me to do, Adela?"

"I only want you to tell me the truth, Evelyn," said Adela deliberately. She was again complete mistress of herself. "That is the only way in which I can prove——" She stopped, touched me with her cold blue eyes, and resumed, "We have no need to fear the truth."

Evelyn's clear eyes went to me, too. She took off her gloves, stripping them off her brown hands with two quick gestures, touched her straight gold hair to be sure it was smooth and said:

"I've just been up at the house. There was a letter from the boys. And one from Aunt Hetty. Allen and Hilary drove over with me; they are outside. They'll be in, in a moment—here they are now."

"Good Lord, it's hot," said Hilary. He was pink and coatless, with dampish spots on his shirt.

Allen took Adela's hand gently.

"Sit down, Allen," said Adela. "You have come in good time. I want you—all of you—to help me."

Something in her voice caught Hilary's quick attention. He stopped wiping his face with his handkerchief, glanced swiftly at Adela and sharply at me, and said at once:

"Certainly, Adela. Certainly."

"You see," said Adela, "I think we owe it to ourselves to prevent—any talk there may be about—Bayard's death."

The last two words came out rather jerkily, as if with tremendous effort on Adela's part. The room was very still for a moment—still, yet echoing those two words: Bayard's death. Bayard's death. It was as if it said: I know which of you killed him; are you going to tell? Are you going to be trapped?

"Any unpleasant talk," said Adela rather stiffly and stuck again, looking rather helplessly at Evelyn. And Evelyn, blessedly direct, said:

"You mean people are apt to hint that one of us killed Bayard? Why, of course, they will. Probably have already. People aren't going to pass up such a chance for talk. I think that's very wise of you, Adela. It's a good thing to prove to our own or any outsider's satisfaction that none of us killed him. Isn't that what you mean?"

"Why—why, yes," said Adela, taken rather off her feet, I think, by Evelyn's blunt stating of the situation.

"Go right ahead, Adela," said Hilary a bit pompously. "I am ready for any inquiry you—or anyone else—choose to make." He addressed Adela and looked at me. I'm sure that even if I had not overheard that family conference I would have known what they were attempting to do. Well, I might spare Janice if I could; I might even keep the affair of the diamonds a secret. But Hilary was, so to speak, a horse of another color.

"Indeed," continued Hilary. "You might like me to undertake this—er—inquiry. I'm more accustomed to matters of this sort."

"Thank you, Hilary," said Adela tartly. "I'll do it myself. The point just now is to get you all to tell me the truth. Not to try to hide things from me. We don't fear the truth. Hilary, where was Bayard when you last talked to him?"

"Here in the library."

"What did you talk of?"

"Why, nothing much. I asked him how he felt. If there was anything I could do for him. Ah, here's Emmeline with some iced tea. It certainly looks good." It seemed to me his gusto was a little forced.

Ice tinkled in the tall glasses. Emmeline, tall and black and spotlessly aproned, passed the tray. The interruption gave us all a little rest from the growing tension. Adela sipped her tea delicately, slowly. As Emmeline put the tray on the table and went away, she said:

"You and Bayard had had no trouble, had you, Hilary? If you had, you know, someone is bound to have heard of it. There are no secrets in C——."

"No, of course not," said Hilary. He gulped some tea and continued: "That is, no more than we'd always had, and you know all about that. He wanted more money, but you knew that. He always wanted money. He'd been bleeding us white for years."

"Hilary! Don't use such coarse expressions." Adela was chalk gray. She set her glass carefully on the table and touched the turquoise beads. "It's quite true, Miss Keate. I suppose everyone in the county knows that Bayard was—a source of much anxiety and trouble to us. He——"

"He was an out-and-out scoundrel," said Hilary, flushing as if the bare memory infuriated him. "Time after time we gave him money, started him in some kind of business, tried to establish him. He always failed, squandered the money, came back for more. And he always worked around us somehow to get it. If he couldn't appeal to our sympathies he——" Hilary stopped abruptly, the frightened look coming into his eyes as they went quickly to Evelyn.

"Perhaps you don't know, Miss Keate," said Evelyn, "how difficult it is to have someone like that in the family. We couldn't permit him to disgrace our name. To do the things he would threaten to do. And then besides—I think we may as well tell her the whole truth about it, Hilary."

"Nonsense. There's no need."

"I think there is. You see, Miss Keate, when Hilary was a boy he did something very silly. It was when he and Dave and Bayard were all in prep school together."

"Do you think there's really any need to tell that, Evelyn?" asked Adela, her face looking old and shrunken, her blunt white hands pulling the beads back and forth, back and forth.

"Yes," said Evelyn sensibly. "It can't do us any harm. We all know about it, and Hilary found the check in Bayard's things and destroyed it. And if we don't tell Miss Keate the truth after having gone so far, she'll think it was something much worse than it is. It was only a boyish scrape, Miss Keate. Hilary had to have some money for something—something that seemed terribly urgent to him then."

"We'd been playing cards—gambling a little," said Hilary, looking pompous and blustering and as shamefaced as if he were a boy in his teens again. "I lost, and the kid I owed threatened to tell the Head if I didn't pay him. He—this kid—was leaving school anyhow, so he didn't care. But I knew I'd be expelled. And I didn't have a cent, and Adela would never send checks between our allowance checks unless she knew why we wanted extra money and approved of it. Bayard—how I don't know—had some money in the bank, and I—well, I forged his name to a check." He wiped his face again. It was strange to hear that man, with sons of his own, confessing the boyhood scrape. "It was only a small amount. We'd often amused ourselves—you know how kids are—writing and imitating each other's signatures. But Bayard—Bayard kept the check. It was written in pencil; he erased the date and amount and kept it all these years, threatening to fill it in for a larger amount, a recent date, and prosecute. He couldn't have got far with it—still I'm not sure. It would have raised an awful stink."

"Hilary!" said Adela in faint protest.

"Well, you know, Adela, there'd have been plenty of people to jump at the chance to discredit me. For a banker it would have been——"

"Then he was using that check to bring pressure just now?" I said.

Hilary looked at me uncomfortably.

"Yes. He wanted a large sum of money. Larger than I could give him. He thought it was a good time to squeeze."

"But Hilary, you didn't quarrel with him. That last afternoon."

"No, Adela," said Hilary heavily. "I didn't quarrel with him."

"You didn't——" it was Allen, standing at the window, his back to us, speaking rather softly. "You didn't shoot him. For that."

Hilary leaped to his feet, his plump face crimson again.

"God, no! He was a scoundrel. A disgrace to the family. But I wouldn't have killed him. Good God, I couldn't do that."

"You left him alive," said Evelyn quickly. "As I found him. Remember, Allen, that I was the last one to see Bayard alive. That was after Hilary had talked to him."

Allen turned suddenly away from the window, walked to Evelyn, and put his hand under her chin, looking down at her upturned face and smiling a little into the steady dark blue eyes so like his own. The two bright heads shone above the two brown faces.

"That's all right then," he said. "We all know you didn't shoot him."

"Then," said Hilary, "Bayard was alive when Evelyn left him.

Dead when Emmeline found him not an hour later. No one of the family saw him during that time——"

"You are wrong, Hilary," said Janice. "I have just told Adela that when I returned from the farm and came into the house a few moments ahead of Adela I found him dead. I saw him dead before Emmeline found him."

"Janice——" Allen was at her side. We'd have been blind, all of us, not to have seen the love and fear in his face. But she pushed him away with steady hands.

"No, I didn't shoot him. But I'm glad he's dead. I think we ought to stop this talk. We ought not to try to discover who did it. If it was one of the family, how much better not to——"

"But, Janice," said Adela hoarsely, as if her throat and mouth were numb, "it was not one of the family. It was the burglar. We are only proving——"

"You ought not to have started this, Adela," said Hilary agitatedly. "Better let sleeping dogs lie."

"You'll have to let me do as I think best," said Adela. "You were going to tell me, Janice, about the revolver."

"The revolver!" cried Hilary, bouncing to his feet again. "What revolver? What about it?"

"I—I warned you not to ask me, Adela," said Janice. Allen's hands were out to hers.

"Don't talk, Janice. Don't say anything——"

"Hush, Allen. The revolver—was on the floor—beside Bayard. I put it in the egg basket—to hide it."

"The egg basket!" cried Hilary, quite frantic with bewilderment. "What on earth are you talking about? What do you mean? For heaven's sake, speak up! Why did you hide it?"

"Why did I hide it?" repeated Janice, as if we should have known. "Why, you see," she said helplessly, "it was *Dave's*. *Dave's* revolver. He'd already shot Bayard once with it."

"*Janice—Dave didn't kill Bayard.*" Adela was on her feet, her eyes like ice, her thickish body swaying a little. "You are out of your senses."

"Now, Adela, wait. It was natural for Janice to think it might have been Dave who shot him." Allen was speaking rapidly, trying to get Adela's attention. Giving them all time, I thought. "If she came in, saw Bayard had been shot, was dead, saw Dave's revolver, of course her first thought would be that Dave might have shot him. She's not saying he did. She doesn't think Dave killed Bayard. She only acted hurriedly. Her first thought was to hide the revolver. To conceal the fact. She acted," said Allen gravely and rather sadly, "only as a loyal wife. You ought to be the last to reproach her for it."

Evelyn stood.

"I think we are letting things get away from us," she said bluntly. "There's no need of making a scene. We are talking too much and not getting any place. The burglar could have picked up Dave's revolver and used it. Just because it was Dave's revolver, there on the floor, doesn't prove anything. Doesn't prove Dave used it. Doesn't even prove Bayard was killed by a bullet from that gun. Doesn't prove anything. Janice was frightened and shocked and acted hurriedly. The burglar must have just escaped. I think we ought to concentrate on finding the burglar. When I left, Bayard was alive. And Dave and Allen were together."

"Not all the afternoon, Evelyn," said Adela. "I have just discovered that Dave took a walk alone, and Allen went for a drive, met Janice near the east farm, and they talked awhile. Mrs. Steadway happened to mention it. Janice and Allen thought it unwise to tell that, after all, Dave and Allen did not each have the complete alibi we all thought they had. Janice and Allen acted as they thought best. But it makes it difficult."

"But didn't you meet again, Allen? You returned together. You came into the library together," said Evelyn.

"Yes," replied Allen. "After leaving Janice I drove directly back to the lake, and Dave was there. We fished for quite a while and then came home together."

"Why, then, that's all right," said Evelyn, relieved. "You see, Adela, they were together from—what time, Allen?"

"About four, or a little earlier," said Allen. "And you left Bayard alive at ten after four. So you see, Adela, Dave's alibi is still good."

"And yours too, incidentally, Allen," said Hilary rather bitterly.

Allen shrugged.

"I can't help that."

"That is right," I said, addressing Evelyn. "You were here after four. I am sure of that, for I saw you. The burglar must have come after you were here. You just came to the door of the library, here, and glanced in?"

"Yes," said Evelyn.

"Bayard was here?"

"Yes. I didn't speak to him. He didn't see me."

"Oh, yes, I remember you said that. The burglar must have come in directly after. When you were here, was the safe open?"

"Why, no," said Evelyn, frowning. "I remember distinctly. It was closed."

"*Evelyn!*" shouted Hilary. "Good God, don't you know what you've done? That woman has tricked you." He was purple with rage. "She's tricked you. You've admitted that Bayard was——" He stopped, thoroughly frightened now, staring at me, on the verge of apoplexy.

"Why, no—I——" said Evelyn.

"The safe," I said, watching Hilary, "is in Dave's study. Bayard was actually killed there. There was blood on the rug by the desk. He was killed in Dave's study. He was dead—" I looked at Evelyn—"when you saw him."

Evelyn stared back at me. She was not a liar by inspiration; she had to be coached, and there was no time for that.

She nodded slowly.

Hilary sucked in his breath with a sort of groan and sat down as if his knees had weakened under him.

I heard Allen say under his breath, "Dave's study."

Adela's face was granite. I met their eyes—all of them, it seemed to me, hating me. And perhaps fearing me.

"Janice," said Adela, "call Dave. I think we must question him."

The room was so still that Janice's small heels made tap-taps of sound along the floor. She knocked on the door of the study. There was no answer, and she put her hand on the doorknob, opened the door, and stepped inside. No one spoke. There was no sound from the study.

It seemed a long time before she stood in the doorway again. She just stood there, her back to the room beyond, facing us, swaying a little. We were all standing. She said:

"You can't question Dave. You can't ask him anything— ever—again."

CHAPTER XIV

FROM THE FIRST IT was not so much a question of Dave's having been murdered as it was a question of whether he had taken the veronal accidentally or intentionally. In other words, whether or not he was a suicide. And if he had committed suicide, was it a confession of guilt? Had he murdered Bayard?

For Dave was dead. And he died of an overdose of veronal. Dr. Bouligny established that fact within twenty minutes of Janice's shocking announcement.

I do not remember much of the few moments immediately following her words as she stood there at the door of the little study, nor of how we crowded into that room, nor of what we said and did and how we looked. I do remember kneeling at the long couch where that silent body lay and making sure that Janice was not mistaken, that Dave was actually dead. And I remember how peaceful his face looked. It is true, of course, that most faces of the dead look peaceful, but there was a look about Dave's face as of one who seeks his rest with the tranquillity of complete surrender.

Singularly enough, while we were all thinking of Adela and trying to spare her, it was Hilary who went to pieces and collapsed on a chair in the library where Allen led him and sat there shivering and shaking with his hands over his face trying to hide dreadful man hysteria. Adela was like a woman carved in stone. She stood at the foot of Dave's couch and looked at him with a still hard face and told Evelyn to telephone for the doctor, and told Allen to take Hilary away and Janice to bring her a chair.

"I intend to stay here," said Adela stiffly. "Thank you, Janice."

Janice looked and moved as if she were in a daze. It was only when Adela reached out and took one of Dave's hands that Janice sank down on the floor beside Adela and buried her head in her arms. The toe of her slim white slipper rested exactly over the spot on the Sarouk rug where I had discovered that damp crimson patch.

Evelyn turned away from the telephone.

"He will be here right away," she said. "Don't look like that, Adela. You know how sick Dave has been. For such a long time he has not been himself. Perhaps it is better."

"Death," said Adela, "is never better."

And Janice lifted her dark head and looked at Evelyn as if she were a creature of a different world. I am sure that, then, Janice only felt a great pity for Dave and for Adela; she had not yet thought of her own freedom. There was nothing hypocritical about her grief; it was the sorrow of affection and pity. She might not have loved Dave, but she had not tried to escape any of the responsibilities of her marriage. And then, she must have loved him once. Even an unsentimental and an honest woman may weep at the end of a marriage which has failed or at the grave of a forgotten love. And Dave was much more than that: he was her husband, an integral part of her world, a vital and important factor in her life.

Dr. Bouligny came very soon: his thick black hair ruffled, his coat baggy, his face growing somber and troubled as he listened to what we said and looked at Dave. He took Adela's pulse, I remember, and sent Evelyn for some wine, and got us all out of the study and into the library with the door closed between. Adela never resisted him, and she did not do so then; she put Dave's poor limp hand carefully on the edge of the couch and obeyed Dr. Bouligny. At his request I closed the door and followed them. The examination had taken only a few quiet moments.

"You'd better," he said to Adela, "go straight to bed and take a bromide. You can't stand this."

Adela was sipping the wine Evelyn had brought. I have always marveled at Adela's fortitude at that dreadful time; but then all of them behaved rather well. All but Hilary, and perhaps Hilary had more for which to reproach himself; he must have drifted far from Dave during recent years.

"Why did Dave die?" asked Adela directly, brushing aside his suggestion as if it had not been made.

Dr. Bouligny looked worried. He ran his fingers through his thick hair, further disheveling it.

"We'd better all of us sit down and talk quietly. Here, Hilary—give him some wine, Miss Keate, please. If you are determined to thresh this thing out here and now——" He paused, looking anxiously at Adela. "Well, perhaps it is best. You are sure you can bear it all?"

"What do you mean, Daniel? Dave is dead—my little brother——" Adela's mouth twisted a little over the words. They were her only audible expression of the turmoil of grief and pain and desolation in her heart. It was a moment before she could continue. Presently she said, her face gray and blank and set, and her eyes like a cold blue wall between us and her thoughts, and her voice rather harshly deliberate: "Why did Dave die? Tell me, Daniel."

Dr. Bouligny sighed heavily. I gave the small glass to Hilary, who took it and gulped the wine in a dazed fashion. I don't think he realized what he was doing or that I, whom he disliked so fervently, had given him the drink. He did seem to come to himself, however; he rose and approached the small tragic group and, I believe, began to consider the matter of Dave's death in its possible relation to our dreadful problem.

"Dave died," said Dr. Bouligny, "of an overdose of veronal."

"Veronal," said Hilary in a breathless way. He was still very pale and had none of his usual self-assurance. "How did Dave get veronal? Why did he take it?"

"I don't know where he got it," Dr. Bouligny said. "Janice, my dear, do you mind answering a few questions? You see, I've got to sign my coroner's certificate."

"What is it?" The girl was like a pale, still little statue in her white gown; her hands were clasped rather desperately together as if to restrain their trembling, but otherwise she held herself with amazing courage.

"About Dave," he said. "How's he been feeling lately?"

"About as usual, I think," said Janice slowly.

"Has he been sleeping well?"

"I don't know. He never sleeps well, but I've not heard him complain recently. You see, he spends so much of his time here in his study. And we never disturb him. I think, though, that he——" She stopped.

"That he's been taking something to make him sleep?" asked Dr. Bouligny.

"Why, yes, I think so," she said. "But he never told me, and I've seen nothing, though I've watched."

"He hasn't said anything about having any difficulty with his eyesight lately?"

"Yes," said Janice, "a little. He didn't care to read. And once or twice he said things blurred."

"What about his speech? And his walk? Has he been a little

slow of speech? Has he seemed to lack a certain exactness of movement?"

I longed to reply to Dr. Bouligny, as I saw what he meant and marveled that I had not seen it in Dave days earlier.

But Janice said hesitantly:

"Yes. A little. He—oh, he's not been himself at all, Dr. Dan."

Dr. Bouligny stared at the rug for a moment, running his fingers through his thick hair.

"I don't know why I didn't see it," he said slowly. "You should have told me—I didn't realize——"

"What is it, Daniel?" said Adela.

He looked at her slowly.

"It's going to go hard with you, Adela," he said. "But I suppose you've got to know. You see Dave's been—Dave was a drug addict."

"Drug," said Adela, as if she were merely repeating words without any comprehension at all of their meaning. "Addict."

"Yes," said Dr. Bouligny miserably. "He took veronal. He must have taken too much at last. Poor fellow. I could have cured him if I'd known it in time."

Adela was on her feet. Her eyes were no longer blank and cold; they were blazing blue fire. There was a very fury in her eyes and in her broken voice as she said harshly:

"Veronal! Veronal! And you could have cured it!"

Dr. Bouligny, his eyes pitying, nodded his great head.

"I could have cured it, Adela," he said gently. "But I didn't know. Dave has been vaguely unwell for so long—I didn't see it, and none of you knew. If it had been morphine or cocaine or any of those drugs, I wouldn't have been at all sure of success. But veronal—I could have cured him of that habit."

That was the second time I saw Adela falter. All that rocklike strength suddenly left her; she sagged down into her chair again, her thick body loose and old, her face flabby, her eyes closed.

"She's fainting," said Dr. Bouligny. "Evelyn, help me."

Adela motioned them back with her blunt white hands.

"No. No. Let me alone."

There was such vehement command in her gesture that Evelyn and Dr. Bouligny and I paused involuntarily. After watching Adela for a moment, Dr. Bouligny sat down again in his chair, and Evelyn went back to stand beside Janice. Allen, tall and brown and grave, stood a little in the background and scarcely took his eyes from Janice during the whole time.

"It's always that way," said Dr. Bouligny. "That is the danger of veronal. It is, in a manner of speaking, a perfectly harmless drug. But taken over a period of time it does not induce tolerance on the part of the patient, as, for instance, morphine does. At the same time veronal tends to lose something of its effect when taken habitually. Thus the patient is apt to increase the dose, and since his system has not grown tolerant any heavy increase is usually fatal. That is why we hear of so many deaths from veronal." He was talking nervously, rubbing his heavy chin with his hand and watching Adela.

Hilary cleared his throat.

"It's a peaceful death, isn't it, Dan?"

"Why, yes, Hilary," said Dr. Bouligny with a sigh. "Dave didn't suffer. Don't worry about that."

"Peaceful," said Hilary slowly. "That is why it is so often used for suicide."

It was the first time the word had been spoken. Janice started to her feet, dreadfully white and horrified, and then sank slowly back again, her wide dark eyes on Dr. Bouligny; Evelyn put out her brown hands as if in reproach and denial, and Adela in her chair stiffened. Slowly her body became firm and erect. She lifted her face. It was no longer flabby and sunken and old; it was granite again, set with resolve. From that moment on to the last it was as if Adela were consumed with a white fever of energy and resolve; as if she could not rest, could not wait, could not even permit herself sorrow until she had cleared Dave's memory of the dreadful imputation. That was the thing that kept her from collapse; that was the purpose that animated her every move. That was, of course, the driving reason for her insistence in continuing that extraordinary inquiry which Dave's death had so unexpectedly and terribly interrupted. For she did just that, incredible though it is.

Now she turned her blue eyes upon Hilary and said rather hoarsely:

"Suicide. Did you say suicide? What do you mean?"

Hilary shrugged helplessly.

"I meant suicide, Adela."

"Do you dare sit there before my very eyes and say that your own brother is a suicide?"

Hilary looked too unhappy to be further disconcerted by Adela's scathing tone. He said:

"Suicide has been a confession of guilt before now."

I heard Janice catch her breath as if it hurt her. Adela's face did not alter.

"I knew that was in your mind," said Adela with relentless scorn. "I knew when you said suicide exactly what you meant. You want us to believe, all of us, that Dave killed Bayard and then killed himself to escape the consequences. That's what you want us to believe." She leaned forward, terribly still, talking in a broken, cold way. "It is an easy way out for you. For all of us. But we are not going to take that way. Hilary, Hilary, how can you! And Dave—only just dead."

"I'm sorry, Adela," said Hilary. He was gradually reassuming the slightly pompous air that was natural with him, although he still looked shaken; his fat hands were unsteady, and his eyes had a tendency to dart about the room and avoid directly meeting other eyes. "I'm sorry. But I don't see any other thing to believe. It is painfully evident. We have all known how Dave has brooded lately; especially since Bayard's death. How depressed he has been. Why, we have scarcely seen him; he's done nothing but sit in his study there and brood. I don't want to think that he killed Bayard and then committed suicide. You may not think it, Adela, but I—I loved Dave, too. But I can't escape the fact. I can't close my eyes to it from sentiment. To me it is as good as proved. Dave killed Bayard."

Dr. Bouligny, anxious eyes on Adela's cold face, moved restlessly.

"That depression of Dave's meant nothing, Hilary," he said. "It is one of the symptoms of his condition. Veronal addicts are subject to periods of extreme mental depression. His depression was no sign that he was brooding over Bayard's death. All those things we talked of were symptoms. I must have been blind not to see it. But it came very gradually."

"It dated," said Adela cruelly, "from his last illness. When you, Daniel, gave him things to make him sleep."

Dr. Bouligny's large fingers rubbed his chin worriedly.

"Adela," he said, "you don't mean that. I would never do a thing like that. I——"

"Forgive me," said Adela more gently. "No, I didn't mean that you contributed to this dreadful habit of Dave's. To Dave's death. No, I did not mean that, Daniel. Dave has always been weak. Has always needed help. And I failed him. I failed him, but I'll prove he did not murder. I'll prove——" Her eyes fell on me, and perhaps it was then that she remembered what Dave's death had interrupted, and resolved to continue that inquiry. Only now there was a more pressing reason to prove her family's innocence.

"You can't prove that, Adela," said Hilary wearily. "It is best to leave things as they are. We'll bury Dave, and we'll remember the things we loved him for. We'll remember him as he was before his—" Hilary paused and then said rather sadly and kindly—"his illness. I'll telephone to Frank Whiting now. We'd better say—what shall we say, Dan?"

"You'll have to tell the truth," said Dr. Bouligny.

"The truth," repeated Adela quickly. "You mean that Dave died of an overdose of veronal? That he died right in the next room while we were all here talking? But people will say what Hilary says! Everyone will say he murdered Bayard and then killed himself. That it was a confession of his guilt. Can't you say something else? Anything?"

"No, Adela. I'm sorry. That is all I can say."

"But wasn't it heart failure in the end? Couldn't you say that?"

Dr. Bouligny smiled sadly.

"All deaths are heart failure in the end, Adela," he said gently. "But I can say with honesty that it was a culmination of a lone period of illness. Everyone knows that he has not been well in a long time. I'll do what I can, I promise you."

It struck me that Hilary was a little eager to shift the blame onto Dave's defenseless shoulders and to close the matter of Bayard's murder once and for all. Impulsively, and thereby, I have no doubt, incurring Hilary's undying hatred, I said:

"If you left Bayard alive at ten minutes after four the afternoon of his death and your wife found him dead not more than ten minutes later at the most, it could not have been Dave who killed him. For Dave and Mr. Carick were together at that time."

The shock of Dave's death had apparently driven from Hilary's thoughts the moments immediately preceding its discovery.

I could almost see him grope about in his memory, while his face hardened suspiciously. He darted a swift look toward Evelyn.

"Bayard was alive when I left him," he said stubbornly. "I don't care what you have taken it in your head to say, Evelyn, he was alive when I left him."

"Evelyn," said Adela slowly, "why did you say what you did? Why did you say Bayard was alive when you left him? Did you really find him dead? There in the study?"

Evelyn's dark blue eyes went from her husband's worried, frightened face to Allen's. I don't know what she found there, some source of strength, I suppose, for she said bluntly:

"I didn't tell the truth, Adela. You see, I knew that Hilary had just left Bayard. I never had liked Bayard, you all know that, so it wasn't such a shock to find him dead as it might have been. Oh, it was terrible, of course, to find him like that, but it wasn't as if it had been someone I loved. The dreadful part of it, to me, was the fact that Hilary, if he had kept his appointment with me, as I soon found he had, must have just left the house. I was afraid they had quarreled. I was afraid——" She stopped, looking in some anxiety at Hilary.

"Oh, go on," said Hilary bitterly. "You are as good as accusing me of murder. Don't stop on my account."

Evelyn's blue eyes looked troubled. But she was always impervious to even the broadest irony. To Evelyn people said what they meant. She continued at once and rather sensibly:

"What else was there for me to think, Hilary? Oh, I know *now* that you didn't kill him. But *then* I was afraid. I thought of everything. Of the boys. Of you. I knew how Bayard goaded you. Even a word or a look or a smile from Bayard could always enrage Hilary——"

"Evelyn, for God's sake, stop," groaned Hilary. "Stop her, Allen. Can't you see what she is doing——"

"So I thought," continued Evelyn inexorably, "that I'd better not tell that I found Bayard dead when I came here to meet Hilary. And Hilary agreed with me about it. He said there were times when a lie is——"

Hilary was on his feet.

"Evelyn, will you stop talking! Will you——"

"Evelyn," said Allen, crisply breaking through Hilary's frenzied protest, "you say you know *now* that Hilary didn't kill Bayard. How do you know it? Don't be frightened."

"I'm not frightened," said Evelyn calmly, and I'm sure she spoke the truth. "I know Hilary didn't kill Bayard because he told me he didn't."

"Because I told—— Oh, my God, Evelyn, are you trying to make things worse than they are already?"

"Why, no, Hilary," said Evelyn. "I'm just telling the truth. I never felt right about that lie, but I told it after I'd promised you I would. I could see why it was so necessary, but now the truth is out we may as well make the best——"

I stepped forward. My uniform rustled in the sudden silence. I suppose they saw something in my face, for no one spoke, and I was conscious of their combined gaze.

"Did you close Bayard's eyes?" I asked Evelyn.

"No," she said. "No. His eyes were closed when I found him. I was glad of that. His eyes were closed."

"His eyes were closed," I repeated slowly. Dr. Bouligny started to speak and checked himself.

"The eyes of those who die a violent death do not close voluntarily." I turned squarely to Hilary.

"Did you close Bayard's eyes?"

CHAPTER XV

HILARY WAS, I BELIEVE, an excellent and levelheaded man of business. It was only owing to the fact that Bayard's murder so nearly concerned him that he found it so difficult to keep his head. Found it, in fact, impossible to behave with the assurance and foresight with which, in all likelihood, he would have advised his bank's client. Perhaps, too, as Evelyn had hinted, he had become supersensitive to Bayard or anything connected with Bayard; I myself had seen how easily and swiftly Bayard's smiling, edged remarks could penetrate Hilary's complacency.

Besides that, his own feelings were deeply involved; everything he had worked for, everything he held dear was threatened. He had been under a protracted nervous strain, he was harassed on all sides by worries, and Dave's death was the final blow.

My question was patently unwelcome. But then, almost anything I might have said would be unwelcome to Hilary.

He gave me a harassed, quick look, fumbled for a cigarette, selected one with jerky fingers, and said:

"No. No, I didn't close his eyes. How could I? Bayard was alive, I tell you, when I came here that afternoon. I'm going to telephone to Frank Whiting right now, Adela. It won't do to wait."

He started for the study. Almost at the door he stopped suddenly, as if he couldn't bear to see Dave's body again, turned abruptly, and went to the hall.

"That's right," said Dr. Bouligny. "Frank will have to be told sooner or later, and it's better sooner."

It was so quiet in the long shadowed room that we could hear Hilary's voice from the telephone in Adela's morning room, and his footsteps back along the hall. He was wiping his face with his handkerchief when he entered the room again.

"This is going to be bad," he said. "Frank Whiting—well, he didn't say much, but I could feel what he thought. God, it's such a mess!" He dropped heavily into a chair and sat there, staring at the rug.

"Is he coming right away?" asked Dr. Bouligny.

"Soon. He couldn't come immediately."

I am never one to put my hand to the plow and look back. And I did not like Hilary's evasion.

"Someone," I said, "closed Bayard's eyes. And if Bayard was alive when you left the house that afternoon, Mr. Thatcher, and dead when your wife came so soon after and no one entered the house in that interval—how did Bayard die?"

"What do you mean by that?" cried Hilary. "Are you accusing me of murder? What business is it of yours?"

"Hilary, I asked Miss Keate to do exactly what she is doing." It was Adela, of course, stiff and cold and straight and marvelously composed.

"I think you would do well to answer the nurse," said Allen dryly. "It is a reasonable question. You see, Hilary, you don't seem to realize that you are in a rather questionable position. You appear to be the last one known to have been with Bayard before his death. You say you didn't kill him, and we are only too ready to believe you. But Miss Keate, quite reasonably, wants further proof."

There was a short silence. It was so quiet I could hear Pansy, withdrawn to a corner and forgotten, panting asthmatically. Hilary continued to stare with narrowed eyes at the rug. Finally he said sulkily:

"I don't know who killed Bayard. I hate to seem cowardly, but I think Dave did it. But I don't know how it happened."

"Suppose we go at this in a more orderly way," said Allen. He went to the table. There was a pad of paper there and a heavy bronze inkwell and pens. "Now then, Miss Keate, you were sitting out in the arbor all that afternoon. About what time did you go out there?"

"About two o'clock. I left Bayard resting in his own room. It was perhaps ten minutes after you and Dave Thatcher had left the house."

"And you say Higby was mowing the lawn?"

"Yes; he had already started by the time I had reached the arbor. He didn't stop except very briefly, when he would turn a corner—so briefly as scarcely to be noted—during the whole afternoon. I could hear the lawn-mower very plainly."

"That ought to let Higby out, then. He couldn't mow the lawn and crawl in the library window and shoot Bayard simultaneously. Now, then, when you took up your somewhat observatory position in the arbor, who were still in the house?"

"Bayard, of course. And Emmeline. And Florrie." I hesitated.

"And I was there," said Janice at once. "And Adela."

"What time did you leave the house, Janice?"

"It must have been about twenty minutes to three." She looked inquiringly at me.

"Yes," I agreed. "It was just two-thirty when Florrie left.

And you came out of the house not more than ten minutes later."

"Janice, where was Bayard when you left the house?" His question was very gentle.

"Bayard was there in Dave's study. Alone," said Janice steadily. "He must have come downstairs again as soon as Miss Keate left him."

"What was he doing?"

"Nothing in particular."

"Did you speak to him?"

"Yes," said Janice slowly, her dark eyes meeting Allen's intent look. "But only for a moment. I only talked to him for a moment, and then I left the house."

"Two-forty, then, Janice leaves the house. Bayard is alive then." Allen was making notes as he talked. "What happened next, Miss Keate?"

"I saw Bayard," interposed Adela. "I came downstairs ready to go to the Benevolent Aid Society. Bayard was there at the door of the study, and I spoke to him a moment before I left."

"Was he alone then, Adela?"

"Certainly."

"What time was that?"

"I don't know exactly," said Adela. "I think it was close to three o'clock."

"But, Adela, you didn't say you had spoken to Bayard just before you left home," said Evelyn in a puzzled way.

"Didn't I?" said Adela calmly. "Well, I spoke to him. So you see, I was one of the last to see him alive."

I caught the flicker of her set blue gaze toward Hilary.

"It was exactly three o'clock when Miss Thatcher left the house," I said. "I happened to glance at my watch. And it was four o'clock when Mr. Thatcher arrived. And no one came near the house in the meantime."

"You are sure of that?" asked Allen. "You didn't drop into sleep during that time?"

"No," I replied, so decidedly that he did not pursue the matter.

"Then at four o'clock Hilary arrives. About how long were you in the house, Hilary?"

"Ten minutes," I said, before I could check myself. Hilary gave me a look of rage and nodded.

"I suppose she is right," he said. "It was probably ten minutes or so. I didn't realize," he added bitterly, "that she was holding a stopwatch on us all afternoon."

"Hilary," said Adela swiftly, "I asked Miss Keate to help me inquire into Bayard's death. Please remember that."

Please remember, she might as well have said, that we must keep Miss Keate friendly to us. That we must convince her that no Thatcher has done murder. That we must answer every question she may wish to ask.

Hilary mumbled something which sounded near enough to an apology, and Allen said rather hastily:

"Four-ten, Hilary leaves." His pen sputtered as he wrote it. "Then Evelyn arrives." He looked questioningly at me.

"It was only a few moments after Mr. Thatcher left," I said. "She must have actually entered the house at close to four-fifteen and left no later than four-twenty."

"Then, after Evelyn left, you saw no one until Janice and Adela returned together?"

"No one," I said positively.

"And Emmeline is perfectly sure that no one came near the back of the house during the time between Hilary's departure and Evelyn's arrival?"

"She is perfectly sure," said Adela stiffly. That was to protect Dave, I thought to myself; I began to wonder what she would do with her burglar theory.

Allen was frowning at the paper.

"You aren't very helpful, Hilary," he said. "According to Miss Keate you were scarcely out of the house before Evelyn arrived. There's at best only four or five minutes between the time when you say you left Bayard alive and Evelyn says she found him dead."

I looked at Hilary. We all looked at Hilary. Hilary, so fatally trapped in his own words.

His plump face was pink and glistening. His eyes were frightened, evading our gaze, looking everywhere but at Allen. He got out his handkerchief and wiped his face again. He had not lighted the cigarette he had selected and had rolled it in his nervous fingers until it was limp and crushed and shedding small shreds of tobacco on his neat gray trousers. He did not speak, and Allen finally said softly:

"You say you found him alive. You talked to him. Are you sure of that, Hilary? Are you sure he was still alive when you left?"

"Allen!" cried Evelyn in a shocked tone. She turned quickly to her husband. "Hilary, they are blaming you for Bayard's death. They are making you a murderer. How can you talk like that, Allen! You know Hilary didn't kill him."

"I don't know anything about this until it is proved, Evelyn. I only know somebody certainly killed Bayard. And I think we'd better have the truth."

The little pause gave Hilary time to rally. I suppose with desperation courage returned; and with it a measure of ingenuity. The wary, frightened look left his face, and he looked openly at Allen and at all of us.

"I think you're going off half-cocked," he said. "And I'd like to know who constituted you private inquiry agent, Allen. You make a damn poor one, if you ask me. Look here. I'm not the only one known to have been in this house with Bayard just before he was killed. Even aside from the burglar—and there must have been a burglar, for the diamonds were certainly stolen—there were two other people, either one of whom had as much reason to kill him as I had. There was Higby. And there was Emmeline."

There was a short silence. Somehow I had been so certain that one of the Thatchers had killed Bayard that Emmeline's possible culpability or Higby's had not presented itself to me as a sensible line of inquiry.

"But Higby," I said out of my thoughts, and not quite realizing that I was speaking aloud and rather decidedly, "Higby was mowing the lawn all afternoon. I heard him."

Hilary looked at me scornfully.

"If that's his only alibi, it's a poor one."

"But Emmeline said she kept an eye on him all afternoon to be sure he worked along——"

"Emmeline says," said Hilary, as if that didn't mean much. "Everybody knows that Higby is as poor as a church mouse. And lazy into the bargain. What more likely than that he's been planning to steal the diamonds for months? Everybody knows about them, probably everyone in town knows exactly where we keep them. Higby thought everyone was out of the house, fixed up some contrivance to keep the mower moving—he's of a mechanical turn of mind, and could amount to something in that line if he wasn't so good-for-nothing—he got into the study, stole the diamonds. Bayard was downstairs and caught Higby in the act, and Higby snatched up Dave's revolver and shot Bayard dead.

Then Higby went back to his lawn-mowing, the diamonds in his pocket or hidden in some safe place, and nobody even searched him. And there you are."

There was another rather curious silence; I saw Evelyn give her husband an admiring but a rather puzzled look; Adela was staring bleakly at Hilary, and even Janice seemed to have put aside for the moment the thought of Dave's death and was watching Hilary with wide, perplexed eyes. I could not tell what Allen or Dr. Bouligny thought of Hilary's suddenly evolved theory.

"How could he have got into the safe?" asked Allen.

Hilary shrugged his plump shoulders.

"We didn't even keep it locked, half the time. It has always been so safe here in C——. Anyway, it is an old-fashioned safe, even an amateur thief could open it, I should think."

"Why is Higby waiting around here, then? Why doesn't he get away?"

"That's easy," said Hilary. "He doesn't want to attract suspicion. Mind you," he went on, as if to be entirely just and fair. "I'm not saying Higby did it."

"I hope not," murmured Allen rather cynically. "There are too many holes in that notion."

"I'm not saying Higby did it. We could only prove that by finding the diamonds on him. Or hidden by him. But he could have done it. You all know that. We can't say he did it without proof. But you can't say I did it without much more convincing proof than you have now. It is only circumstantial evidence against me now, and mighty slim evidence at that. I'll not speak of the rather unusual matter of a man's own family trying to make him out a murderer——"

"Hilary," said Adela faintly. "We are not doing that. But Dave didn't kill Bayard. Dave couldn't have killed him. I won't let Dave be thought——"

Hilary continued. As he noted the effect of his words upon us he was becoming more natural, a bit pompous.

"I'll not talk of that," he repeated, failing to reproach his family for their lack of faith in him with a noble restraint which was a little too obvious to be exactly impressive. "But I will bring some other things to your attention. Here's another point about Higby. Higby could easily have been bribed."

He paused to give his suggestion its due dramatic emphasis, and then went on, and this time even Allen looked as if he might consider the matter seriously.

"Higby has never had enough money. He's distinctly the get-rich-quick type; he never wants to work and earn, he always hopes for some windfall. He's not particularly devoted to us; there's no reason why he should be. If a thief came along and offered him, say, five hundred dollars, a thousand even, to let him cross the lawn, get into the library windows, and to be silent about it afterward, don't you think Higby would be tempted? He might hesitate, but not for long. He's weak and lazy. And it would have been such an easy way to get some money. Higby would be afraid to tell it once he found that Bayard had been killed. He would only know enough to stick to his story that nobody crossed the lawn all the afternoon."

He paused in barely veiled triumph. Adela looked at him with the first shade of approval I had seen her offer him.

"I must say, Hilary," she said, "that is quite possible."

Allen was drawing idle circles on the paper before him, his brown face enigmatic, and Dr. Bouligny looked mottled and uneasy.

"I think," said Dr. Bouligny, "the sooner we let this thing

drop the better. Call it a burglar—as, of course, it was," he inter-polated swiftly as he met Adela's cold gaze, "and forget it."

"Then," said Hilary, without even looking at Dr. Bouligny, "here's another possibility. Emmeline."

"Emmeline!" cried Adela. "Hilary, you are mad. I would nev-er be convinced that Emmeline would do such a thing."

"Emmeline," repeated Hilary firmly. "She was out in the summer kitchen the entire afternoon. No one was watching her. She was only a few steps from the back door of the house. It seems to me that she insists that she never left that window a bit too fervently. Why should she be so determined that we should believe that——"

"Emmeline is always determined," said Adela, but Hilary swept on.

"She could have entered the house and shot Bayard as easily as not. And she could have done it during those few moments between my departure and Evelyn's arrival."

"But the motive," said Allen, still drawing circles on the pa-per and not looking up.

"Motive?" Hilary made an expansive gesture with his fat pink hands. "The motive is the most convincing thing about it. Em-meline knows all the family affairs. She can hardly help know-ing. She's not so deaf as she seems to be, and besides, she has been with us for years. To all practical purposes she is one of the family. She is devoted to Adela and to Dave. She's known, of course, what a source of trouble and anxiety Bayard has always been. She must have known of his frequent demands for money, threatening all kinds of things, making Adela's life hell. Emme-line is direct, blunt, has no qualms about anything she considers her duty. Besides, she has a strong religious bias."

"But that," said Evelyn in a bewildered way, "would keep her from—" she shivered a little and said—"murder," in a muffled voice.

"No." Hilary shook his head. "No. It has often occurred to me that Emmeline's religion has a strongly hysterical flavor. You know yourself how emotional she is."

"Emmeline," said Janice incredulously, "emotional!"

"Certainly," said Hilary. There was just the faintest air of a savant, instructing. "Certainly. Don't you remember the old-time revival meetings, Adela? How regularly Emmeline was converted? How she wept? How she sang? How she went around for days in a trance? There haven't been any real old-time revivals for years now; probably she's missed them——"

"Hilary," interrupted Adela, "you are preposterous. Are you seriously intimating that Emmeline killed Bayard because she didn't get to go to a revival meeting this winter?"

"Certainly not, Adela. You just don't understand these things. Isn't what I've suggested possible, Dan?"

Dr. Bouligny looked up slowly and shook his great head rather sadly.

"Hilary," he said, "I've doctored Thatcher county for thirty years. I've brought over eight hundred babies into the world. I've waited at practically every deathbed in the county. I've dosed my people and I've listened to their troubles as if they were so many children. I am old-fashioned, I know. But I don't know what you are talking about."

"Look here, Dan, you'll admit that you remember Emmeline's fervent love for revivals?"

The doctor smiled faintly.

"Yes. Nobody could get a stroke of work out of Emmeline while one of them was going on. And then she'd turn around and threaten us all with hell-fire and tell us we were lost. Remember, Adela?"

"It was very trying," admitted Adela, "but nothing to do with this."

"Wait, Adela. It proves that Emmeline has a very fervid emotional nature, doesn't it?"

"It proves she was a fool," said Adela. "But go on."

"Well, all that emotionalism, tangled up with religion and duty and hell-fire, has been denied any outlet for years. Now then, suppose Emmeline gets it into her head that Bayard was threatening the peace and welfare of this family. Her family. Not only the welfare but the family itself. Suppose she gets it into her head that she ought to remove him. Those religiously and emotionally warped natures get crazy notions and——"

"You are talking as if you thought Emmeline was crazy," said Adela tartly. "You sound nearer it yourself, Hilary Thatcher."

"Perhaps she knew that Dave had already shot Bayard once and had wounded his——" Hilary stopped so suddenly he nearly choked himself and looked at me.

"Go right ahead," I said coolly. "I've known that Dave fired the shot that wounded Bayard's shoulder for some time."

Hilary's look sharpened to suspicion, but he did not stop to discover the source of my information. Which was just as well. He went on:

"She was always devoted to Dave. Loved him more than the rest of the family put together. Like you, Adela. If Emmeline thought Dave was determined to kill Bayard, don't you think she'd rather do the murder herself than let Dave do it? She would far rather martyr herself than let Dave kill him. She——" Another thought seemed to strike Hilary. He stopped, considered it, and added thoughtfully and in a meditative tone far different to the pompous voice in which he'd been addressing us, "For that matter, if Emmeline saw Dave coming into the house that afternoon she'd die before she'd tell he was here."

"There you go again, Hilary, accusing your brother of murder. Dave—so recently dead—you might at least wait——" Adela's thick white hands clenched tightly about the shining blue beads. "Your theory that Higby might have been bribed is your only contribution to our problem. I think that quite possible. He will never admit it, but it is quite possible that that is the way the thief got into the house. And there was a thief, of course; all this talk of Emmeline and Dave and Hilary is absurd. There was a thief. And he stole our diamonds. And he killed Bayard."

I had heard enough talk of the thief and the diamonds. Enough and too much. I said wearily:

"There was no thief. Nobody stole the diamonds. They are in the house. Hidden."

CHAPTER XVI

THE LONG ROOM HELD only silence and eyes looking at me. Everyone was looking at me, and no one spoke. The silence grew until it was actually thick and tangible, as if it were some entangling, impenetrable blanket laid fold on fold all about me.

As it deepened and prolonged itself, as I met that combined gaze, I began to regret my rash words. After all, what business was it of mine? Why hadn't I continued to keep a discreet silence on that delicate point? Why had I ever come to that house? And above all, once having got there, why had I remained? Why had I not taken to my heels, willy-nilly? In what moment of mental aberration had I permitted myself to be persuaded to remain?

Even Janice's dark eyes were unfriendly; unfriendly and frightened. And Evelyn gave me a long and singularly cold and penetrating look before her eyes went in a significant and communicative way to Adela, who returned the glance.

But it was Hilary who burst into speech, who finally broke that sinister silence. His words, however, were not calculated to make me easier in my mind. For he shouted:

"Arrest that woman for murder!"

And as no one moved, he repeated furiously:

"Arrest her. Call Strove. She knows where the diamonds are. She was here with no one to watch her the afternoon Bayard was killed. She killed him herself. She took the diamonds. And now she's trying to blackmail us. She thinks she'll have an income for life from us. Arrest her——"

By this time Dr. Bouligny had got heavily to his feet.

"Hilary, stop shouting like that. You are out of your head. Stop telling us to arrest her. For one thing we can't. And Jim Strove isn't here to do it. And for another thing," concluded Dr. Bouligny a little wearily, "she didn't murder Bayard. You are making a fool of yourself."

Hilary, quite purple, whirled to Allen.

"She's guilty. It's as plain as the nose on your face. She killed Bayard. She——"

Allen had risen and had taken Hilary by the arm. He said something, I don't know what, in Hilary's agitated ear. Hilary lapsed rather suddenly into a red and volcanic silence from which one felt he might erupt at any moment, and Allen turned to me.

"What, exactly, do you mean, Miss Keate? That is an extraordinary statement to make."

"I mean," I said, wishing I had bitten out my tongue long before it had behaved with such alarming indiscretion, "I mean that the diamonds were never stolen. They are upstairs."

"Where are they hidden? How long have you known this?"

Well, I told them. I told them just as Florrie had told it to me. I added rather lamely, my eyes on Janice's suddenly stricken face, that it may have been merely servant's gossip.

But it wasn't. The diamonds were still in that jar of green bath salts in Janice's shining little bathroom with its water lilies and pale green frogs.

Evelyn and Allen and Janice went to see, and returned after only a few moments of silent waiting on the part of the rest of us. Someone spread a newspaper on the table and pushed the rose bowl aside, and I think we all held our breath while Evelyn's firm brown hands pulled the stopper from the large crystal jar and let the shower of green rattle softly on the paper. All of us, clustered around that table, saw the first jewel come out—it was the sunburst brooch Adela had talked of—and I think we all gasped as it caught a light from the window and glittered and shone like a live thing. The others came out, too. Hilary counted in a husky whisper and reached for each one avidly, as if someone might snatch it from him.

It had grown late during that feverish talk, but no one realized that it was dusk in the long, old room until Allen reached out to the shaded table lamp and snapped on the electric light in order to see the diamonds more distinctly. In my memory his turning on the light is the period to that strange and terrible afternoon; not Hilary's excited comments about the diamonds, nor Frank Whiting's arrival, nor Janice's slow turning toward the door of the study as if, for the moment, her thought had been driven away from Dave's death and that now she must return to sorrow and regret and tragedy.

For Hilary had scarcely said in a relieved way, "Well, they are all here, every one of them," when Emmeline, followed by Frank Whiting—intense curiosity back of the tactfully sober look in his face—appeared in the doorway.

And I gave the faces about that table, all thrown into bright relief by the table lamp, a last searching look. No one had admitted hiding the diamonds. And not one face revealed any previous knowledge of the whereabouts of the jewels; I could not point to anyone there and say: This face shows guilt; this one shows no surprise; this one shows fear lest it be detected.

Then Emmeline was advancing, horrified question in her face, and Adela was turning bleak blue eyes rather helplessly to Evelyn.

"Emmeline doesn't know," she said to Evelyn. "She doesn't know why Frank Whiting is here." She looked puzzled, as if it seemed strange to her that all the world did not know of Dave's death. "Emmeline doesn't know. I must tell her——"

"Go on up to your room, Adela," said Dr. Bouligny, stepping forward. "I'll see to things. This way, Frank."

I followed Evelyn and Adela. At the door I glanced back to see Hilary carefully recounting and sorting the diamonds which made bright sparkles of iridescent light in his fingers. Dr. Bouligny and Frank Whiting disappeared into Dave's study. Janice had dropped into a chair near the window, and Allen was standing beside her, looking at the bent dark head as if he longed to take her into his arms and comfort her sadness.

The patch of pale green crystals on the table sparkled softly in the light. Outside, the shadows had grown long, and the soft summer night was on the way.

Then Emmeline came swiftly from the study. Her face was stiff and unnatural, and she stared straight ahead as if she saw nothing but perhaps a memory of Dave's face. It might be true, what Hilary had said. It might be true that Emmeline had loved Dave more than any of them. I felt an impulse of pity for the gaunt dark woman, and I stepped toward her, about to speak, although I don't know what I could have said. But she brushed past as if she didn't see me.

Bayard's death had been, as far as possible, ignored. Dave's death disrupted the household.

It did more than that. It brought things to their climax. It could not be ignored. It could not be thrust for one moment out of our consciousness. Hilary, so determined to prove it was a suicide, Adela, equally determined to prove it was no suicide, between them pushed things on to that strange and unexpected end. If either had been content to let things rest it might have been different.

I remember that I stood there at the foot of the stairway for a moment, looking up its polished length—rather dark since no one had thought to turn on the hall light—striving to reorient myself, so to speak. So much had happened since I had come down those stairs at Adela's request to meet her in the library. Was it only a few hours ago that Mrs. Steadway had called? That Adela had begun her amazing inquiry? That I had left Florrie sitting up in her ugly silk dressing-gown?

Since then Dave had died.

Evelyn had admitted that she had found Bayard dead, Hilary had been all too ready to say that Dave had killed him, Dave had been discovered to be a veronal addict and had at last died of the drug—and I was no nearer knowing who had actually murdered Bayard than I ever was.

And death and tragedy and the horror of suspicion had again visited that shadowed, spacious old house.

Florrie was still sitting up. Her boasted second sight must have failed her, for she said nothing of the stirring events that had been taking place downstairs and, I'm sure, knew nothing of them. I stayed with her only a moment, to be sure she was all right, and then returned slowly to the lower hall. I reached it in time to see the ambulance, gray and ghostly in the dusk, drive carefully away. Hilary and Allen and Dr. Bouligny had apparently helped carry the stretcher, and they turned toward the house again, walking slowly across the smooth lawn. Hilary was brushing the back of his hand across his eyes, and Allen had thrown one arm over Hilary's shoulders, and Dr. Bouligny, a little behind, walked slowly and heavily, his head bent wearily and his body sagging as if the Thatcher burdens were too heavy for him.

Well, somehow we got through the dreadful night.

It was that night that I had my momentous talk with Janice: a weary, ineffably saddened Janice who was only a slender shape with a pale face and dusky hair in the shadows of the rose garden. I had gone quietly out of the house about ten, as much to escape the horror and death and fear that lurked in every shadow of the silent house, as to seek my ostensible objective, fresh air and exercise. Adela and Evelyn had disappeared; Hilary and Allen and Dr. Bouligny were in the library, smoking innumerable cigarettes and, in the glimpse I had from the hall, talking not at all.

I did not know that Janice, too, had taken refuge in the friendly, fragrant shadows of the rose garden until I met her face to face when I rounded a curve in the silent, dark path. The moon was barely touching the trees, and the shadows were still dense, and I think we were both startled—indeed, rather frightened just for an instant—until we recognized each other. Then she said, "Oh, it's you, Miss Keate," with a kind of sob in her throat.

I have never known exactly how we began to talk or why she confided so freely in me. Perhaps she had to talk to someone. But I remember very well how we sat on the curved stone bench just in front of a rose tree that hung out and over our heads and made the soft dusk sweet with its fragrance, how white her dress and face looked, and how her hair seemed to blend imperceptibly with the shadows, and how, presently, the moonlight began to stretch gently along the path before us and then gradually to touch the tips of her white slippers.

I believe she began to speak of Dave, for I remember that she asked me a number of questions about veronal and the effects of the drug when taken as a habit. I answered as far as I could.

"His death, then, was peaceful," she said at last. And when

I told her yes, that he had died in his sleep, she seemed a little relieved.

"He looked peaceful," she said, as if to herself. "So peaceful that one might almost envy him." And as I made some startled expostulatory comment, she said, "Oh, no, I didn't mean that, of course. One never really means that. But it has been a dreadful, dreadful time, Miss Keate. I should never want to live these days over again. I wonder if ever in my life I shall be able to forget them. Forget any of it"—she paused and added in a low voice which held a note of horror which gave me suddenly a measure of the nightmare her days and nights had been since Bayard's death—*"forget Bayard's blood on my hand."*

She lifted her hand as if to see whether, even in the shadows, the stain still was visible, and I reached out and took the slim white blur in my own clasp. Her fingers were cold and clung to mine as those of a child caught in some bad dream might cling. And all at once she was telling me what happened.

"I moved Bayard. I moved him. He was in the study, you see, there on the small Sarouk rug by the desk. I didn't know what to do. All I thought was that he must not be found there in Dave's study. We all knew that Dave had tried once before to kill him; had actually shot at him and Bayard's shoulder was wounded. That's when you came. I knew, too, that I had no time; that Adela would be coming into the house in just a moment or two. I had glanced into the library as I was about to pass the door; I saw the study door open and went to look to see if Dave was there, and there was Bayard. Dead, on the rug."

She took a long tremulous breath and almost visibly steadied herself.

"It took only a second to be sure he was dead. And I thought, 'He must not be found here in Dave's study. The room that is Dave's. He must not be found here.' So I—I set the baskets down, and I bent over, and I had to drag him—drag him, hold him by the arms and drag him out of the study and into the library. It was terribly difficult. And I had to hurry. I got as far as that table, and I left him there on the floor, and I ran back and straightened the rugs that had been pulled up and took the baskets and ran to the kitchen and left them there. I didn't know what was on my hand until I had reached my own room. I don't remember why I took off my hat; habit, I suppose. But I looked at it and saw the stain. And just then Emmeline, downstairs, began to scream, and I knew she had found Bayard. I hid the hat and washed my hand and ran down the front stairs. And there you all were in the library."

She shuddered and stopped.

"You'll feel better now," I said. "It is a good thing to talk of it to someone. I suppose Dave must have returned and got into the house somehow and—shot Bayard."

"I don't know," she said. "I don't know. I don't want to know."

"Didn't you say Bayard was downstairs when you left the house early in the afternoon and that you spoke to him?"

"Yes. He was downstairs. I had gone to the kitchen to get the baskets for the eggs and butter, and I thought I would take Mrs. Steadway some flowers. I stopped in the library to get some scissors I had accidentally left there that morning, and Bayard was there."

"Did Dave keep the door to his study locked?"

"Not as a rule. It was a set rule in the household, you see, that he was not to be disturbed. There was no need to lock the door."

"And you spoke to Bayard?"

"Yes. But only a word or two. Not," said Janice, "a pleasant conversation. He said he would give us till night to decide what we would do about the letter. My letter. I took the scissors and put them in my basket and left. I was nearly frantic, but there was nothing I could do. Bayard thought that in the end Allen would give him the money he wanted in order to protect me, and I suppose Allen would have done just that, but I so hoped we could discover a way out of it without that."

"But if Dave killed Bayard, what about the diamonds?"

"I don't know. I don't understand about the diamonds. But I think that someone in the family put them in that jar of bath salts merely because they would be thought to be quite safe there. It would have to be someone who knew I don't use bath salts."

"You don't think, then, that it was a deliberate attempt to make it look as though you had taken the diamonds?"

I could feel her astonishment.

"Oh, no," she said after a moment. "Why should anyone do that? There would be no point in my taking the family diamonds. Many of them were to come to Dave's wife anyway—were, in fact, already mine. Oh, no, it wasn't that. I think—perhaps I ought not to tell you this, Miss Keate, but I think that Adela or Evelyn somehow managed to get the diamonds out of the safe merely to give an appearance of burglary. I know," she said sadly, "that we all feared Dave had killed Bayard and tried to shield him."

"What were the circumstances of Dave's first attack upon Bayard? You told me you didn't know why they quarreled, but can't you think of anything that might have caused trouble between them?"

"I didn't know when I talked to you before, Miss Keate, but now I believe I know. I think Bayard was supplying Dave with veronal. The drug is hard to get in this state, you know. And there's nothing Bayard would have liked better than to ruin Dave—or Hilary, or both. He's always hated them. I suppose he was jealous of them. Or perhaps the whole thing dated back to something in their childhood. And Bayard was thoroughly bad. He was unbelievably bad."

"Why do you think Bayard was supplying Dave with veronal?"

"I'm not sure that he was. I only heard a few words of their quarrel. But there's nothing else they could have quarreled so dreadfully about. Dave hasn't been well in a long time, and lately he's been growing more and more unlike himself. Of course, Adela and I knew, though we never talked of it, that he was taking some drug. I thought it was morphine, though I could never be sure. We did everything we could to distract and amuse him. We watched him so carefully. We tried everything. It's been rather bad here for the last two years, Miss Keate."

She paused, staring thoughtfully into the shadows for a moment before she continued sadly:

"I don't know whether Hilary knew or not. It was nothing we liked openly to discuss. I suspected Bayard, but not for any definite reasons; it was a sort of instinct. I dreaded his visits here. But when Florrie took veronal by mistake, and you said you had had no veronal, and I knew that Bayard had hidden my letter in your bag, I felt sure that he had also hidden the veronal in your bag. He had had access to it, and he would know it was not safe to keep the drug openly about the room while he was ill. If he was furnishing veronal to Dave he would undoubtedly ask a large price for it. What more likely than that he asked more than Dave would pay? Or held back a supply of the drug? If poor Dave was like drug addicts usually are, he would be frantic for it. That's my explanation for Dave's frenzied quarrel with Bayard. I think Bayard goaded Dave until Dave was beside himself. Poor Dave—he must have hated himself, and he must have hated Bayard for the hold he had. Do you think I am right?"

"It sounds quite likely that Bayard supplied him with veronal," I said. "And if Bayard hid your letter in my bag, which is the only reasonable thing to suppose, he could easily have hidden the veronal he had with him in the same place. He would think it a safe place in case anyone searched his room. But, of course, if this has been going on for two years or more, they must have had some systematic system of supply. Just what happened the night Bayard was shot and Dr. Bouligny called me?"

"I don't know exactly. They were in Bayard's room, Dave and Bayard. I couldn't sleep that night, and I had heard Dave moving about in his room and the door into the hall closing as I supposed he left the room. In a short time I heard him come back, and pull open a drawer, and then leave again. He seemed hurried, and I don't know why I immediately thought he'd come back for his revolver. But that's what I thought, and I hurried out of bed and after him. It had taken me a moment to get into a dressing gown and slippers, and Dave was already in Bayard's room when I reached the hall. Adela must have been awake, too, for just as I passed her door it opened, and she came out, and before we had time to speak we heard——"

Again she steadied herself.

"We heard a revolver shot. It was so loud—I can't tell you how dreadful it was. We ran to Bayard's room, and Dave was standing there aiming the revolver again, and Bayard was swearing terribly and had his hand over his shoulder, and it was bleeding all on his pajama coat. And Dave looked white and dazed, as if he didn't know what he was doing. As if he were another person. Adela ran and seized his arm and I managed to get the revolver away from him and out of sight while Adela talked to him. When I came back Dave was beginning to look less queer, and Adela took him to his room, and I looked at Bayard's shoulder and put cold water on it, and by that time Emmeline and

Florrie were in the hall, and Adela was back, and she told them what we told everyone. That Bayard had had an accident. It was foolish, of course, but we couldn't say Dave shot him. Adela sent Florrie to telephone to Dr. Dan, and he came right away and dressed the wound and said Bayard would recover. That he was not seriously wounded. What a relief that was!"

"But didn't Dave explain why he had tried to kill Bayard?"

"No. No. He said nothing. That made it worse, somehow. You must have seen how frightened Adela and I were. We were desperately afraid Dave would attack Bayard again. We tried to hide our fear, act as if there was nothing. We tried to keep the two men apart. Adela insisted on a nurse coming in the hope that she would—that your presence would in a measure protect Bayard. And thus protect Dave; it was Dave we cared for. Poor Dave."

She sighed, and after a moment said thoughtfully:

"I was very young, you know, when I married. I didn't know. I didn't know anything about love. I didn't know——"

She paused, her face turned a little away from me as if the darkness were kind to her. The moonlight lay, by that time, white on the roses, and the fragrance was heavy and sweet, and the shadow over the bench black and soft and cool. Janice said in a voice that was not steady:

"You are very good to me, Miss Keate."

"I? Nonsense!" I said brusquely. And repeated, "Nonsense!"

She moved, took a long breath, and said gravely:

"Is there anything else, Miss Keate? I want you to know the whole truth."

"Well, yes, there is," I said promptly. "There are several things, in fact. It was you who tried to enter Bayard's room from the hall that first night I was here, wasn't it? You tried the doorknob, and while I was unlocking the door returned to your room and watched me in the mirror?"

"Yes," she admitted at once. "I didn't think Bayard would need night care, so I supposed you were in your own room. I hoped, of course, that I could get into the room and by some lucky chance discover my letter while Bayard was asleep. I knew that Dr. Dan must have given him a bromide, and I thought there might be some small chance of my success. I was desperate, or I wouldn't have tried."

"Who then was on the balcony that night?"

"What do you mean? Was someone on the balcony?"

I did not explain. At a sudden memory I said:

"Had the dog followed you to Bayard's door? I thought I heard a sort of panting sound. Like a dog on a hot day."

"Yes," said Janice and added, "It was rather horrible, wasn't it? I felt so furtive. Stealthy. Ashamed. It seemed to me even Pansy must know what I was doing and why."

The moonlight was so clear on us then that I could see her face quite definitely. Her lovely sad face, and her slender white arms, and the soft outlines of her frock. She was twisting a fold of the white silk nervously in her fingers, twisting and folding it tightly. I watched her idly for a moment. Then I jumped to my feet.

A new and amazing theory had flashed into my mind.

That piece of tightly folded paper that I had found on the Sarouk rug there in Dave's study—had found there immediately after Bayard's death was discovered.

Could it possibly mean what I thought it might mean?

CHAPTER XVII

JANICE MURMURED SOMETHING IN surprise at my abrupt motion, and I suppose I replied. I don't know what I said, for I was only anxious to get to my room. I left her sitting there among the roses, with the moonlight soft on her beauty. As I reached the lawn I met Allen. He looked grave but very tall and cool and resourceful, and his eyes were shining.

As I emerged from the shadows of the shrubbery he said quickly and eagerly:

"Is it you——" and in a different tone, "Oh, Miss Keate. I caught the flash of your white skirt there in the shadow. I thought—" he stopped abruptly, and I did something that, considering the circumstances, was in very bad taste. I said, "She's in the rose garden," and walked rapidly toward the house.

I had no romantic notion that Janice and Allen would fall promptly into each other's arms. Thoughts travel swiftly, and they could not have failed to realize what Dave's death meant to them. But Janice was a sensitive woman; she had temperament and pride. All Allen could do then was give her the comfort of his presence; talk to her of the things that must be done; love her and protect her and try to shield her.

In my unwontedly tender mood I found myself strolling with slower and slower steps across the moonlit lawn, thinking

214

of the two in the rose garden and of the soft dusky shadows and of what they might be saying and feeling.

Once at the door, however, I walked hurriedly through the still, polished spaces of the hall, up the dim stairway with its gleaming handrail, and toward my own room. As I passed Adela's door it opened and Dr. Bouligny emerged.

"Ah, Miss Keate," he said. "We have finally got Miss Thatcher to sleep. I think she'll rest all night, but you'd better take your room next to hers here, in case she needs you during the night. I've left a sedative if she needs it. Florrie is quite recovered; I just went up to see her; she can be up and about her work tomorrow."

I assented and watched his thick figure move along the hall toward the stairway. He looked old and weary; his shoulders were stooped, and his body sagged, and he went slowly down the stairs.

I turned into my own room.

Owing to the delay there had been about getting my supply of fresh uniforms the wrinkled and soiled uniforms I had worn had still not been sent down to be laundered. I hunted feverishly among them, diving into the pockets rapidly, and in only a moment or two found what I sought, the little tightly folded piece of paper I had picked up there in the study immediately after we had found Bayard dead.

Adela had been telephoning, I remembered. And I remembered, too, how she had first asked me to telephone for the doctor and then had changed her mind suddenly and said, "No, I'll go." And I had followed her into the small room and had picked up almost at her feet that tiny folded paper.

There was one way to attempt a proof of the amazing explanation that had occurred to me.

I glanced at my watch. It was something after eleven, and the house had been very silent when I came upstairs. In all probability I could do what I wished to do without being seen, and an inner voice cautioned me that it would not be well for me to be seen.

I waited for a long time. I heard Janice's light step go past my door. I thought I heard Evelyn's voice speaking to Hilary and his reply before another door closed with a decisiveness which led me to think that Evelyn's hand had propelled it. I waited until the moon was high and white and the whole house had sunk into complete stillness—as complete a silence as if there were not another living soul besides myself in its dark, wide old walls.

When I finally ventured from the comparative safety of my own room into the silent gleaming spaces of the hall, the rustle of my uniform sounded loud and sharp through the stillness. I felt uneasy, as if eyes were watching me from some place, and it was difficult to plunge into the dark stair well. And yet I was going on no errand of positive danger. I was not, I certainly hoped, going to meet Bayard's murderer. I was only going to the telephone in Dave's study.

The lower hall was as usual dimly lighted, but the drawing rooms, so peaceful by day, were by night great black caverns, and at the door of the library I hesitated. It was all so silent. So black. The room so large. And over there by the table we had found Bayard's body.

I sought for but did not find the button which would turn on the electric light. Finally, my eyes becoming more accustomed to the darkness, and finding that the reflected moonlight from the white lawn actually served faintly to dispel the blackness in the room, I gave up trying to find the light and groped my way across to the study door. The furniture along the way loomed up dimly black and solid, and I felt, absurdly perhaps, that almost any dreadful thing might be crouching behind the davenport or in the shadow of the great leather chairs, or even behind the carved oak screen at the fireplace. But I did reach the study door, opened it, and entered.

There I had no difficulty in discovering the light switch, although a moment of panic caught me and brought my heart pounding to my throat as I brushed against the foot of the couch where Dave's body had lain.

The desk light, shaded with green, sprang into view and lighted softly the small room. The telephone stood beside it on the desk.

I took a long breath. A moment more, and my errand would be accomplished, and I would be free to take to my heels if I wished and fly from those horror-laden shadows.

I took the tightly folded paper from my pocket and bent over the telephone.

After an absorbed moment or two I straightened up. I did not know whether I felt sad or triumphant. But I did know the truth about the telephone.

The instrument was an old-fashioned desk set, with a mouthpiece on a standard and a separate receiver which hangs on its hook when the telephone is not in use and which, on being lifted, automatically connects the telephone. That tightly folded wad of paper fitted exactly into the narrow slot along which the hook moves up and down.

I sank into a chair near the desk and sat there staring at the telephone. I inserted the paper above the hook and took down the receiver as if about to telephone, and there was, of course, no connection: I might dial as long as I liked and get no one.

I inserted the paper below the hook; the receiver might, in that case, be left on the hook, but, since it was an automatic telephone, anyone might call that number indefinitely and still get the busy signal.

But when I entered the study, following Adela, just after the discovery of Bayard's death, she had been using the telephone, and the wad of paper was at my feet. And I had heard from Janice and Evelyn no mention at all of the telephone; they had not said that Bayard had the telephone in his hand; had not, in the shock of discovery, appeared to have so much as looked at the telephone.

There was only one thing that was clear in my mind, but it was highly significant. And that was that Adela's telephone conversation with Bayard—which, in my mind, and I'm sure in others, had gone so far to establish a conviction that Bayard had been murdered after Adela and Janice had left the house—might possibly have been no conversation at all. I had heard the telephone ring, it is true, and I had so distinctly heard it break off in the middle of one of its peals that I was sure someone had answered it. But a child would have known that if the connection at the other telephone had been suddenly broken, the bell of this telephone would instantaneously stop ringing.

If that folded piece of paper meant what I thought it meant, Adela's story of the telephone conversation with Bayard *after every one of the Thatchers was out of the house* meant precisely nothing.

Or, rather, it meant that Bayard was dead before Adela left the house. Before Adela, clad in her dainty lavender frock with her eyeglasses dangling from their ribbon and her parasol carefully lifted to shield her from the sun, had walked composedly along the broad turf path on her way to the Benevolent Aid Society.

It was not possible. It was not, I repeated to myself, possible.

But if it were true we must reconstruct the whole story of the crime. In the first place, it automatically released Hilary from suspicion. But then, if Bayard was already dead when Adela left the house that afternoon and she had arranged that contrivance on the telephone—what did that mean? I leaned my head on my hand and stared at the rich tones of the small Sarouk rug. The rug which still bore, hidden in its thick nap and concealed by the small, tightly interwoven figures, the stain of Bayard's blood.

If Bayard was dead when Adela left the house that afternoon, the field of suspects was thereby still more limited. With my own eyes I had seen Allen and Dave leave the house. Bayard had sent me to the arbor. Only Janice and Adela were in the house with him. And Florrie.

Florrie. But Florrie had left the house before Janice came out of it with her baskets over her arms and her small white hat on her head, and from Janice's story, as I had heard it that night, I had received a distinct impression that Janice had come directly from her brief and unpleasant interview with Bayard out of the house, into the garden to cut the flowers for Mrs. Steadway, and thence to the garage and away. If Janice had come directly from Bayard she had talked to him after Florrie had left the house.

There were still Higby and Emmeline; they were always to be included among that extremely short list of possible suspects, but in spite of Hilary's spirited and rather ingenuous defense of himself that very afternoon—a defense which, of course, was based upon the possible guilt of either Emmeline or Higby—I did not feel that either of the two was guilty. The small incident of the silver spoon on the floor of the library, upside down with a sticky little pool of purple jelly under it, went a long way in my mind toward proving Emmeline's innocence of the crime. It was too trivial a thing to have been deliberately evolved; if Emmeline had been set upon proving her innocence of Bayard's death she would have arrived at some far more ambitious a plan.

I was equally reluctant to suspect Higby; it was barely possible that he had arranged some highly unusual and ingenuous method by which to keep the lawnmower running while he crawled into the library windows, entered Dave's study, and shot Bayard with Dave's revolver—the only revolver in the house, hadn't Janice said?—but since the diamonds had not been stolen at all, what could have been Higby's purpose? With the memory of that monotonous whir of the lawnmower in my mind I did not think it a likely solution. Besides, the little I had seen of Higby did not lead me to believe that he could, by any stretch of the imagination, accomplish any undertaking which involved much use of brain cells.

But by excluding Florrie, Higby, and Emmeline, and granting which was only supposition, after all that the telephone incident was as I reasoned it to be, only Adela and Janice were left as possible suspects. And while I could readily have believed that Adela would undertake almost any subterfuge in order to turn suspicion from her family, or any task to protect and further their interests, still I could scarcely suspect her of out-and-out murder. And Janice, to me at least, was equally inculpable.

But what, exactly, had been done with that tightly folded piece of paper and why? The trick of breaking the connection from the other end could have been accomplished without plugging the slot of the telephone hook. Perhaps Adela had wanted to leave the telephone there, with the receiver off the hook as if Bayard was in the very act of telephoning when he was killed; yes, that might easily have been the way of it. If Bayard was actually dead before Adela left the house, and she knew it and wished it to look as though he'd been killed after every member of her family was safely out of the house, she might have done exactly that. Then her story of the telephone conversation (which, no doubt, she had taken care the druggist should hear) would be even more convincing if Bayard were found with the telephone as if he had been talking through it. It would be, in fact, all but conclusive as an alibi for her family.

But Bayard had not been found there on the rug in the study with the receiver off the hook of the telephone and the instrument perhaps near his hand. He had been found in the library, sprawled hideously on the floor. Janice had moved him. Janice, her slender muscles pulling with all their strength, her white hands reddened by their grisly task, had pulled that shattered body across the library floor. And Evelyn had seen Bayard dead in the study. And, if my surmise was correct, Hilary, too, had been in Dave's study while Bayard lay dead on the rug. Any of them might have picked up that telephone and replaced it.

And the train of supposition which I had built from that tiny wad of paper might be entirely wrong.

I sighed wearily and took the paper in my fingers and looked at it again and at that very instant heard a rustle back of me.

I find I cannot adequately describe my feelings as I sat there in that small study, my back to the dark door of the cavernous library, and realized that someone stood in that doorway watching me. Had been watching me perhaps while I fitted that damning piece of paper into the telephone slot. Two men had already come to their deaths in that small room. One death had been a murder. The other death had been so nearly induced by that sad and tragic train of circumstances that in its fundamentals it was murder, too.

Deaths go in threes. Deaths go in threes. It is an old superstition and an unreasonable one. But it has more than a little element of truth in it. I have seen it happen more times in my nursing career than I cared, at that moment, to recall.

Who stood there behind me? I could not turn. I could not breathe.

Was it Adela, Hilary, Evelyn, Janice? Might it be, even, Allen? Or Emmeline?

It was strange that, though I felt no fear of any one of those people, at the same time I felt a very definite and terrifying fear of whoever it was in the doorway. I suppose that paralyzing feeling of terror was owing to some sixth sense; some deeply primitive warning of danger.

Then there was another sound of motion. And a voice said: "Don't move. I'll shoot."

It was Hilary's voice. But a Hilary I had not known before.

Perhaps it is unnecessary to state that I did not move. Indeed, I sat so still that the very beating of my heart seemed for the moment suspended. And it is as well that I did so. For Hilary advanced from behind me and stepped just in the circle of light cast by the green-shaded desk lamp, and I saw that he held a revolver in his hand. And his hand was not very steady. And the revolver was aimed directly at me.

His hair was disheveled, his eyes red and bloodshot, his face pale and puffy, and he wore a dark dressing gown. I never knew how long he had watched me, nor how he had happened to follow me to the study. His voice too, was unnatural; husky and threatening.

"What are you doing here, when the whole household is asleep?"

I did not like the way his nervous hands caressed the revolver.

"Nothing," I said. "Nothing."

"Answer me! You had some purpose here."

The bit of folded paper rolled from my numb fingers, and his quick eyes caught it. I decided rapidly on a half truth.

"I found that piece of folded paper here on the rug just after Bayard's death," I said rather weakly. "I came to try to discover whether or not it was a clue to the murderer."

His eyes wavered. I felt sure he had not seen the paper before and had no idea as to its possible significance.

"And what did you discover?" he asked in an unpleasant way.

"Nothing." And as I thought he looked faintly undecided as to whether or not to believe me, I added nervously, "Don't you want to put the revolver down? Is it Dave's gun?"

He glanced then at the revolver, as if he had forgotten he was holding it, and back at me.

"I don't believe you," he said. "But if you'll keep quiet I won't shoot."

As a matter of fact, I am inclined to think I was rather nearer an abrupt and complete end than is exactly pleasant to recall, much less experience, during those few moments while Hilary's unsteady fingers touched that revolver. He did not, I am sure, think that it would better conditions to dispose of me in such a manner; he couldn't have meant cold-bloodedly to shoot; but he was in a frame of mind not to know exactly what he was doing. Perhaps my rather obvious and certainly acute discomfort recalled him to himself. He put down the revolver, looked at it rather strangely, said in an absent way, "Yes, it's Dave's gun. It's the only one in the house," and then went on with an abrupt change of tone:

"Look here, Miss Keate. I don't know what you know of this affair of Bayard's murder, or what you don't know. But I'm going to put my cards flat on the table, face up. I'm not by any means a rich man. But I'll give you ten thousand dollars in cash to leave this house tomorrow morning and forget you've ever been here."

Afterward I was glad the interruption came before I could find my voice. Otherwise I would have said far too much, and the revolver was still conveniently near Hilary's right hand. It was Evelyn who interrupted: she must have heard the whole thing. She said crisply:

"Hilary, you are a fool. Go away. Take that revolver with you." And when he'd gone—and somehow it was not an ignominious departure; there were threat and menace in the solid lines of his shoulders and his thick red neck—she said to me, "Miss Keate, if you have any kind and generous womanly instincts you will forget this—this extraordinary scene." And then she too was gone, and I could hear her firm footsteps crossing the library.

Well, somehow I reached my own room. Somehow I spent the night, imagining every whisper of sound I heard was Hilary trying to get into my room, with Dave's revolver, which Adela must have given into his keeping, in his unsteady pink hand. It seemed to me that Evelyn was asking rather too much of womanly instincts.

After a night of restless dreams and wakeful hours I resolved to see the druggist in the morning and get his impression of Adela's telephone conversation with Bayard. But if it was, as I thought it might well be, a fiction on Adela's part, then Hilary could not have killed Bayard.

When morning came, however, I did not immediately have an opportunity to leave the house, and it soon developed there was to be no need for the druggist's testimony. Shortly after breakfast Adela summoned us into the library again. She had had only the night to survey the situation, and that had been spent for the most part in drugged slumber. But like any keen-sighted general, she knew what her next move would be; she knew that in trying to extricate Dave she had placed her other brother under suspicion.

We were all there except Dr. Bouligny; all of us tired and hollow-eyed and ill at ease. I think we all knew something was coming. Her first words, however, were such as to shock us into strained attention. For she said calmly:

"The Thatchers appear to have taken to lies. Evelyn did not tell the truth when she said she found Bayard alive. Hilary did not tell the truth when he said he found Bayard alive. And I did not tell the truth." She faltered a little there but resumed, her blue eyes daring us to doubt, her face gray and stern. "I lied when I said I talked to Bayard over the telephone. I did not. He was dead before I left the house."

Hilary was the only one who dared speak. He started forward with a smothered exclamation. Adela silenced him with an imperious motion of her wide white hand.

"Wait, Hilary. Let me tell it. I came downstairs and found Bayard dead in the study. I was afraid Dave would be blamed for shooting him. We all knew Dave had made one attempt upon his life. I was frightened. I knew I must hurry and plan something to draw any possible suspicion from Dave. I thought if I telephoned from town and seemed to talk to Bayard from a place where people could hear me, that might make it appear that Bayard had actually been shot after the time I telephoned, which would be, of course, after the members of the family were out of the house. I even—" she faltered briefly here again, smoothing the white ruffle on one wrist and looking at it with unseeing eyes—"I even arranged the telephone so it would ring with the receiver actually off the hook—" I suppose I made some gesture there, for Evelyn glanced sharply at me and then back to Adela—"and placed the receiver near Bayard's—Bayard's hand as if he had been using it. I hoped it would look as if he'd been killed after I talked to him and this after everyone who might be thought to be concerned in his death was away from the house."

She stopped, looked at us coldly, and finished: "I went to the drug store and telephoned. I let it ring just once, and at the beginning of another peal I broke the connection. No one could see my left arm, but I leaned against the telephone and talked so

Mr. Lelly could hear me. Then I thanked him and went to the Aid Society."

There was a complete silence. Then Hilary said jerkily:

"Adela, you are trying to shield me. I was going to stick to what I'd said in the first place. But it's true. Bayard was dead when I came."

I leaned forward.

"Where was the gun?" I asked.

Adela looked at me in a perplexed way.

"I don't know," she said slowly. "I don't remember the gun."

I turned to Hilary.

"When you entered the study and found Bayard dead, did you see the revolver? What did you do with it?"

"I didn't have it. I didn't see it. There was no gun." He had answered quickly with an air of defense as if I had accused him of something. He turned to Evelyn. "There was no gun, was there, Evelyn?"

"No," she said at once and very decisively. "I'm sure there was no revolver there. I feel sure Dave's gun was not——" Perhaps the look on my face stopped her.

Janice had hidden the gun in the egg basket. She had had the egg basket over her arm while she had her last brief words with Bayard. She had told us she hid the revolver *on her return* to the house late in the afternoon. That she had found Bayard dead then and had hidden Dave's revolver in the basket and carried it to the kitchen in order to protect Dave.

But only a few moments after Janice had left the house with the presumably empty baskets, Adela had found Bayard. Had found Bayard dead. And she had seen no revolver.

Hilary had seen no revolver. Evelyn had seen no revolver. And it had been found late that night in the egg basket.

Too late I saw how dreadfully my injudicious questions had involved Janice. Hilary saw, too, and Allen.

"I refuse to permit Janice to be questioned until she has seen a lawyer," said Allen. He was standing at the side of Janice's chair. He put his firm brown hand on her arm. "Been advised by someone, I mean," added Allen, "who is not a member of this family."

CHAPTER XVIII

It took Hilary an incredulous moment or two to comprehend the full enormity of Allen's suggestion. It was rather alarming to watch his face grow slowly purple with rage. But instead of venting it on Allen, as one might justly have expected, he whirled to me, pointing a forefinger that was literally trembling with anger.

"This is your doing, Nurse," he all but shouted. "If it wasn't for you we wouldn't have got into this damn fix."

"Hilary——" warned Evelyn.

He gave his wife a look of fury, but stopped, and Janice said rather sadly:

"But I don't need a lawyer, Allen. I'm perfectly willing to tell the whole truth about the thing. I have already told the truth. I told Miss Keate last night."

"I'm not sure," said Adela slowly, "that any of you have been telling the truth. But I didn't mean—I didn't realize—I had no intention of bringing suspicion upon Janice. Janice had nothing to do with Bayard's death. That is not to be thought of."

"Look here," said Allen. "That's what's the trouble. That's why we are so frightfully entangled. We've all been trying to shield each other. Or rather to shield Dave. Suppose Dave did kill Bayard. He's gone now, and the truth can't hurt him. Why don't we all tell exactly the truth about Bayard's death? If we prove that Dave killed him, it can't hurt——"

"No, no!" cried Janice. "I don't want to know. I don't want you to prove that Dave killed him."

"You are all so determined that it was Dave," said Adela coldly. "Why not Allen? Or Hilary? Or any of you, as well as Dave?"

Hilary had barely subsided, and the mention of his name as a possible suspect was like a match to gunpowder.

"I'm not afraid of the truth," he cried. "I've admitted that I found Bayard dead. You all probably know why I said he was alive when I saw him last. It was because I knew people might blame me for his death. Might say I killed him. I thought Dave had killed him, and I still think so. I think Dave's death is an admission that he killed Bayard."

"Dave was not a suicide," said Adela. "I will not let you say that."

Hilary shrugged.

"Call it what you will, Adela. We know he took that veronal. No one else could have given it to him. He knew it for what it was; took it as a habit. Dan explained all that. What easier than for Dave to take the overdose intentionally? Especially since he could readily have overheard our conversation in the library by merely opening the door of the study a trifle—the inquiry you insisted upon, Adela—and would have known that we all realized he must have killed Bayard. But I think, too, that it might be better to forget the whole business."

"That is like you, Hilary," said Adela. "You never like to face anything disagreeable. But I will finish what I've begun. Miss Keate has brought up the question of the gun. I think any questions she wishes to ask ought to be answered. Miss Keate——?"

Her voice was lifted in inquiry. There was a complete silence in the library. The long room was cool and shady. Someone had removed the pale green heap of bath salts and had rearranged the table, and there were fresh crimson roses in the bowl. Dr. Bouligny was not there, nor Emmeline. But there was Adela, stately in her high-backed chair; Evelyn, cool and matter-of-fact; Janice, very quiet and grave but with a certain anxious, tight-drawn look erased from her lovely face. Allen was standing near her, watchful; it was rather curious to note the slight but very definite difference the night had brought to Allen. Yesterday his bearing toward Janice had been removed, careful, withdrawn; today, while he was exactly as unobtrusive, there was a certainty about him, a kind of authority. It was as if he felt, as I suppose he did, that he had a right to protect Janice openly and frankly.

Hilary stirred impatiently and I realized that they were still waiting for me to speak.

"Was Dave's revolver the only one in the house?" I asked.

"Yes," said Adela definitely. "We all know that. Even Hilary has no revolver now."

Evelyn smiled faintly. "Not since the boys left for school this last term," she explained. "They appropriated Hilary's revolver. He didn't replace it. We have no use for revolvers in C——."

I repressed a desire to say that they seemed to have discovered a use for them, and said instead:

"It seems to me, then, that the possession of the revolver is a rather important part of the evidence."

I suppose no one liked to say, "Janice, explain. Explain where the gun was when Adela found Bayard dead. Where it was when Evelyn and Hilary saw that shattered body. When did you put the gun in the egg basket?" But they all looked at her. Even I, who felt so certain that she was innocent of Bayard's murder— so certain that I dared inquire further about the revolver when, if I had left it to the Thatchers, it would probably have never been mentioned again—even I felt a qualm of doubt as we waited for her to speak. And it was just then, to add to my anxiety, that I recalled what she'd said when she told me of the quarrel between Dave and Bayard when Bayard was wounded, and she and Adela had interfered in time to save Bayard's life.

Janice had said, "I managed to get the revolver away from him and out of sight." Had it remained, then, in her possession?

"Don't say anything, Janice," said Allen again. "There's no need to. They can't make you talk."

"But I'm quite willing to talk," said Janice. Her dark, troubled eyes met our combined gaze openly. "I want to tell exactly what I know of this."

"Then do so, my dear," said Adela rather crisply. She sat very stiff and straight, her blunt white fingers fumbling with her eyeglasses, and the arrogant curve of her nose rather sharp.

"Where was the gun when you picked it up, Janice?" asked Allen.

"It was on the rug. On the small Sarouk in Dave's study."

The lines about Allen's eyes tightened a bit.

"But Adela, Evelyn, and Hilary all say there was no gun when each of them entered the study during the afternoon. And you found the gun, remember, late in the afternoon after all three of them had visited the study." Allen was speaking very deliberately, as if to give Janice time to word her answer carefully. I suppose, after warning her not to talk, and seeing that she meant to do so in spite of his warning, he had resolved quickly to question her himself and thus give her a measure of protection.

A moment of utter silence followed his inquiry. We were all watching Janice, waiting a bit breathlessly for her reply. It was only then I think that she knew she was trapped. For I saw the horror flare into her eyes. She sprang out of her chair.

"Oh, I see," she cried with a sort of incredulous gasp. "The basket! That is what you mean, the basket! I could have taken the revolver out of the house in the basket, couldn't I! I could have shot Bayard myself with Dave's revolver and hidden it in the egg basket and left Bayard's body there in the study. Left his body there for Adela to find when she came downstairs only a few moments later. I know now why you are all looking at me so strangely. How stupid I was not to see it at once. Oh, how can you! How can you think that of me!"

A half sob caught in her throat, and Allen put out his hand, and she brushed it away and flung up her little white chin and cried, "I did not! I did not shoot Bayard. I did not kill him. When I left the house that afternoon Bayard was still alive. I spoke to him. But I did not kill him with Dave's revolver and then hide the revolver in the basket and leave. It all happened just as I told you. I never dreamed Bayard was dead until I returned from the farm and walked into the house just ahead of Adela and found Bayard dead. And moved him. I moved him, you know. I moved him from the study into the library."

Hilary cried out something incoherent, but Adela did not speak. And Evelyn said directly, "But the revolver, Janice. When did you hide the revolver?"

Janice's eyes went slowly around the group, traveled deliberately from one intent face to another before she walked gracefully out of the trap.

"The revolver," she said quietly, "was under Bayard's body."

It was Hilary, of course, who exploded into the silence.

"Under Bayard's—— And you moved him, Janice? It was you who moved him?"

"Yes, yes, Hilary. I moved him. I thought Dave had killed him. I moved him out of Dave's study into the library, and I found the revolver and hid it in the egg basket."

"I hope," said Allen with a rather grim look around his mouth, "that that satisfies all of you. And now that you've hounded Janice into telling 'exactly what happened,' no matter how painful, suppose the rest of you tell a few things. Who, for instance, put those diamonds among Janice's things? And why?"

"Allen!" Adela made an expostulatory gesture. "Don't speak so. We didn't try to make a victim of Janice. You can see for yourself how much better it is now that she has explained about the revolver. And as to the diamonds—I put them in the jar of bath salts myself. You didn't give me time to finish my story. I had only a few moments, you see, there in the study to make it look as though no one in the family had murdered——"

"You mean Dave?" asked Allen sharply.

"Dave," conceded Adela. "That Dave had not murdered Bayard. The safe caught my eyes, and I remembered the diamonds were in it, so I opened the safe and took the diamonds out and dropped them into one of the lower drawers of the table there, and left the safe open. The next morning after the murder I took them upstairs, and since I feared there might be considerable search for them, I hid them in what I thought was a safe place and one that was unlikely to be looked in, no matter what happened. I imagine the rather frenzied things I did may seem foolish and disconnected to you—" Adela adjusted her eyeglasses carefully and looked bleakly at us through them—"but I thought that with the telephone to establish a sort of alibi for Dave. and the safe open, and the diamonds actually gone, there would be little chance of anyone suspecting that any of the family had killed Bayard. I cannot tell you what a shock it was to find that everything I had planned had gone wrong. The worst thing—" she faltered a second and touched her gray-blue lips with a delicately laced handkerchief—"the worst thing was finding Bayard in the library. Not in the study." She paused again, regained her resolute manner, and said with just a touch of her former blandness, "not that I am admitting that Dave killed Bayard. I only knew that he would be thought to have killed him. I am convinced it was a burglar, in spite of everything you say. I am trying to prove it."

"Adela, it is so hopeless," said Hilary despairingly. Don't you see that what you are actually doing is to involve every one of us in the affair? Since we all know that Dave tried once to kill Bayard, why don't we let it——"

"Did you know why Bayard and Dave quarreled?" I asked Adela directly, breaking in upon Hilary's rambling reproaches, which threatened to involve us all in one of those long family discussions which told so little and so much and were consistent and so dreadfully cruel.

A gray shadow passed over Adela's face, but she answered with a barely perceptible evidence of the effort it must have been to force the words from her tongue.

"Yes. I know. It is a very terrible thing, but we all know now that Dave was a drug addict. Bayard had been furnishing Dave with veronal. They quarreled somehow over that; I do not know exactly why it reached such a shocking climax that night, but I believe Bayard was trying to get more money from Dave and was keeping a new supply from him. Bayard, of course, had ways to provide the drug, and Dave depended upon him for it. I heard only a word or two of it while Janice had slipped out of the room to hide the revolver."

The revolver again, and Janice. Allen said quickly:

"When you took the gun from Dave's hand that night what did you do with it, Janice?"

"I put it in my own room. In the drawer of my desk."

"Do you keep the drawer locked?"

"No."

"Then anyone in the house had access to the gun by merely walking into your room and helping himself?"

"Why, yes, I suppose so. But, Allen, I don't think that anyone would——"

"When did you last see the gun in your desk?"

"I'm not sure. Wait, let me think. I didn't look at it again at all. I didn't see it again until I found it under Bayard's body there in the study, when I found him dead. Why do you question me like this, Allen?"

Allen's grim face softened a little as he looked down at the slim girl shrunk into the corner of the chair. It seemed to me then that with Dave's death a certain air of maturity had left Janice; she was younger, less rigidly controlled and poised now that she was released from the tragic load of care and anxiety and responsibility she had carried so resolutely.

"For your own protection, Janice," said Allen.

Hilary flared immediately.

"I don't like your tone, Allen. I don't like your implications. We are not trying to blame Janice. None of us has even hinted that things looked rather black for her——"

"Hilary——" Allen had taken a step forward so quickly and suggestively that Hilary backed off a little. But Allen checked himself abruptly and said more quietly, "Look here. Janice has been everything that is good and fine. She's stayed by Dave and tried to take care of him and help him, and has been a loyal wife to him when most women would have simply walked out. And it's because she tried to protect Dave and thought nothing of herself that she has become involved in this murder. This," said Allen grimly, "this family murder."

Hilary had been swelling and empurpling with every word, and I really thought for a moment or two that we were about to witness an out-and-out fight between the two men. But Evelyn said quickly:

"Allen, what are you saying! You must not talk like that!"

And Adela in her stately manner said with cold reproof:

"I think you two are forgetting yourselves. Certainly you have forgotten the rest of us."

Hilary cast his wife and sister an outraged glance and returned to Allen.

"While you are defending others who don't need your defense," he said hotly, "why don't you defend yourself? Or do you think you are above suspicion? Because, if you think that, I must undeceive you. Your quarrel with Bayard was overheard. Your—" Hilary paused as if to give his words more emphasis—"your threat to kill Bayard was overheard."

If Hilary's knowledge was a blow to Allen, he gave no evidence of it. And if it was news to the others I could see no evidence of that either; I dare say there were family conferences at which I was not in uninvited attendance.

"If you accept Emmeline's statement that no one approached the house during the afternoon as exculpating Dave, you've got to accept it for me," said Allen coolly. "And if you accept it as conclusive proof that Dave was not near the house that afternoon, then why all this talk of protecting Dave from suspicion? No matter how many times he tried to kill Bayard, if he wasn't near the house at the time when Bayard was actually murdered, then he couldn't have killed him."

Which was true enough, of course. That was one of their most trying inconsistencies; they accepted Emmeline's statement, which released Dave from suspicion, and at the same time in their hearts they firmly believed that he had murdered Bayard. They wanted it proved, and they didn't want it proved. They wanted, I thought somewhat shrewishly to myself, to establish Dave's guilt as a belief, for that released the rest of them from that grisly suspicion; yet it was not to be established as a fact so conclusively and formally proved that it made their brother a murderer, Janice's husband a murderer. A Thatcher can do no wrong: that was their standing ground. They would thrust the ugliness of the affair deep down into their consciousness and hide it; gradually they would begin to speak of Dave gently, with tenderness. Subtly the non-existent burglar would be reinstituted. Before many years had passed it would be an accepted family fiction that Bayard had been killed by a marauding burglar and that Dave had died of an illness. Most families maintain certain fictions: that would be one of the Thatchers'.

"You are trying to divert our interest, Allen," said Hilary. "Clever of you, but suppose you do some telling of the truth yourself. Didn't you threaten to kill Bayard? The very night Dave shot him in the shoulder?"

"So it was you walking so conveniently in the shadows of the shrubbery that night. Were you taking an after-dinner stroll?"

"Never mind what I was doing. I heard you tell Bayard you'd kill him. You didn't make any secret about it. You were telling the world. Emmeline in the kitchen above you could have heard it all if she wasn't deaf."

I resisted an impulse to say Florrie had heard them, and Evelyn said in a stricken way:

"Allen, you didn't threaten to kill Bayard! You didn't!"

"Why, yes," said Allen calmly. "Yes, I threatened to kill him. He had taken a—paper—that was mine. And I'm not sure I wouldn't have kept my word if someone else hadn't got him first."

I saw Adela's bleak blue eyes go swiftly to Allen as if she were thinking, "What is this? What does this mean? Does it threaten us? How shall we meet this?"

"Allen, Allen, you must not talk like that." Evelyn's brown face looked suddenly thin and sharp with anxiety, and her blue eyes were dark and full of fear. She went to her brother and put her hand on his arm. "You don't really mean that, Allen. It's just your hot temper. All of us disliked Bayard. It was his own fault; he was everything that is despicable. And there was scarcely one of us who did not have some reason to wish him out of the way. His very presence goaded us. But you didn't really mean that you would kill him."

It seemed to me that they were launching upon another mass of conversation that might get nowhere at all. I said dryly:

"The point is, are we to accept Emmeline's statement that no one entered the house from the back? If we do, that excludes Dave and Mr. Carick from suspicion, no matter what either of them felt for Bayard."

Hilary looked petulantly at me.

"The nurse is right," he said grudgingly. "We can't seem to talk of this matter without letting our own feelings and fears distract us from the logical trend of inquiry. It doesn't matter what we feel to be the solution of this trouble or who we feel to have murdered Bayard. We must stick to the plain facts of the matter. And just now the thing is to consider who could have come into the house and shot Bayard during those few moments after Janice left him and Adela found him dead. Could a burglar or some intruder have got into the house unobserved? Could Higby have killed him during that time? Could Emmeline have done so? And I think she could and possibly did——"

"Hilary," murmured Adela in an expostulatory way, and Hilary continued without looking at her:

"Or could Dave or Allen have returned to the house at that time unobserved? No, Allen, I'm not trying to blame you. But those are the facts of the matter."

I felt the first shade of approval for Hilary that I had yet experienced. At the same time, it seemed to me that there was a certain alacrity about his willingness to pursue the matter now that Adela's unexpected confession had automatically removed Hilary himself from possible suspicion.

"The farther we go the more difficult it becomes," Evelyn said in a hopeless way that was unusual with her. "None of those questions can be answered. It all depends upon whether or not Higby and Emmeline are telling the truth, and I don't know what infallible test we can make of that. Oh, why can't we just drop the whole thing? There isn't any proof. There never can be any proof. We have done everything we can do. If Dave somehow got past Emmeline into the house and killed Bayard, I, for one, don't want to know it. Don't want it proved."

"Dave didn't kill Bayard before three o'clock," said Allen definitely. "He was with me until then. And—" he fumbled in his pocket and drew out the paper on which he had made a sort of chart the previous afternoon. "According to Miss Keate it was exactly three o'clock when Adela left the house *after* having found Bayard dead and made her hurried efforts to make it look like robbery. What Adela has told us has upset all our previous calculations. We shall have to rearrange everything to discover the time of Bayard's death. Florrie left the house at two-thirty; Janice possibly ten minutes later. Two-forty, then. Adela left at three. What time was it, Adela, when you found Bayard dead?"

"I don't know exactly. But it would have taken at least fifteen minutes to do what I had to do. One thinks rapidly in an emergency; still, it takes a few moments to recover from the shock and outline a sort of plan. But Janice had been out of the house and gone at least five or ten minutes before I came downstairs. And five minutes would be long enough for anyone to kill Bayard."

"But, Adela," said Allen more gently, "don't you see that while five minutes might be long enough for some member of the family who knew his way about the place to take the gun from Janice's desk and shoot Bayard and escape, it couldn't possibly give time enough for an intruder. And we all know it was Dave's revolver."

I need have felt no sympathy for Adela. She was more than a match for Allen. She said with unruffled dignity and a sincerity that was inescapable, so that I did not in the least doubt her story:

"My dear Allen, I have told now the exact truth. You may make of it what you will. If anyone wishes to believe that I committed a murder he may do so. But I shall be glad that I have been the means of clearing Dave's name. Of proving that he did not kill Bayard."

"You've proved nothing," said Hilary rather cruelly. "Dave is dead. Don't look at me like that, Adela. That margin of time is too small. Five minutes more or less is not enough. Our watches might not have coincided. Allen might have been mistaken about the time when he and Dave separated."

"Hilary, I refuse to listen. You are determined to make it appear that Dave killed Bayard and then killed himself."

"Now, Adela, wait. The thing I'm trying to show is that this inquiry is hopeless. We can't prove anything conclusively. But if we don't settle on something we'll spend the rest of our lives wondering. Suspecting each other. Not sure. And since Dave was obviously a suicide and we know he had tried once to kill Bayard, why not——"

"But you aren't at all sure he was a suicide," I said wearily, wishing I had never seen these baffling, inconsistent, illogical Thatchers with their pride and their selfishness and their undeniable courage. "You aren't even sure he was not murdered, too. Where did he get the veronal that killed him?"

CHAPTER XIX

IT WAS JUST AT that moment that Dr. Bouligny opened the door to the long room and entered, pausing in a worried fashion, for I suppose our very attitudes gave him some warning of the suspense the moment held. Then he advanced toward Adela. His face looked old and very tired, there were pouches under his eyes, and his cheeks and heavy chin were flabby.

"Good-morning, good-morning," he said with an obvious and not very successful attempt at a professionally cheery greeting. "How are you this morning, Adela?"

Almost visibly she thrust aside any hidden reference to her grief over Dave's death; it was as if she were reserving her sorrow.

"You are in good time, Daniel," she said. "The nurse has just hinted that Dave, too, was murdered."

Dr. Bouligny gave me a sharp look from under his bushy eyebrows.

"*Dave* murdered!" he said in surprise. "Oh, no, Miss Keate. There is no question of that. Dave was a veronal addict. I have proved that beyond a doubt. Adela and Janice have known it for some time. I don't know whether or not he took an overdose intentionally but I do know that no one could have given it to him without his knowledge. Florrie's mistake came from ignorance; she knew nothing of veronal, and besides, was under the firm conviction that she was taking some kind of aspirin. It was an entirely different matter with Dave, as you can readily understand. The dose he took yesterday was his own doing. There's no doubt of that. But, of course, I can't say that it was with suicidal intent. I wish you had told me of Dave's—illness."

"I wish I had, Daniel," said Adela sadly, but she returned resolutely to me. "Does that answer your question, Miss Keate?"

Well, it did in a measure; that is, I agreed with Dr. Bouligny and had agreed from the beginning. But that was not all of my question.

"In part," I said with dignity. "But where did he get the veronal?"

Adela looked blankly at me, and Janice said slowly:

"I suppose he must have got it from Bayard."

"But if Bayard was withholding a supply of veronal when they quarreled, and Dave needed it so badly that he was ready to kill Bayard for tantalizing him by not giving him the drug, why, Dave must have had none then. And I am sure Bayard and Dave were together only once, from the time I arrived until Bayard was found dead. And that one time was at the lunch table the afternoon Bayard was killed."

Allen said meditatively, "But you were not with Bayard every moment of the time, Miss Keate."

"His door was locked when I left him alone."

Hilary made an impatient gesture.

"We are running up against something else we can't possibly prove. But what became of the veronal in the box Florrie had?"

"Evelyn took it," said Dr. Bouligny. "Where is it, Evelyn?"

"I don't know," said Evelyn. "I didn't like to speak of it after Dave had died of veronal. You see, I don't know what happened to it."

"What do you mean?" said Adela crisply. "Do try to speak

plainly, Evelyn. I don't understand you. Do you mean you had in your possession the remaining veronal tablets from the box Florrie had?"

"Why, yes," said Evelyn. "I saw the box lying there on the table by Florrie's bed, and I thought that was a poor place for it. So I took it and left it on the dressing table in my room. But it—" she seemed to speak with an effort and avoided Hilary's look— "it disappeared that night. Sunday night. And I don't know who took it. I suppose it must have been Dave."

"Why on earth didn't you tell me about that, Evelyn!" exploded Hilary.

"Well," said Evelyn, glancing at Allen as if for support, "I didn't think it was the thing to do. I guessed, of course, that someone must take the drug habitually or it wouldn't have been in the house. But I thought it would only make matters worse to try to discover who had taken it from my room and why. Things were bad enough," said Evelyn rather miserably, "as they were."

"Now we'll never know," said Hilary impatiently. "You should have told me about it sooner, Evelyn. We'll just have to suppose that Dave found the veronal and took it. That's as near as we can come to it, and it must be the truth. I don't think anyone will accuse Evelyn of inducing Dave to swallow the overdose of veronal——" He paused, rather in the fashion, half threatening, half suggestive, that a minister pauses when he says if anyone has a just objection to a marriage will "speak now or forever hold his peace."

Then he continued, "As Dan says, Dave must have taken the overdose himself. By his own hand. Couldn't be any other way. We know he must have been out of the drug when he shot Bayard the first time, and that he certainly had it when he died. And that a rather large supply of veronal disappeared from Evelyn's dressing table last Sunday. And that we have scarcely seen

Dave during these four days. Those facts, put together, seem to me conclusive. I'm in favor of letting the whole thing drop. Now. Let Miss Keate go," concluded Hilary, forgetting discretion just for an instant, "and drop the whole matter."

"But, Hilary," said Adela, "you know what people will say. They'll say Dave killed Bayard and then himself."

"Let them," said Hilary grimly. "I only hope that's what they'll say. It's the kindest thing we can hope for."

"I am leaving tomorrow morning," I said. "I can be of no more assistance here, Dr. Bouligny, and I must go."

Dr. Bouligny looked uneasy but murmured, "Yes, yes, certainly, Miss Keate." And Adela looked at me thoughtfully. I could almost see her revolving in her mind some plan for keeping me on until she was convinced that I would never be a danger to them. I said firmly:

"I must go. It is quite impossible for me to remain any longer."

Adela glanced at Hilary and then at Evelyn. Apparently she received no help from either of them, and she said, "Certainly, Miss Keate. It's been very good of you to stay with us this long. Especially under the—er—sad and trying circumstances."

Momentarily I wondered if she would actually give up her project or if she hoped yet, either to convince me of her burglar theory, or to induce me to give her more time. Or perhaps she hoped to prove to me that there was no solution; that it was impossible to arrive at the real truth of the matter and thus the murderer's identity.

"That," repeated Hilary, harking back, "is the kindest thing people could say. That is, that Dave killed Bayard and then himself. It is hopeless to try to prove anything further. We could never prove anything to a jury. God knows I hope we'll never have to try."

"You are right that far," said Allen soberly. "The more we talk of it, the worse the tangle grows. We say the same things over and over again. Or we deny what we have already said. Now that Adela says Bayard was dead when she left the house and——— But you didn't hear all that, Dan, did you?"

"All what?" asked Dr. Bouligny, and Hilary briefly explained.

"You ought to have told the truth about it from the beginning, Adela," said Dr. Bouligny, when Hilary had finished. "But I don't see that it makes things any clearer. The question is, could Dave have got back into the house during that five minutes, and I don't see how we could ever prove that. I think it's best to drop the whole thing. Let people think what they will. It will never be brought to a jury. You can be sure of that."

"*Can* we?" said Adela.

Dr. Bouligny looked thoughtfully at me.

"I think so, Adela. It isn't likely there will be any new evidence. Miss Keate is the only stranger here. It isn't likely she will interest herself further in the matter."

It was an invitation for me to promise to keep still. Hilary had openly tried to bribe me. Dr. Bouligny appealed, not too subtly, to my better nature.

"I'm sure I have no particular interest in this deplorable affair," I said with some spirit. "But if it's evidence you want, I know of several rather singular matters which might lead to the discovery of the real murderer."

"What do you mean, Miss Keate?" said Adela.

"For one thing, you said you left the safe open after you had removed the diamonds, so as to call attention to the presumable burglary. The safe was closed when Mrs. Thatcher entered the study. Who closed it?"

Hilary cleared his throat.

"I did," he said. "I closed it."

"Why?"

"I don't know exactly," said Hilary. "You see, I had come to see Bayard about the old check he had. I hoped we could arrive at some conclusion. I did not expect a pleasant interview. When Evelyn said Bayard goaded us, she used the correct word, for that is exactly what he did. He nearly drove us all to a frenzy. Well, dreading that interview as I did, you can imagine what a shock it was to discover that someone had been there before me. Had killed Bayard. There were just two things in my mind. I've made them clear already, but Miss Keate seems to want things in black and white. I was sure Dave had killed Bayard. But I knew people would think I had killed him. Everyone knows that Bayard and I were never friends. That's all clear, surely. Even to the nurse."

"Very clear, indeed," I said crisply. "But you haven't told why you closed the safe."

"But I tell you, I don't know why," he said in a peevish way. "I just saw it open and reached out and closed it. I really didn't think what I was doing. And Adela's notion of a burglary had not occurred to me."

"I wish," said Adela coldly, "that you had never come near here that afternoon. Otherwise——"

"Otherwise your scheme would have worked," finished Hilary. "Well, if it's any comfort to you, Adela, I heartily agree with you."

"But the telephone. I suppose you picked that up and replaced it, too, without knowing what you were doing."

"Yes. That is, I mean no," said Hilary, looking further annoyed. "I did that purposely. I thought—" his pink face grew a richer crimson—"I thought Dave hadn't even given Bayard a chance. Shot him without warning while he was at the telephone. That part of it sort of got under my skin."

"Hilary's like that," said Evelyn. "I mean," she added hurriedly, "I mean he is very neat. He likes things to be tidy. Everything in its place."

"Why, then," I said at a sudden thought, "was it you on the balcony? In the rain? The night before Bayard was killed. It must have been you trying to get into the room through the darkness."

I had scarcely spoken before I regretted it; in view of Hilary's extremely susceptible sensibilities it was rather unwise on my part. After all, I was to spend one more night in that silent, knowing house. At the moment all Hilary could do was to bluster a bit unconvincingly and incoherently, but with something in the narrowed eyes that I did not like. I reminded myself that a barking dog never bites, but unfortunately recalled at the same time that I'd never had much faith in the adage. I dislike cats and do not understand dogs, with the result that cats follow me about as if I were a can of sardines and dogs growl at me. Indeed, at that very instant Pansy, curled in a fat brown-and-white bundle under Adela's chair, winked slyly at me and ran her tongue out of her mouth in a threatening manner. Pansy: what had she seen, I wondered, there in the library? What had she heard?

"Was Pansy in the room when you last talked to Bayard?" I asked Janice, unheeding Hilary.

"Yes," said Janice. "I had to shut her in the library to keep her from following Dave and Allen when they drove away. She had got over her indignation about it by the time I came downstairs again, and when I talked to Bayard she was curled up on the couch in the study."

I turned to Adela.

"Was Pansy still on the couch in the study when you found Bayard dead?"

"Yes," said Adela vaguely, her eyes on Hilary. "Asleep. Now, Hilary—there's no need to become so excited."

"I wish you would stay on the subject, Miss Keate," said Dr.

Bouligny rather testily. "You have accused Hilary of something, heaven knows what, and now, instead of listening to him, you start talking of dogs. Why did you say Hilary was on the balcony in the rain?"

"Because I think he was there," I replied promptly. "But I have no reason," I added, for I pride myself on being fair, "to suggest that he tried, then, to kill my patient."

"*Then!*" exploded Hilary, and Dr. Bouligny said, "Explain what you mean."

I did so briefly.

"And I think it was Mr. Thatcher," I concluded. "Because he seems to have a passion for setting things straight. And whoever was on the balcony had very carefully folded up the steamer chair to protect it from the rain. I've never felt that an ordinary burglar would have done that."

Hilary had got out his handkerchief and was wiping his face as if it felt very warm and uncomfortable.

"Well, I was there," he said grudgingly. "But I didn't do anything except get tangled up in the roses and tear my clothes off, to say nothing of my skin. There are," he added viciously, "millions of thorns on those damn roses."

The gray granite look of resolution on Adela's face had given way to a rather singular look of mingled anxiety and alarm and irritation. The irritation was uppermost.

"Really, Hilary," she said in a sort of what-next way, "it seems to me you have deliberately tried to bring suspicion on yourself. What exactly were you doing on the balcony of Bayard's room? After midnight? Secretly?"

CHAPTER XX

IT ADDED, NOT UNNATURALLY, to my increasing feeling of blind groping in the dark that Hilary's explanation should be so simple. That was the trouble: every explanation was simple and natural. All the things I had stored up in my memory as possible clues seemed to turn upon explanation into simple and natural acts which left me no closer to a solution of the ugly mystery. Perhaps the murderer had left no clues. Or perhaps the explanations were merely adroit and suave fabrications. Or again, perhaps there was no solution and the Thatcher case would remain forever a closed and sealed puzzle.

I had felt from the beginning that the man on the balcony had had some sinister purpose there; there is a kind of primitive sense which warns one of danger, and I had felt, that night, shaken and terrified. But Hilary said simply that he had hoped to discover and take the check with which Bayard had threatened him for so long. And when I asked about the blank piece of paper he said merely that he'd thought possibly he could outwit Bayard; if Bayard awakened while Hilary was searching the room he would give him the envelope in exchange for the old check and induce Bayard to think it held a check for the sum of money he wanted.

Allen listened with open derision.

"Did you really think you could put that over?" he asked when Hilary had finished.

"I hoped to, certainly," said Hilary with a touch of his old pomposity. It wilted suddenly as he continued: "You see, I knew Dan would give Bayard something to make him sleep. And I thought it possible that Bayard, not being quite himself, if he waked, would be more—amenable to reason. You can't deal honorably with dishonorable men. I had hoped Bayard would not wake at all and that I could search the room at my leisure. But I didn't expect the nurse to be in the room. And in getting away in a hurry I suppose I lost the envelope." Hilary looked darkly at me. "What was it you threw at me?"

"I didn't throw anything at you," I replied stiffly.

"You certainly did," insisted Hilary with heat. "I heard it crash."

"I accidentally knocked over a lamp," I said with dignity. "Then—was it you who searched Bayard's room immediately following the murder? Someone went through it like a cyclone while I was in the very next room."

"You would be there," muttered Hilary, favoring me with another bitter look. "No, I didn't search his room. He had the old check in his pocket when I found him dead. I looked for it then and there and found it: that's why I was in the house for ten minutes or so. But I didn't have to touch his body."

"Then was it you?" I asked Allen.

But I had reached apparently another blind alley. It was not Allen who had searched the room. It was not any of them. I explained as much as I knew of the incident, and Evelyn finally advanced the theory that it was Dave looking for the veronal. That seemed as likely an explanation as any, particularly in view of the fact that Bayard had undoubtedly hidden the veronal in my bag, but it was one that in a moment or so we were to prove. For Evelyn had scarcely spoken when Emmeline appeared in the doorway with several telegrams. Adela took the telegrams, adjusted her eyeglasses as if to read them, and said to Emmeline:

"Emmeline, Miss Keate says someone searched Mr. Bayard's room immediately after his death. That it was left in shocking confusion. Do you know anything about it?"

Emmeline looked narrowly at me. Tall and gaunt, with her hands working and her eyes unfathomable, the woman looked quite capable of keeping any number of dark secrets. Just for an instant I wondered if Hilary's accusation could have had a measure of truth. Then I remembered the testimony of the jelly spoon, and Emmeline said:

"Yes, ma'am. It was Mr. Dave. I saw him. And if he wanted to search that room he had a perfect right to do it."

"By all means," said Adela. "You may go, Emmeline."

"No, wait, Emmeline," cried Hilary. And as the gaunt woman turned to watch his mouth, he went on: "Can you swear that Mr. Dave did not return to the house the afternoon Bayard was killed?"

Well, she was sure that Dave had not returned. That there had been no one at the back of the house. Nothing had occurred to distract her attention; she was all the time within full view of the house and lawn. When they let her go at last she stopped in the doorway and said something that actually made a cold shiver creep up my back. She said, her somber eyes on Hilary's mouth, and her gaunt dark hands working hungrily:

"I'm telling you the truth. Mr. Dave wasn't here. He couldn't have murdered Mr. Bayard. But I'll say this, and when I've done I'll leave this house, if you want, Miss Adela. The murderer is here. Right now. In this room. And if you'd buried Mr. Bayard with his face down like I said to do the murderer would have confessed long before this. But now you'll never know. You'll never know whose hand is stained with blood."

"Emmeline!" gasped Adela. But Emmeline, a tall black ram-rod, had vanished on the heels of her grisly pronouncement, leaving us, I must say, more than a little shaken. I wondered momentarily when and where she had told them to bury Bayard with his face down.

There was a note of grim truth in her words that was unpleasant in the extreme. The case that seemed in retrospection loose and full of loopholes was actually very tight and rigidly limited. According to the evidence we now had, Janice was the last one to see Bayard alive. And while it had been at the beginning a tangle of lies, evasions, cross-purposes, we were at last, I was convinced, as near the truth as we might ever approach.

"The thing is, can we believe Emmeline?" said Hilary at last breaking into that heavy, thoughtful, anxious silence. "I say no. She would shield Dave with her last breath."

"You don't want to believe Emmeline," said Adela coldly. "As usual, you prefer not to face the truth. You know as well as I that in all the years Emmeline has been with us we have never known her to lie. Which is more than I can say for my own family. Oh, there, there, Hilary! I know you are going to say you did it with the best of intentions. So did I—I had the best of intentions when I concealed what I knew of the time of Bayard's death. When I tried to draw attention from my family."

"Well, the truth is out now," said Hilary. "And I don't see that we have accomplished anything. Unless we are to agree that it must have been Dave and let the whole thing drop. Forget it as soon as we may. Aren't you going to read your telegrams, Adela?"

Adela looked bleakly at the telegrams and put them on the table, where they remained, a vivid yellow patch on the polished table top.

"Not now," she said. "I can't bear to read them yet. We must decide what to do. I can't go on like this much longer. I am not afraid of the truth, but the physical strain of indecision is almost more than I can bear."

"Miss Keate," said Allen directly, "you can see how matters stand. Do believe me when I say that we are not keeping some fact from you. You know as much as we know about this affair. In your career as a nurse you must have seen various family skeletons exposed, and you must have kept sad and tragic secrets. If I were to consider only myself I would prefer digging away at this thing until we proved that Dave did it, rather than assume that he did it in the face of what seems to be proof to the contrary. Perhaps we would all prefer that except Janice, and we know why Janice does not want it proved that Dave was a murderer. But I believe that we can go no farther, as things stand. I think it is best to do as Hilary suggests. Forget the whole thing. Is it too much to ask you to forget it, too?"

I hesitated. They were all watching me anxiously, and in the little waiting silence Adela leaned forward.

"Is there still something unanswered, Miss Keate?" she asked.

"Yes," I said promptly. "Who was Nita Thatcher, and why did Bayard talk of Nita's grave in his sleep, and why did I meet Dave in the cemetery right at the foot of a grave marked Nita Thatcher?"

There was another silence. Adela looked at me steadily, and while I could feel the gaze of the others, I could not tell what their expressions were. I was sure, however, that Adela knew the answer to my question, and I was surprised and incredulous when she replied with just a tinge of her former blandness:

"Can anyone answer Miss Keate?" And as no one spoke she said in a faintly disapproving manner, "If Bayard was talking in his sleep his mention of Nita Thatcher's grave could mean nothing. And your meeting Dave at that place in the cemetery was merely accident, I imagine, Miss Keate."

I resisted an impulse to ask her if it was merely accident that she roused herself so early the morning after Bayard's murder and walked to the cemetery.

"Nita Thatcher's been dead and gone for years," said Hilary. "She had nothing to do with this, Miss Keate, if that's what you're driving at."

"This means nothing at all to me, Mr. Thatcher," I said with spirit. "If I had known what I was to be involved in when I came here, do you think I would have set foot in this house? But I've ears and eyes and can't help seeing and hearing——"

"Have you tried very hard not to?" interrupted Hilary rudely, and Adela said swiftly, "You must forgive my brother, Miss Keate. This has been a great strain to him, and he is not himself. I'm sorry I can't tell you anything about Nita's grave, although it does not seem exactly an important point to me. I realize that I made a mistake in undertaking this informal inquiry, but I thought we could at least settle our minds about Bayard's death. As Allen says, it begins to look hopeless. But can you think of anything else, Miss Keate, that you believe might bring the truth to light?"

I could. There was one thing yet that must be answered, and I was convinced that one of them could answer it.

But I paused for a long moment before speaking. The strain of the prolonged talk was beginning to be felt by everyone. Even Evelyn was looking tired and anxious, her brown features sharp and taut below her smooth gold hair, and she had taken a red rose from the bowl on the table and was pulling it absently to pieces between her strong brown fingers, staring at the thing without seeing it.

Allen was standing near Janice as if he dared not leave her, and Janice, weary and sad, yet somehow with her beauty poignantly in flame, was huddled in a corner of the large chair in which she sat. Dr. Bouligny was rubbing his chin with his heavy hand, back and forth nervously; watching me, watching Adela, watching us all. Adela looked older but was still dignified, unapproachable, determined. Those two long talks with me as an alien audience, and with their frequent lapses into ugly bickering and hideous accusation and—which were probably even more trying to her—occasional harrowing self-revelations, must have been inexpressibly painful to her.

"Well, what is it, Nurse?" asked Hilary impatiently.

But I took my time to look at every one of them; perhaps my question would bring at least some illuminating change of expression.

"Who," I said, "closed Bayard's eyes?"

There was a complete silence. Dr. Bouligny stopped rubbing his chin, and no one else moved.

And no one spoke.

"You see," I went on, after searching those still, masked faces in vain, "a burglar or any outsider would not have stopped to close his eyes. It must have been some member of the family."

"Take care, Nurse," said Hilary. "Don't go too far."

"Don't be silly, Hilary," said Evelyn, looking up suddenly from her shattered rose. "Miss Keate knows very well you all think it was Dave. She undoubtedly thinks so, too. And since no one of us here closed Bayard's eyes, then it must have been Dave who did it."

Again there was silence in that long room. That long, quiet room with its ancestral portraits and its books and its secrets. I had reached a complete impasse. It was like groping blindly along a stone wall; at every turn I reached that wall and could never penetrate its thickness.

I could, of course, bring the matter as it stood to the proper authorities, but that would be only to involve Janice. To give her up for arrest for the murder of Bayard Thatcher. To drag her through the ignominy of trial. To publish and forever tarnish her love for Allen. It would ruin her life, and there was no reason to believe that it would result in the proof that someone else had murdered Bayard.

Every inquiry I had made had led to exactly nothing so far as solving the mystery of Bayard's death was concerned. It was not a matter of surrender on my part; it was simply that I could go no further.

They had proved that Dave had not entered that quiet, shadowy house the afternoon of Bayard's death. And illogically, driven by their instinct rather than their reason, they yet believed that Dave had killed Bayard.

Well, let them believe so. And if any of them ever doubted, no one would know. After all, most families have their secrets.

"I am only too ready to forget this," I said slowly. "I am a nurse and I am accustomed to holding my tongue. I will finish out my day and night and then leave. And I promise you," I paused, conscious of Hilary's eager yet skeptical eyes, "I promise you that the whole affair will remain a secret so far as I am concerned."

It seemed to take them a moment or two to comprehend that I really meant what I had said. It was strange to hear the singular kind of sigh that went over the room. Much as I knew of their feeling toward me, I had not perceived until then the real depth and extent of their urgent fear. Evelyn and Adela came to me and took my hand, and Dr. Bouligny murmured something approving, and Janice's dark eyes looked gratefully into mine. Allen said briefly that they were in my debt. Only Hilary remained in the background, his eyes still wary and guarded.

It was done, then, the Thatcher case. Tomorrow I would be out of that silent, secretive house with its darkly polished spaces and its air of knowledge; out of the house and gone. Probably I should never see the Thatchers again. And I would never know the truth of that murder; it would remain an unsolved mystery and an ugly and harrowing memory.

I remember that, as I took their hands and heard their thanks, something back in my mind was saying, "Which hand? Which hand? Everyone of you had a motive for wishing Bayard dead."

Finally I escaped to my own room. I remember ascending those wide, gleaming stairs and thinking of my first night in that silent house, and being glad that I was leaving, inexpressibly eager to get away. To return to the hospital where shadows did not threaten and night noises meant nothing.

Somehow my last day in the Thatcher house dragged along. I saw little of the family; I suppose they all felt exhausted with the continued strain and perhaps had relaxed with the assurance of my silence. Evelyn, I believe, undertook the arrangements Dave's death had made necessary, and she and Hilary conferred for a long time with Adela, in Adela's little morning room, and more briefly with Janice.

It was warm that day and very quiet. There seemed to be only a few callers. Sometime during the afternoon Florrie, chastened and pale from her experience, but perfectly well and able to be about the house again, brought me a note from Adela. It enclosed a check and a brief and formal word of thanks. The check, I was glad to see, was for not one penny more than the amount of my professional services.

They believed in my promise, then, and were willing to let me leave. Either that or they knew that they, too, had reached a place whence they could go no further.

Somehow I ate my last dinner in that stately dining room.

Somehow I listened to Adela's occasional word and Evelyn's efforts to prevent the meal from being a ghastly, silent horror. How well I remember, even now, the gentle flicker of the tall candles, the heavy fragrance of the roses and Janice's face above the soft white lace of her gown and the way her eyes kept going to Allen.

For the Thatchers kept up the pretense to the last. To the last they preserved the surface of things. And to the last they were— and how well I remember Bayard's bitter word—aristocrats.

I went directly from dinner to my own room. I don't know just when Hilary evolved his brilliant idea. I was packing uniforms when Emmeline summoned me again to the library. They were all there when I entered, obviously waiting for me. Hilary was holding Dave's revolver in his hand.

"Miss Keate," said Evelyn at once, "Hilary thinks he can prove that it was not Dave's revolver that killed Bayard, in spite of the circumstances that seem to prove it. He says it is too large a caliber to have been fired even in a soundproof room and not heard. He has asked us to remain here in the library while he goes into Dave's study and, with the door closed, fires the revolver. He thinks we will be able to hear it very plainly."

"Not only that, Evelyn. I think you can hear it out on the lawn. But you can judge something of that from here. If you can't hear it, we are still in the position in which we have left things. If we can hear the sound as loudly as I predict, we shall be obliged to reconsider the whole thing on the basis that Dave's gun had nothing to do with the murder. That it was, after all, an intruder with a revolver of smaller caliber than this one."

"That will involve a rather belated autopsy, Hilary," said Dr. Bouligny rather wearily. "You don't want that, do you?"

"We'll do that, of course, if there's a chance to prove it was not Dave," said Adela.

"Go ahead, Hilary," said Allen dryly.

We all watched while Hilary walked to the study, entered it, and closed the door.

The lamp cast long shadows into the corners of the long old room. Adela's gray chiffon trailed on the polished floor; her face was in shadow, but I could see the long strand of bright turquoise beads which hung from her blunt white fingers and caught sharp blue high lights. Janice shrank closer to Allen, and I think, in the shadow by the window curtain, his arm went protectingly around her. Evelyn was sitting directly under the light, and her firm brown profile was in sharp relief. Dr. Bouligny rubbed his chin and watched the door to the study.

Then we heard the muffled sound of the detonation. We heard it distinctly enough to recognize it for what it was. But out on the lawn with the whirring sound of the lawn-mower it could not have been heard. I was sure of that. The situation, then, was left unchanged.

There was a frenzied sound of scratching at the study door. Hilary opened it, and a brown and white streak catapulted between his ankles and hurled itself out of the door and fled through the library and into the hall. It was Pansy, of course, ears hugging her head, legs flying, tail hidden.

"Confound that dog!" cried Hilary. "She's nearly upset me. I didn't see her there on the couch. She nearly goes crazy when she hears a gunshot. Did you hear it?"

"Pansy still gunshy?" asked Dr. Bouligny. "I thought she'd get over that when she grew so old. Yes, Hilary, we heard it. But it was too muffled to be heard on the lawn. You've not proved anything at all. Of course, if you want an autopsy after all this time—but I don't advise it."

I heard no more of their futile discussion. I was moving rather dazedly toward the door. For I knew who killed Bayard Thatcher.

Adela approached me. She started to speak, but my face must have told her what I knew, for she checked the words on her lips and leaned forward to search my face. At that instant Dr. Bouligny came forward.

"Well, Miss Keate," he said, extending his hand, "I must say good-bye for a time. I won't see you again before you leave in the morning. But as a member of the Thatcher family I must thank you for your——" He stopped. He could not say silence, I suppose, nor promise. While he hesitated Adela said, "Good-night, Miss Keate."

I don't believe I took Dr. Bouligny's hand. I murmured something and escaped.

I ran up the stairs. I whirled into my own room and locked the door.

That long night will never leave my memory.

After a time I roused to the realization that the house had sunk into its familiar night quiet. Perhaps if I busied myself I could escape the horror that had clutched me. I remember that I packed my things and then deliberately took them out of the bag and repacked them. How silent the house was!

It was shortly after midnight, though it seemed much later, when something at the door caught my eyes. It was a bit of white. It moved almost imperceptibly. Became larger and larger. Finally lay there, a square white envelope. I heard no sound in the hall outside; there was not a whisper of motion. But I waited a long time before I moved and approached that envelope and finally took it in my shrinking fingers. It was not addressed, and I slipped out the paper it held, and read it. Read it there in that silent, waiting house that had guarded its secret so well.

"*Dear Miss Keate,*" it began. It was written very neatly in a small, delicate handwriting.

"*You know, now, who killed Bayard. I want you to know the*

whole truth as I know it. I think it likely you are in some doubt as to what to do with your knowledge, and I want you to know all of it rather than the bare fact. You will understand that I am in great anxiety as to what your decision will be after reading this letter. You will not, I believe, think it too hasty if I ask you to tell me at the breakfast table if you have decided to keep this dreadful thing a secret or to bring Bayard's murderer to justice. That gives you until morning to decide, and I can wait no longer to know. I am sure you will understand the strain I am under and why I make this request.

"First, let me answer your two questions. Dave kept his supply of veronal in a small, hollowed-out place under the headstone of Nita Thatcher's grave; he did it because in a house like ours it is impossible to keep anything concealed for long. If I hadn't discovered it, someone else would have. Bayard would leave the drug there when he didn't give it to Dave directly. If I had known it earlier I might have saved Dave, but I knew nothing of it until Bayard mentioned it the night Dave shot him. I went to the grave early in the morning after Bayard's death in the hope of removing any drug that might have been left there. I did not tell you this when you asked, because it seemed to me the last drop of humiliation in the story of Dave's sad affliction.

"And your other question: I myself closed Bayard's eyes. I had to do that much for him.

"What you know of Bayard's death is the whole truth. We have kept nothing back. When Pansy—poor old Pansy, who would never betray her friend if she knew—ran out of the study tonight and I met your eyes I remembered. I knew then that you knew exactly what had happened. Pansy was on the couch in Dave's study. When she heard the sound of the shot she nearly went mad with fright. I opened the door, and she ran outdoors, and of course you saw her.

"But I must tell you why.

"Dave was murdered as surely as Bayard. Bayard murdered him; deliberately debauched him; cold-bloodedly and intentionally led poor

weak Dave into the habit that ended in his death. Bayard threatened all I held dear. There was no use in trying any longer to pay for peace. He had to die to save Dave, and then it was too late. There was no saving for Dave. Dave took the last dose of veronal, as Dr. Bouligny has said. But actually and really Bayard murdered him. So I have no pity for Bayard.

"And I have none for Bayard's murderer, whose remaining life—which as your trained eyes must have seen will not be long—can only serve to uphold and preserve for others that family tradition which has meant so much to generations of Thatchers.

"How difficult it is for me to say it openly and frankly—yet my hand was very steady when I took that revolver from Janice's desk and went downstairs and leveled it at Bayard's wicked heart. It was only when I had pulled the trigger and sent the bullet that my hand weakened and dropped the revolver and Bayard, dying, fell upon it.

"For I killed Bayard. You know it. You know I was the only person in the house with Bayard when Pansy fled from the sound of the gunshot.

"I can't say any more. It is not for myself that I ask your mercy."

It was signed very neatly and carefully: "*Adela Thatcher.*"

AMERICAN MYSTERY CLASSICS *from*

*Available now
in hardcover and paperback:*

Charlotte Armstrong
The Unsuspected

Introduction by Otto Penzler

To catch a murderous theater impresario, a young woman takes a deadly new role ...

The note discovered beside Rosaleen Wright's hanged body is full of reasons justifying her suicide—but it lacks her trademark vitality and wit, and, most importantly, her signature. So the note alone is far from enough to convince her best friend Jane that Rosaleen was her own murderer, even if the police quickly accept the possibility as fact. Instead, Jane suspects Rosaleen's boss, Luther Grandison. To the world at large, he's a powerful and charismatic figure, directing for stage and screen, but Rosaleen's letters to Jane described a duplicitous, greedy man who would no doubt kill to protect his secrets. Jane and her friend Francis set out to infiltrate Grandy's world and collect evidence, employing manipulation, impersonation, and even gaslighting to break into his inner circle. But will they recognize what dangers lie therein before it's too late?

CHARLOTTE ARMSTRONG (1905-1969) was an American author of mystery short stories and novels. Having started her writing career as a poet and dramatist, she wrote a few novels before *The Unsuspected*, which was her first to achieve outstanding success, going on to be adapted for film by Michael Curtiz.

"Psychologically rich, intricately plotted and full of dark surprises, Charlotte Armstrong's suspense tales feel as vivid and fresh today as a half century ago."
—Megan Abbott

Paperback, $15.95 / ISBN 978-1-61316-123-4
Hardcover, $25.95 / ISBN 978-1-61316-122-7

OTTO PENZLER PRESENTS
===AMERICAN MYSTERY CLASSICS===

John Dickson Carr
The Mad Hatter Mystery

Introduction by Otto Penzler

*A murdered man in a top hat leads Dr. Gideon Fell
to a killer with a sick sense of humor*

At the hand of an outrageous prankster, top hats are going missing all over London, snatched from the heads of some of the city's most powerful people. But is the hat thief the same as the person responsible for stealing the lost story by Edgar Allan Poe, purloined from a private collection, which Dr. Gideon Fell has just been hired to retrieve? Unlike the manuscript, the hats don't stay stolen for long; each one reappears in unexpected and conspicuous places shortly after being taken. When the most recently-vanished hat is found atop a corpse in the foggy depths of the Tower of London, the seemingly-harmless pranks become much more serious; and when the dead man is identified as the nephew of the book collector, Fell's search for the missing story becomes a search for a murderer as well.

John Dickson Carr (1906-1977) was one of the greatest writers of the American Golden Age mystery, and the only American author to be included in England's legendary Detection Club during his lifetime. Under his own name and various pseudonyms, he wrote more than seventy novels and numerous short stories, and is best known today for his locked-room mysteries.

"Very few detective stories baffle me nowadays, but Mr.
Carr's always do."—Agatha Christie

Paperback, $15.95 / ISBN 978-1-61316-125-8
Hardcover, $25.95 / ISBN 978-1-61316-124-1

Erle Stanley Gardner
The Case of the
Careless Kitten

Introduction by Otto Penzler

Perry Mason seeks the link between a poisoned kitten and a mysterious voice from the past

Soon after Helen Kendal receives a mysterious phone call from her vanished uncle Franklin, long presumed dead, urging her to make contact with criminal defense attorney Perry Mason, she finds herself the main suspect in the murder of an unfamiliar man. Her kitten has just survived a poisoning attempt—as has her aunt Matilda, who always maintained that Franklin was alive in spite of his disappearance. Certain of his client's innocence, Mason gets to work outwitting the police to solve the crime; to do so, he'll enlist the help of his secretary Della Street, his private eye Paul Drake, and the unlikely but invaluable aid of a careless but very clever kitten.

ERLE STANLEY GARDNER (1889-1970) was the best-selling American author of the 20th century, mainly due to the enormous success of his Perry Mason series. For more than a quarter of a century he wrote more than a million words a year under his own name and numerous pseudonyms, the most famous being A.A. Fair. His series books can be read in any order.

"[Erle Stanley Gardner's] Mason books remain tantalizing on every page and brilliant."
—Scott Turow

Paperback, $15.95 / ISBN 978-1-61316-116-6
Hardcover, $25.95 / ISBN 978-1-61316-115-9

Dorothy B. Hughes
The So Blue Marble

Introduction by Otto Penzler

Three well-heeled villains terrorize New York's high society in pursuit of a rare and powerful gem

The society pages announce it before she even arrives: Griselda Satterlee, daughter of the princess of Rome, has left her career as an actress behind and is traveling to Manhattan to reinvent herself as a fashion designer. They also announce the return of the dashing Montefierrow twins to New York after a twelve-year sojourn in Europe. But there is more to this story than what's reported: The twins are seeking a rare and powerful gem they believe to be stashed in the unused apartment where Griselda is staying, and they won't take no for an answer. When they return, accompanied by Griselda's long-estranged younger sister, the murders begin . . . Drenched in the glamour and luxury of the New York elite, *The So Blue Marble* is a perfectly Art Deco suspense novel in which nothing is quite as it seems.

DOROTHY B. HUGHES (1904-1993) was a mystery author and literary critic. Several of her novels were adapted for film, including *In a Lonely Place* and *Ride the Pink Horse*, and in 1978, the Mystery Writers of America presented her with the Grand Master Award.

"Readers new to this forgotten classic are in for a treat."—*Publishers Weekly*

Paperback, $15.95 / ISBN 978-1-61316-105-0

Hardcover, $25.95 / ISBN 978-1-61316-111-1

OTTO PENZLER PRESENTS
AMERICAN MYSTERY CLASSICS

Frances & Richard Lockridge
Death on the Aisle
A Mr. & Mrs. North Mystery

Introduction by Otto Penzler

Broadway may be a graveyard of hopes and dreams, but someone's adding corpses to its tombs...

Mr. and Mrs. North live as quiet a life as a couple can amidst the bustle of New York City. For Jerry, a publisher, and Pamela, a homemaker, the only threat to their domestic equilibrium comes in the form of Mrs. North's relentless efforts as an amateur sleuth, which repeatedly find the duo investigating crimes. So when the wealthy backer of a play is found dead in the seats of the West 45th Street Theatre, the Norths aren't far behind, led by Pam's customary flair for murders that turn eccentric and, yes, humorous. A light mystery set in a classic Broadway locale, *Death on the Aisle* is the fourth novel and one of the best in the saga of this charming, witty couple, which can be enjoyed in any order.

FRANCES AND RICHARD LOCKRIDGE were two of the most popular names in mystery during the forties and fifties, collaborating to write twenty-six mystery novels about the Mr. & Mrs. North couple, which, in turn, became the subject of a Broadway play, a movie, and series for both radio and television.

"Masters of misdirection."
—The New York Times

Paperback, $15.95 / ISBN 978-1-61316-118-0
Hardcover, $25.95 / ISBN 978-1-61316-117-3

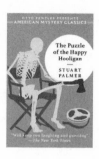

Stuart Palmer
The Puzzle of the Happy Hooligan
Introduction by Otto Penzler

After a screenwriter is murdered on a film set, a street-smart school teacher searches for the killer

Hildegarde Withers is just your average school teacher—with above-average skills in the art of deduction. The New Yorker often finds herself investigating crimes led only by her own meddlesome curiosity, though her friends on the NYPD don't mind when she solves their cases for them. After plans for a grand tour of Europe are interrupted by Germany's invasion of Poland, Miss Withers heads to sunny Los Angeles instead, where her vacation finds her working as a technical advisor on the set of a film adaptation of the Lizzie Borden story. The producer has plans for an epic retelling of the historical killer's patricidal spree—plans which are derailed when a screenwriter turns up dead. While the local authorities quickly deem his death accidental, Withers suspects otherwise and calls up a detective back home for advice. The two soon team up to catch a wily killer.

STUART PALMER (1905–1968) was an American author of mysteries. Born in Baraboo, Wisconsin, Palmer worked a number of odd jobs—including apple picking, journalism, and copywriting—before publishing his first novel, the crime drama *Ace of Jades*, in 1931.

"Will keep you laughing and guessing from the first page to the last."—*The New York Times*

Paperback, $15.95 / ISBN 978-1-61316-104-3

Hardcover, $25.95 / ISBN 978-1-61316-114-2

Ellery Queen
The Dutch Shoe Mystery

Introduction by Otto Penzler

After a wealthy woman is strangled in a hospital full of friends, Ellery Queen seeks her deadly enemy

When millionaire and philanthropist Abigail Doorn falls into a coma, she is taken to the hospital she funds for an emergency operation at the hands of her protégé, one of the leading surgeons on the East Coast. Her friends and family flock to the scene, anxious to hear of the outcome; also in attendance is mystery writer and amateur detective Ellery Queen, invited by a member of the hospital staff. Covered in a white sheet, her form is wheeled into the main operating theater—but when the sheet is pulled back, it reveals a grim display: the garroted corpse of the patient, murdered before the chance at survival. Who among the attendees was ruthless enough to carry out this gruesome act? As the list of suspects grows, and the murders continue, it's up to Queen—and the most perceptive of readers—to uncover the clues and find out.

ELLERY QUEEN was a pen name created and shared by two cousins, Frederic Dannay (1905-1982) and Manfred B. Lee (1905-1971), as well as the name of their most famous detective. Born in Brooklyn, they spent forty-two years writing the greatest puzzle-mysteries of their time, gaining the duo a reputation as the greatest American authors of the "fair play" mystery.

"Ellery Queen *is* the American detective story." —Anthony Boucher

Paperback, $15.95 / ISBN 978-1-61316-127-2
Hardcover, $25.95 / ISBN 978-1-61316-126-5

Craig Rice
Home Sweet Homicide

Introduction by Otto Penzler

The children of a mystery writer play amateur sleuths and matchmakers

Unoccupied and unsupervised while mother is working, the children of widowed crime writer Marion Carstairs find diversion wherever they can. So when the kids hear gunshots at the house next door, they jump at the chance to launch their own amateur investigation—and after all, why shouldn't they? They know everything the cops do about crime scenes, having read about them in mother's novels. They know what her literary detectives would do in such a situation, how they would interpret the clues and handle witnesses. Plus, if the children solve the puzzle before the cops, it will do wonders for the sales of mother's novels. But this crime scene isn't a game at all; the murder is real and, when its details prove more twisted than anything in mother's fiction, they'll eventually have to enlist Marion's help to sort out the clues. Or is that just part of their plan to hook her up with the lead detective on the case?

CRAIG RICE (1908–1957), born Georgiana Ann Randolph Craig, was an American author of mystery novels, short stories, and screenplays. Rice's writing style was unique in its ability to mix gritty, hard-boiled writing with the entertainment of a screwball comedy.

"A genuine midcentury classic."—*Booklist*

Paperback, $15.95 / ISBN 978-1-61316-103-6

Hardcover, $25.95 / ISBN 978-1-61316-112-8

Mary Roberts Rinehart
The Red Lamp

Introduction by Otto Penzler

A professor tries to stop a murder spree, uncertain whether the culprit is man or ghost

An all-around skeptic when it comes to the supernatural, literature professor William Porter gives no credence to claims that Twin Towers, the seaside manor he's just inherited, might be haunted. He finds nothing mysterious about the conditions in which his Uncle Horace died, leaving the property behind; it was a simple case of cardiac arrest, nothing more. Though his wife, more attuned to spiritual disturbance, refuses to occupy the main house, Porter convinces her to spend a summer at the estate and stay in the lodge elsewhere on the grounds. But, not long after they arrive, Porter sees the apparition that the townspeople speak of. And though he isn't convinced that it is a spirit and not a man, Porter knows that, whichever it is, the figure is responsible for the rash of murders—first of sheep, then of people—that breaks out across the countryside. But caught up in the pursuit, Porter risks implicating himself in the very crimes he hopes to solve.

MARY ROBERTS RINEHART (1876-1958) was the most beloved and best-selling mystery writer in America in the first half of the twentieth century.

"Fans of eerie whodunits with a supernatural tinge will relish this reissue."—*Publishers Weekly*

Paperback, $15.95 / ISBN 978-1-61316-102-9

Hardcover, $25.95 / ISBN 978-1-61316-113-5

Mary Roberts Rinehart
Miss Pinkerton

Introduction by Carolyn Hart

After a suspicious death at a mansion, a brave nurse joins the household to see behind closed doors

Miss Adams is a nurse, not a detective—at least, not technically speaking. But while working as a nurse, one does have the opportunity to see things police can't see and an observant set of eyes can be quite an asset when crimes happen behind closed doors. Sometimes Detective Inspector Patton rings Miss Adams when he needs an agent on the inside. And when he does, he calls her "Miss Pinkerton" after the famous detective agency.

Everyone involved seems to agree that mild-mannered Herbert Wynne wasn't the type to commit suicide but, after he is found shot dead, with the only other possible killer being his ailing, bedridden aunt, no other explanation makes sense. Now the elderly woman is left without a caretaker and Patton sees the perfect opportunity to employ Miss Pinkerton's abilities. But when she arrives at the isolated country mansion to ply her trade, she soon finds more intrigue than anyone outside could have imagined and—when she realizes a killer is on the loose—more terror as well.

MARY ROBERTS RINEHART (1876-1958) was the most beloved and best-selling mystery writer in America in the first half of the twentieth century.

"An entertaining puzzle mystery that stands the test of time."—*Publishers Weekly*

Paperback, $15.95 / ISBN 978-1-61316-269-9

Hardcover, $25.95 / ISBN 978-1-61316-138-8